Duck!

An Avian Shifters Novel

By Kim Dare

Duck! (Avian Shifter Series, Book 1)
ISBN # 978-1-910081-13-6

Published by Kim Dare
Edited by Christine Allen-Riley and Shannon Leeper
Cover Art by Kris Norris

First Edition – August 2010
Second Edition – August 2015

Dedication

To everyone who has yet to discover who they really are.

Chapter One

"Duck!"

Instinct took over. Ori dropped to his knees, taking cover behind the waist-high partition that separated the dining area from the adjacent corridor. A plate smashed against the wall to his right—just where his head would have been, if his reactions hadn't been so quick.

Ori's grip on his tray of dirty plates faltered as he hunched over them in an effort to stay low and out of range. They slid forward. Scrabbling at the china, he desperately tried to catch more than a dozen fragile pieces of crockery at the same time.

Two hands were never going to be enough. The dishes and glasses spilled leftover food and wine across the floor as they tumbled out of his grasp. Ori made one last attempt to catch a wine glass. Success! His fingers wrapped tightly around the delicate stem as the rest of the plates and silverware plummeted toward the dark oak floorboards.

As the clatter peaked, then faded away, Ori's attention flickered from one piece of expensive china to another, from one lead crystal glass to the next. Each item stared back at him, miraculously unscathed.

"What the hell...?" Highly polished black shoes stopped at the edge of the debris.

"I'm sorry, sir. I'll clean it up immediately," Ori rushed out, scrambling to pick up the mess of scattered crockery and utensils, and move them out of the man's way.

Clearing one side of the hallway first, Ori quickly made a path through the wreckage for the higher-ranking man. As soon as he was sure the man could walk by without soiling his shoes, Ori paused and politely waited for the man to pass.

The shoes didn't move.

Ori sprung back into action, working even more frantically, as he realised the man had no intention of taking another step until every scrap vanished from his sight.

Ori didn't waste precious time peering up at the stranger who loomed over him. It didn't matter who he was. He outranked Ori by default, and every second that passed probably added another lash to the whipping Ori's clumsiness must have already earned him.

Damn it, just a few more steps and he'd have reached the safety of the full height section of wall that still kept the stranger out of sight of the dining room. He'd have been out of range then—at least until he had to venture back into the dining room to clear another table. Ori pressed his lips together and kept his curses to himself. It was too late to wish he'd walked quicker now.

Placing the last shard of the plate that had smashed against the wall on the tray next to the surviving dishes, Ori set it to one side of the corridor and knelt neatly behind it, waiting for the other shifter to finally step past him. The shoes remained exactly where they were. Uncertain what else was required, Ori risked a glance up as far as the man's knees.

A hand appeared alongside the neatly tailored trousers. Ori's eyes went to the tattoo on the inside of the man's wrist.

Hawk.

Ori knew he still had a lot to learn about the marks that distinguished each species of avian from the others, but the harsh black lines that decorated the stranger's skin were impossible to mistake.

Hawk.

Ori's stomach turned over as he imagined what angering such a high-ranking man could mean for him.

The stranger's hand stayed exactly where it was until Ori reached up and offered his own wrist up in return. His fingers were still smeared with the food he'd cleaned from the floor. His unmarked wrist looked even barer when held next to the one that properly signalled a man's species.

Ori looked farther up and into a pair of startling amber eyes.

"There's a reason you're not marked?"

"They're waiting until they're sure what I am, sir," Ori blurted out.

"Have you completed a partial shift?"

"Yes, sir."

The hawk looked at Ori's wrist again. "What was the elder's best guess?"

"A rather ugly little duckling, sir."

It was an exact quote. It was also four words longer than his answer needed to be. Such things mattered when speaking to a man whose species endowed him with a rank as high as a hawk's — Ori had learnt that the hard way. He dropped his gaze and waited for the worst.

"Is there a name you're certain of?"

The question was so unexpected, it took Ori a moment to find an answer. "Ori Jones, sir."

"Up on your feet, Ori."

Picking up the tray, Ori rose to his full height without considering anything but the hawk's order.

"Duck!"

Ori dropped heavily to the floor as laughter echoed out of the dining room. His tray spilled from his hands once more. The plates weren't destined to survive two equally spectacular demonstrations of his clumsiness in such quick succession. Fragments of shattering chinaware skidded along the floorboards, colliding with the hawk's shoes and Ori's bare legs.

He looked up just in time to see the hawk step out from behind the wall and into view of the crowd of crows who'd been drinking in the dining room for most of the day.

"All of you — over here. Now!"

Ori started collecting up the fragments of smashed crockery, his hands shaking as he imagined the look that would flash in the chef's eyes when he saw the mess Ori had made of the nest's fine dining service.

Shadows fell across his skin as the crows crossed the room in response to the hawk's command.

"Clean that up."

Ori kept his head down, his eyes on his task. "Yes, sir."

"Not you — them."

Ori looked up. "Sir?"

"You heard me. On your feet."

All Ori could do was stare up at him in horror. "I can —
"

"You'll do as you're told. Stand up."

Ori's body obeyed without consulting his brain. Some sort of mental process clicked into operation when he was half way to his feet. "I could —"

The hawk didn't appear impressed. He pointed to an area of clear floor, just beyond the fallout from the tray. "Take care that you step over the glass."

Ori gave in. Keeping his gaze lowered, not daring to look toward the crows, he took up position where he'd been commanded.

"You expect us to —" one of the crows began.

"I expect you to do what you're told, too," the hawk snapped, as if a crow was no different from a duckling in his eyes.

Ori swallowed rapidly. Perhaps to a man with a hawk's rank, the rungs at the bottom end of the social ladder were very close together. But Ori was well aware that the crows all knew the difference between their station in the nest and his own precarious and unofficial position.

The crows' glares skittered over his skin as they stooped to collect the broken pieces of crockery and pile them on the tray. They didn't have to say a word. Ori knew they all intended to remind him exactly how far above him they were

4

as soon as the hawk stepped out of sight.

"And the rest," the hawk commanded.

Ori looked up. The second plate that the crows had pitched at him hadn't been empty. Food streaked across the wall in a vivid mess of browns and greens.

The hawk caught his eye.

"I'll fetch—" Ori began.

"They can find whatever they need. Just tell them where."

"There's a storeroom behind the kitchens, sir."

A nod from the hawk dismissed one of the crows in that direction.

Ori closed his eyes. His toes clenched against the floorboards as he fought against an almost overwhelming urge to run. He wasn't even sure if he wanted to race away from the crows or from the hawk. The crows were going to give him hell, but the hawk was...

The moment Ori opened his eyes, his gaze went to the bird of prey. He was far larger than either him or the crows; tall and broad across the shoulders. His well-tailored shirt did nothing to hide the muscles beneath the fabric. The dark material only succeeded in making him look more dominant, more aristocratic.

It was only supposed to be a glance, but Ori found himself incapable of looking away. He'd seen a hawk at the nest a few months before, but he had been a much older man whose hair had faded to grey as his back had bent with age.

He'd never seen a hawk like this one. The man was glorious, all strength and certainty.

Ori was still helplessly staring at the hawk when the crows finished their task. The hawk nodded to the tray, finally dismissing Ori from the corridor. Ori stepped forward, making his way between the crows.

The flock's eyes followed him, sending a shiver down his spine. The tiny pair of shorts he'd been provided with when he started serving at the nest had never felt smaller.

He scurried back into the heat and chaos of the kitchens as quickly as possible. A few of the other servants cast glances in his direction as he rushed to his station at the farthest end of the room. Word always travelled quickly through the nest. They would all know what had happened by now. And, no doubt, they knew just as well as he did what would happen next.

Ori took a deep breath as he stared down at the tray full of broken dishes. The crows might not have dared to disobey a hawk, but the hawk would leave at some point, and then…

He let the breath out as a sigh. Perhaps, if he'd already been a fully-fledged shifter, he might have had a chance. Maybe he could have spoken to whoever represented his species and asked him to take his concerns to the nest's elders. But, as it was, Ori knew that he didn't really exist in the eyes of any of the avians who ran the nest. No one would step in and stop whatever the crows had planned for him.

While his mind rushed in circles, Ori automatically resumed the duties that had occupied his time for the last six months. Broken pieces of crockery disposed of, he took up his position in front of two huge Belfast sinks and started working his way through all the trays of dirty dishes that had made it back to the kitchens intact.

Each second dragged out until time stood still around him. His heart raced faster and faster. His hands shook with nerves, making him clumsier than ever. It was almost a relief when the atmosphere in the kitchen changed and he knew his wait was over.

"Get out."

Still facing the sinks, Ori heard the other servants scurrying out of the room, leaving their duties without a word. Even the chef's domineering presence faded from the kitchens as he temporarily relinquished his domain to the flock of crows. Ori stayed very still, his eyes closed tightly, knowing the order didn't apply to him.

Footsteps sounded on the uneven flagstone floor as the flock made its way toward him. A rough hand grabbed Ori's arm, spinning him around to face his long-standing tormentors. Every crow who had been in the dining room was there, fanning out around him, blocking any chance of escape.

Ori's stomach clenched, tying itself in knots around his nerves as his hands formed into fists at his sides.

"Did you really think you'd get away with that?" Jermaine, the somewhat unofficial leader of the ragged flock, demanded.

Ori stayed silent.

The back of Jermaine's hand slammed into Ori's cheek, sending him stumbling toward the countertop adjacent to the sinks. Pain flared through the side of his face. His mind reeled. He fumbled at the edge of the granite in the vain hope that holding onto it might make the world stop weaving in front of his eyes before the next blow landed.

"I asked you a question," Jermaine spat out. "Did you really think you could carry tales back to the hawk and not pay for it?"

"No, sir," Ori whispered.

Another crow grabbed his right arm and pulled him around again. Before Ori could even get his balance, the crow had caught his left arm in an equally painful grip. He dragged Ori back to stand in front of him, his arms wrenched behind him, leaving his torso exposed and vulnerable.

Ori risked another brief glance up from the floor. The crows were looking around the kitchen with interest. Suddenly, it was impossible to see the objects that surrounded him as a simple collection of cooking utensils. It was a room full of sharp blades and scalding liquids.

Ori's gaze flickered over knives, ranges, boiling saucepans, and a dozen other things that would hurt like hell when thrown in his direction.

Survival instinct tried to take over. He pulled at the crow's hold on him. The crow tightened his grip around his arms. Part of Ori knew he was stronger than the man trying to hold him in place, but as the crow's fingers dug into his skin, an even more powerful instinct took over. Ori felt something inside himself willingly yield to the higher-ranking man's wishes. He fell still within the crow's grasp.

"Apologize," Jermaine demanded.

"I'm sorry, sir."

A light appeared in the crow's eyes, and some of Ori's panic eased. He'd become almost used to the flock's casual sadism. Being made to jump through painful hoops for the crows' amusement wasn't new. Getting screwed by one or more of them wasn't such an unusual occurrence either. The idea that the situation might be survivable in spite of the crows' fury began to spread through Ori's mind.

"Again," Jermaine demanded. "Look me in the eye when you say it."

Ori lifted his gaze, but the words died on his tongue as he glanced past the crows and realised they were no longer alone in the kitchen.

Please, not in front of him.

The words flashed up in the forefront of Ori's mind, vivid and desperate. It was a stupid thing to think. Having an audience wasn't so rare a thing. He should have been used to it. It shouldn't have made any difference, but it did — with the new hawk standing there, it did.

Then, he saw the anger in the hawk's eyes.

"Let him go."

All the crows' attention transferred to the hawk.

The hands holding Ori in place jerked away as if the words had turned his skin as hot as any range, as sharp as any knife in the kitchens. The crows fled, colliding with each other in fear as they rushed along the far edges of the kitchen, skirting around out of range of the hawk.

All Ori could do was remain where he was, staring at the hawk. They held each other's gaze as the crows hurried from the room, and Ori couldn't even bring himself to care that they would no doubt be back at some point in the future.

The hawk was right there, and, in some stupid way, that was all that mattered. Ori stared helplessly up at the bird of prey as he realised just how much he'd hoped he might catch another glimpse of him.

The hawk stepped forward, closing the gap between them.

Ori watched him approach, not sure what to do—what the hawk might want him to do. Stopping directly in front of him, the man ran his thumb along Ori's bottom lip.

All confusion disappeared. Lowering himself quickly to his knees, Ori reached for the hawk's fly. It wasn't until the hawk pushed his hand away, that Ori noticed the blood on the man's fingertips.

Ori's lip was bleeding. The sharp metallic taste hadn't really registered until then. Snatching a cloth off the countertop, Ori carefully cleaned the hawk's hand.

That task accomplished, Ori swiped at his own bottom lip. More blood smeared onto the fabric. For a few silent seconds, Ori stared down at the vivid red smudge. It was silly to hope the hawk might want to use his mouth regardless.

"Shall I fetch one of the other servants for you, sir?" he asked, trying to hide his disappointment.

"Stand up."

Ori quickly stumbled to his feet.

"How long have you been serving here?"

"A few months, sir," Ori whispered. When he glanced up, the hawk was still staring at him, a serious expression lingering in the amber eyes.

The silence went on and on.

"Mr. Hamilton offered me a place here."

More silence.

"He said it would keep me out of trouble until I can complete a full shift, and everything can be sorted out properly," Ori added.

"And how old are you now?"

"Twenty, sir. I'll turn twenty-one in June." Ori swallowed. He knew the math. Part of him had been counting down the days ever since he'd stumbled upon the nest and found out how things were arranged among the shifters. It would be another six months before he'd reach his avian maturity and be able to complete a full shift into his avian form—six months before he had any chance of becoming a true part of the shifter community.

The hawk looked him up and down. Without another word, he turned and walked out of the kitchen. All Ori could do was watch him go.

Except, the hawk didn't actually go. He paused in the doorway, looking both ways along the corridor outside the kitchens.

"Everet!"

The hawk remained in the doorway until a younger man, a raven who Ori had spotted in the nest a few times over the previous six months, joined him. "Watch him."

The raven looked into the kitchen. His eyes locked on to Ori. He nodded his acceptance of the order. When the hawk strode away, Everet came closer.

For the third time that day, Ori found himself standing in his usual corner of the kitchen, waiting for a higher-ranking man to reach him. He had no idea what was going on anymore. Any instinct he might have had for fight or flight was too confused to even suggest a course of action.

"Your lip's bleeding."

Ori reached up and touched his mouth.

The raven stood a few feet away from him, watching him, just as the hawk commanded. His curiosity was obvious. "Did Raynard do that to you?"

Ori blinked. The hawk's name was Raynard. Eventually, something more than the knowledge of the hawk's surname sank in. Ori shook his head as he dabbed at his lip with the cloth again. "It was one of the crows, sir."

The raven said nothing more; he merely looked Ori

over as if wondering why the hell a hawk would take any sort of interest in him.

Ori looked down. He should have already asked himself the same question. Now that the query was in his head, the answer wasn't far behind it. Raynard was a hawk and he was an ugly little duckling. Ori might not have been raised among shifters, but since he'd found his way into their company, he'd learnt enough to know that species was rank, and rank was everything to the avians. The only reason a hawk would ask Ori his name, was so he could suggest his dismissal.

Even knowing his position in the nest was about to be snatched away from him, Ori found himself looking back to the dishes. "Shall I...?"

The raven looked to the sinks and the plates piled high around them. He shrugged, causing highly defined muscles to jostle beneath his tight black t-shirt. "Raynard didn't say you couldn't."

Ori silently returned to his duties. The work might not have been enthralling, but there was a certain simplicity to it that he'd learnt to appreciate. There was something comforting about knowing exactly what was expected of him, exactly where his place in the world was.

The raven leaned back against one of the huge cabinets to Ori's right, arms folded across his chest as he stared vacantly into the middle distance. He was so still, so silent, Ori almost forgot he was there. Picking up a stack of the plates, he turned toward the cabinet and only just stopped short of walking into him.

Everet straightened up and opened the cabinet door for Ori.

"Thank you, sir."

Not meeting Everet's eyes, Ori turned back to the sinks. Filling them with fresh water, he looked over his shoulder. The other servants had filed back into the kitchen at some point, but they were giving both him and the raven a wide berth. One of them, a rather bedraggled pigeon, offered Ori a sympathetic smile as their eyes chanced to meet. Ori managed to return the expression, but nothing was said. Even the chef was keeping his orders and tantrums more muted than usual.

"Everet."

For a moment, Ori thought it might have been Raynard's voice that had echoed through the kitchens, but it wasn't. The hawk hadn't come back. Ori stayed very still as he waited for the message to be relayed, but whatever it was, it must have been communicated in nothing more than a look.

Everet stepped away from the cabinet. "Follow me."

Turning off the taps and hastily drying his hands, Ori trailed after the raven. The messenger mumbled something to Everet when he reached the kitchen door, but the words were too hushed for Ori to catch.

"Come on." The raven set off again, occasionally glancing over his shoulder to make sure his charge hadn't fallen too far behind.

Everet led him out of the communal areas of the club that all the species had access to and up a grand staircase toward the more exclusive sections of the establishment. It took more courage than Ori had known he possessed to keep going, to keep wading even farther into increasingly unfamiliar and luxurious territory.

The dining rooms and meeting rooms on the ground floor had taken his breath away when he'd first visited the nest. He wasn't sure what he'd have made of these higher corridors if he'd seen them on that initial visit. On each side of him, portraits stared down. Back then, he'd probably have thought they were of wealthy aristocrats, their tamed birds of prey flying in the background.

Now, it was obvious that each portrait merely showed two sides of the same man, and there was nothing tame about the birds of prey who filled the topmost perches of the shifter hierarchy.

Ori took a deep breath and pushed forward, his bare

feet making no sound on the thick carpeting. Everet reached a mahogany door at the far end of the corridor and knocked firmly on the dark panelling.

"Enter."

Everet pushed the door open and nodded for Ori to step inside. A moment later, the raven pulled the door closed without joining Ori in the room. Ori found himself in what looked like some sort of office, albeit an incredibly expensive one.

Mr. Hamilton sat behind a huge desk on the other side of the room. He glanced across at Ori. Sharp blue eyes pinned him in place until Mr. Hamilton lost interest in him and turned his attention back to where Raynard sat on the opposite side of the desk. The hawk didn't even look over his shoulder to see who had entered the room.

Stepping to one side of the door, Ori waited patiently, inconspicuous and out of everyone's way, until one of the birds of prey had some use for him.

"He's obviously not suited to the position as things stand," Raynard bit out, each word clipped and angry.

Ori had never heard anyone speak to Mr. Hamilton that way. The eagle who ran the club was years older than Raynard, his hair already greying around his temples where Raynard's was still deep brown, but their ranks obviously made them equals.

Then Raynard's actual words sunk in to Ori's mind. *Not suited to the position.* He lowered his gaze to the patch of carpet directly in front of his feet. He had been right then, he was going to be dismissed?

Thoughts tumbled through his head as he tried to work out where he might go. If they paid him off, he could probably find somewhere. But there was no reason to believe they would. They hadn't paid him up to this point, when they'd seemed to find his service at least vaguely acceptable.

"Do you really think he'd do better in your house?" Mr. Hamilton asked, each word tinged with his rich Scottish burr.

13

Ori's gaze snapped up. He stared unbelieving at the back of Raynard's head.

"Yes." No explanation. No justification. Just the answer. Raynard had made his decision, and he obviously didn't expect anyone to argue with him — not even an eagle.

Mr. Hamilton smiled slightly. "Your time away from this nest hasn't changed you in the faintest, has it?"

"Is there any reason why it should have?" Raynard asked.

Mr. Hamilton shook his head at him, but the slight twist of his lips still lingered. It died only when he moved his attention to Ori. "Come here."

Raynard glanced over his shoulder as Ori stepped forward to stand a pace behind the hawk's chair, and two feet to his right.

"Yes, sir?"

"Mr. Raynard is offering you a position in his house. You'd be his personal servant, answerable to him in all matters," the eagle informed him.

"Yes, sir."

"You'd remain under his care until you come back to us to complete your first full shift when you come of age."

"Yes, sir," Ori repeated.

Mr. Hamilton glanced at Raynard before he went on, his accent thickening a little as his tone turned even more serious.

"This isn't an easy position — you'll be expected to work just as hard for Mr. Raynard as you do here — more so, probably. And there would be no limits put upon what Mr. Raynard could expect from you or on the ways he could discipline you if your service is not up to the standard he requires. You'd belong to him completely."

"Yes, sir," Ori managed again.

Mr. Hamilton looked him over one more time. "Your answer, then — you accept the position?"

"Yes, sir." The words were out so quickly, Ori didn't

have time for any second thoughts.

Mr. Hamilton nodded, just once. "The paperwork will be drawn up. Go to your quarters. Change out of your uniform and gather your belongings before returning here."

"Yes, sir."

The two birds of prey turned their attention back to each other, neither bothering to actually dismiss him. Ori backed away as unobtrusively as possible, before turning and walking silently from the room.

Everet still stood outside the door in his seemingly habitual pose — his arms crossed and his back resting against any convenient surface. He stopped staring into the middle distance when he noticed Ori.

Ori hesitated. "I'm to go to my quarters and change my clothes, sir."

The raven nodded and strode off down the corridor. He paused when he realised Ori wasn't following him.

"They didn't say you had to come with me, sir."

"Raynard said to watch you. He hasn't told me to stop."

Ori looked down. Arguing with a raven wouldn't do him any good. The truth was his only option. "I don't have official quarters. I've been staying in the servants' area behind the kitchens, sir."

Everet's expression remained impassive. He stepped to one side of the corridor and nodded for Ori to pass him. "Lead the way."

"Yes, sir."

They soon left the luxury of the upper floors behind. With every step Ori took, his heart raced a little faster, until he was sure it would explode from his chest, no doubt making another mess that would need to be cleaned up before his duties were finished for the day.

"Raynard's taking you with him?" Everet asked as they headed down a white washed corridor behind the kitchens.

Ori nodded. "He's offered me a position in his house,

sir." He opened the door to a store cupboard at the end of the corridor. The clothes he'd been wearing when he arrived at the nest had been tossed in there, but there was no sign of them now.

He rifled through what was there, trying to find something that might fit. It wasn't easy. The clothes were a jumble of bits and pieces and there was no order to the way they'd been stored.

He felt Everet's eyes run up and down his back and guessed he should just be grateful that he wasn't going to be led out of the nest just wearing the tiny black shorts.

A pair of dark blue jeans that looked about the right size finally emerged from the chaos. Ori discovered a light green T-shirt a few minutes later. There was no sign of anything resembling a coat or underwear. Once he'd unearthed a battered pair of trainers from the very back of the disordered space, his wardrobe seemed to be as complete as it was destined to become.

The shorts were part of the uniform that marked him out as a servant belonging to club. He didn't belong to the club anymore. He belonged to Raynard. Ori took off the shorts.

Everet remained in the doorway. Ori kept his back to him, hoping that he wouldn't notice that the idea of becoming Raynard's personal servant was already having an effect on him.

His cock was half hard at the very thought of servicing Raynard the way he had so many of the men in the nest. At the same time, his stomach re-knotted itself with nerves. Taking a deep breath, Ori pulled on the jeans.

It had been months since he'd worn anything more than those miniscule shorts. The crumpled denim tubes felt strange around his legs. The material in the T-shirt was softer, but Ori still shrugged uncomfortably as the garment settled around him, clinging and suffocating every time he moved.

The trainers were a size too big. Ori wasn't sure if that

made them more or less comfortable now that his feet had become accustomed to being bare all day. Laces tied, Ori rose to his full height, such as it was. With the image of the hawk fresh in his mind, he felt far too small to be of any use to anyone.

"Raynard's not a bad guy; he's better than most of the birds of prey. Do as he tells you, and you'll be fine," Everet offered.

Ori nodded, wrapping the hope Everet's words gave him around him as best he could. "Thank you, sir."

As he heard the raven step back, Ori forced himself to turn and walk out of the little storeroom too. Long before he was ready for it, he found himself back in Mr. Hamilton's office, once more standing to one side of the door as he waited for the other men to recognise his presence.

If Mr. Hamilton had seen him return, he made no mention of it. Ori had no idea if Raynard had sensed anyone enter the room behind him.

The birds of prey stood up and shook hands. Raynard turned around. He didn't look surprised to see him. Ori got the distinct impression that there was very little that escaped the hawk's attention, even if he didn't choose to turn around and stare at it.

Raynard walked out of the room without a word, leaving Ori to trail along behind him, scurrying to keep up with the taller man's longer stride as best he could. They were out of the building and standing in the car park before Ori had quite caught up with events. He hesitated as the chill winter air whipped against him.

Closing his eyes, he relished the way the sunlight caressed his face. It had been months since he felt the sun on him. When he looked up, the world above him seemed impossibly big; the wide expanse of sky above him was both immense and terrifying. He instinctively took a half-step back toward the safety of the building.

"When was the last time you left the nest?"

Ori turned his eyes toward the hawk. Raynard stood next to a sleek black sports car, keys already in his hand. Ori blinked at him, unable to make his mind work quickly.

"A few months, sir." That was no excuse for keeping Raynard waiting. Standing on the threshold to the outside world, he waited to be told if he had displeased Raynard so badly he'd be sent back before he had even truly left.

"Come here."

Ori stepped forward. Eyes lowered, he stood before his new employer, waiting for his verdict.

"Get in."

Raynard nodded to the passenger side door. Ori obeyed, fumbling his way into the seat and pulling the door closed after him. The hawk moved around the car and slid behind the wheel, folding his tall frame into the low-slung space as if it were the easiest thing in the world.

A moment later, the engine roared into action. Without another glance at his new servant, Raynard drove them both away from the nest.

Chapter Two

Frederick Raynard changed gears as the car escaped the worst of the traffic in the centre of the city and made its way into a quieter, less built up part of town. The office blocks gradually faded away in favour of the kind of houses the men who owned those office blocks tended to live in.

His newly acquired servant sat silently by his side. Every so often, Raynard felt Ori glance at him, but the duckling didn't go so far as to speak without being spoken to. Raynard wasn't sure if that could be taken as a sign that he'd been trained for silent service, or if the poor little sod was just as nervous as hell.

Raynard mentally shook his head at himself. The last thing he needed was an untrained servant on top of everything else, but there was nothing to be done about it now. He was stuck with him for at least the next six months.

Still, the boy couldn't have been left at the nest — not when he'd have remained a sitting duck to the other men's cruelty. A sitting duck... Raynard held back a sigh as he turned a corner.

He had to wonder if Hamilton's control over the other avians was failing. *He's never made any complaints about his treatment here.* Raynard revved the engine a little more forcefully than he intended as the eagle's words replayed inside his head. Ori probably hadn't complained about the fact that he'd not been let out of the nest for months, either.

"Do you have a family?" Raynard asked.

Ori glanced at him out of the corner of his eye, but quickly dropped his gaze. "I had foster families, sir."

Raynard filed that fact away, in amongst the jumble of

business dealings that had recently taken over his world. If nothing else, it explained why Ori couldn't be certain of the species he'd shift into when he came of age, and why they were relying on the elders' best guess based on a partial shift.

"Have you kept in contact with any of them?"

Ori shook his head. "No, sir."

Raynard glanced at Ori as they stopped at a junction but he made no further comment. There was no point confusing the boy, making him think his employer was going to be his new best friend. A few minutes later, they pulled into the curved drive in front of Raynard Lodge.

Unfolding himself from within the tight confines of the car, Raynard looked up at the building. The expression on the duckling's face as he did the same might have been funny in other circumstances. Awe and horror filled Ori's eyes as he peered up at the dilapidated gothic monstrosity. He was probably regretting accepting a place in Raynard's house already—and he hadn't even seen inside the damn thing yet.

Raynard strode up to the front door. He twisted the heavy iron key back and forth in the lock until he chanced on the right combination of wrist actions to make the bloody contraption cooperate with his inclination to enter what was to be his new home now that he was required to take his uncle's place in the Anderson Nest's hierarchy.

Raynard went in, but Ori hesitated halfway over the threshold.

"There may be a servants' entrance somewhere," Raynard informed him. "But from what I've seen of my uncle's organisational skills, it would take a search team weeks to find the key to it."

Ori stepped inside and attempted to close the front door behind him—with very little success. Reaching over Ori's shoulder, Raynard pushed high up on the edge of the door, forcing it into its frame.

It slammed with a bang. Ori jumped. Springing away from the door, he backed straight into Raynard.

A hawk's reaction time was far faster than a duckling's. Steadying them fell to Raynard. Grabbing Ori's shoulder with one hand, Raynard slid his other arm around Ori's waist and pulled him in safely against his body.

There wasn't much of Ori that Raynard hadn't already inspected. The skimpy black shorts hadn't hidden a lot from those he was serving. Still, seeing something, and having it pressed intimately against him, were two very different things.

The duckling froze, not even drawing a breath as they stood in the gloom of the hallway. It had been far too long since Raynard had made time to bring another man close and enjoy what his body could offer.

Ori wouldn't say no.

Raynard closed his eyes for a moment. Ori wouldn't have said no to the crows in the kitchen or any other man in the nest either. Raynard forced himself to step back and put some distance between them before he forgot why he'd brought the boy home with him in the first place.

Turning his back on his new servant, he looked around the hallway. The place didn't need one servant—it needed an army of them—which was rather what he'd had intended to hire when he went to the nest.

Raynard looked over his shoulder and found Ori watching him very carefully from a position just to the left of the door. He dropped his eyes as Raynard glanced toward him.

"Do you have any questions?"

Ori swallowed rapidly before he attempted to speak. Even then, his words were softly spoken. "How may I serve you, sir?"

Raynard considered the question carefully. The response had probably been taught to him by rote, but there was a hint of true submission in his tone of voice. He wasn't just asking because he'd been taught to—he was asking because he really wanted to know.

21

Ori's attention dropped to the floor. Raynard's followed it. The tiles had probably been magnificent once upon a time. They might be again, when the dust was cleared away.

"It's late," Raynard decided. "We'll discuss your duties tomorrow."

"Yes, sir."

If the rooms Raynard had already investigated were anything to go by, it would probably take them an hour or more to find the servants' quarters and discover what sort of state they were in. By that time, Raynard was sure they'd both be more than ready for bed — for their *separate* beds, Raynard reminded himself.

"Follow me." Without looking over his shoulder to see if his order was being obeyed, Raynard set off toward a door he was reasonably confident led below stairs. The sound of his footsteps actually changed as he left the little pathway his previous footfalls had left in the dust.

He'd made one path to the master bedroom and another to his late uncle's study. The rest of the house hadn't really changed since he arrived a few weeks before.

The little door was tucked away almost out of sight, under the arch of the stairs. Lowering his head to avoid the treads overhead, Raynard pulled it open and groped around in the darkness for a light switch. A bare bulb flickered to life a third of the way down the stairs. Another guttered and promptly died another third of the way down.

As Raynard made his way into an even darker gloom than that which filled the main part of the house, he heard Ori descending a few steps behind him. He could only guess that the younger man was wondering what the hell he'd got himself into.

Reaching the bottom of the flight, Raynard made his way along a dismal, flagstone paved corridor. The kitchen, when they emerged into it, was little better. Everything was still draped in dustsheets after the previous servants closed up this part of the house. The curtains were drawn halfway across the window. There was barely enough light to make out the outlines of the larger items of furniture.

"There should be some sort of butler's quarters somewhere," Raynard said, nodding to one of the corridors leading off the kitchen.

Ori dutifully approached the first door and tried it. Peeking inside, he closed it before moving on to the next one, then the next one.

Working his way along the corridor to the other side of the kitchen, Raynard discovered room after room which would have bustled with dozens of staff when the house was in its heyday, but which now lay abandoned. Finally, he heard Ori call out.

"I think I might have found it, sir."

Raynard strode back into the kitchen and looked around the room. Ori had found the room, now all Raynard had to do was track down the damn duckling. He stood silently in the middle of the kitchen, but Ori made no sound.

"Ori?"

"Yes, sir?"

Raynard strode toward the sound of Ori's voice. Third time lucky, he found an open door that revealed another open door, and finally Ori standing in the middle of yet another shrouded room. One of the dustsheets had been pulled back to reveal the edge of a bed.

"Have to tie a ball of string to you before I let you out of my sight," Raynard muttered to himself.

Ori blinked at him as their eyes chanced to meet.

"Damn place is a maze," Raynard bit out. He reached for one of the other dustsheets, but found Ori there before him. The little fledgling was obviously eager to make a good first impression. Raynard stepped back into the doorway and watched as Ori carefully removed and folded each huge expanse of fabric.

The room had obviously been furnished with the cast

offs from the main part of the house — apparently around the time when deep carving and dark wood had just stopped being the latest fashion.

Raynard looked around the room. It would do. A glance toward Ori found him looking more than a little sceptical. Raynard pushed that aside. He was only a fledgling after all — it couldn't be easy for him having been raised with no understanding of what kind of man his species would lead him to be.

As he stared at Ori, Raynard found himself trying to imagine what it must be like, not knowing who he really was, what his place in the world should be. When Ori failed to speak of his own volition, Raynard saw little choice but to nudge him on. "Ori?"

"I don't need all this, sir. I could just..." He looked back to the kitchen as if he'd have been content to find some draughty little corner and curl up on the flagstone floor, as if that was what the nest had taught him to expect.

Raynard shook his head. There was no such thing as too soon to start showing the boy how he should have been treated at the nest. But at the same time, it was difficult to believe that Ori was in any condition to take anything in at that late hour. "We'll discuss the details tomorrow."

"Yes, sir."

Ori looked to his bed. Raynard followed his gaze then quickly looked away, before the sight of it gave him ideas that had no place in his mind. "Get some sleep."

"Yes, sir."

Raynard forced himself to turn away. He was out in the kitchen before he heard the boy speak again.

"You asked if I had any questions, sir?"

Raynard turned back to him and nodded his permission to ask.

"What would you like for breakfast, sir?"

Raynard looked around the kitchen. It would be far easier to summon up a ghost than a meal in there. "We'll dig out some coffee in the morning," he promised. Then, they'd go and get some real food. He might not have brought the boy into the kind of house he'd have liked to be able to provide to anyone he took under his protection, but at least he could see to it that he was well fed.

As he climbed the last of the stairs to the master bedroom, Raynard pushed his hand through his hair, disordering the brown waves. A suitcase stood open on the ancient chest in the corner of the room. The bed was in the same crumpled mess as he'd left it that morning. Apart from that, it was still very much his uncle's domain.

He'd have to do something about that. Raynard muttered a few well-chosen curses under his breath; he'd been saying as much since he stepped into the damn house. He draped his clothes over the back of the chair by the dressing table as he stripped them off, then strode across to the bed. Collapsing naked against the sheets, he felt his exhaustion in every muscle.

Putting his uncle's financial and business affairs in order wasn't hard physical work, but it was mentally draining. Inheriting such a mess was an embarrassment in itself. Going from place to place and trying to piece together what his cantankerous old relative had been involved with was a special brand of torture. Having to admit his ignorance of what were now his own business deals over and over again was worse than a whipping.

And he hadn't had time to shift in what felt like forever. As he closed his eyes, he waited to see the wide, blue expanse of sky materialise in his mind just as it did every night, reminding him that no shifter could ignore the other side of himself forever.

No blue skies appeared, just a pair of brown eyes, staring back at him with that perfect look of submission. Ori's mottled brown hair was a mess, as if someone had taken a firm grip on the strands at some point, and they'd never quite settled into place since.

As Raynard's mind's eye drew back, his attention trailed down the fledgling's frame, and his body started to react to the sight. His hand had been resting idly against his stomach, now it slid down toward his cock.

Flight wasn't the only thing he hadn't had time for. Raynard opened his eyes, but the temptation to set that right didn't ease. A glance up at the shadow hanging to the right hand side of the bed, and it doubled twice over.

The bell pull's cables led down to the servant's quarters. Ori wasn't stupid. When he heard the bell, he'd realise he was being summoned and follow the paths in the dust like a good servant. He'd soon find his way to Raynard's room, to his bed.

Raynard closed his eyes. The image of Ori couldn't compare to having the actual man there, but if it was all he could permit himself without turning into something as contemptible as the bastards at the nest then…

Raynard stroked his fingers slowly up and down his shaft. His touch was barely more than a tease, but the image of Ori standing in the nest wearing nothing more than that skimpy pair of shorts, still had him quickly hard.

In his private little fantasy, he saw Ori hook his thumbs into the waistband and push the shorts slowly down his legs. He glanced up at Raynard as he stepped out of them, just a little bit shy now he was completely bare before him, hard cock exposed for his inspection.

He stepped forward, coming closer to Raynard, before losing his courage a few feet away from him. An approving nod was all the encouragement he needed to close the last of the gap between them. Ori lowered himself to his knees and glanced up at Raynard through his lashes.

"How may I serve you, sir?" The words were whispered very softly, full of submission and the simple hope that he'd be allowed to display how much he wanted to please his master. And in this version of the world, that is what Raynard would be, not his employer, but his master.

Raynard gasped as he finally wrapped his hand properly around his cock, cocooning the sensitive skin within his palm and fingers. Still keeping his movements slow, he kept most of his attention devoted to the fantasy playing out in his mind.

As Ori stared up at him, waiting patiently for his answer, Raynard watched an image of himself step forward and bury its hand in the fledgling's hair, making the messy strands follow the route his grip created for them and wiping away any previous lover's touch.

A little gasp escaped from Ori as Raynard guided his lips to the tip of his cock, but there was no hint of reluctance. Ori nuzzled gently at his shaft, rubbing his face against his crotch before lapping enthusiastically at the head.

Raynard's free hand tugged at the bed sheet as the image in his mind tightened its grip on Ori's hair, dragging him even closer.

More of his shaft slipped into Ori's mouth. A pleased little sound surrounded the tip with vibrations, sending sparks of pleasure shooting through him as Ori lifted his hands to rest them on Raynard's flanks.

Raynard tightened his hand around his cock as he imagined Ori sucking greedily around him.

The fantasy version of Ori kept its eyes closed, seeming to savour the taste on his tongue. Raynard stared down, watching his shaft disappear into the boy's mouth, then reappear, slicked with saliva as Ori pulled back only to quickly dive down to suck him back past his lips again.

Raynard's hand guided the fledgling's movements, but as Ori blinked his eyes open and looked up, there could be no doubt that he was exactly where he wanted to be. He whimpered his own pleasure as Raynard slid farther into his mouth and strengthened his grip on Raynard's sides, as if he was fighting against the temptation to reach down and take himself in hand.

Rocking his hips, Raynard pushed his cock against his

palm as pre-cum leaked down his shaft, slicking his strokes. It wasn't a hot willing mouth, but inside his head, he saw each perfect detail as Ori held his head still and let him thrust between the thin, pink line of his lips.

Mentally lifting his gaze an inch or two, Raynard let his eyes meet Ori's. He came, hard and fast, arching off the mattress as his cum spilled against his stomach. He worked his shaft more frantically than ever as white-hot pleasure raced through him, coaxing every ounce of bliss out of each available moment until he finally collapsed back against the bed.

His hand was still wrapped around his cock, turning sticky as his semen dried, but Raynard kept his eyes closed as he watched the image of Ori pull away from him. A shy little smile touched Ori's lips as he remained kneeling before his master, waiting to see if it would please Raynard to give him permission to come, too.

No expectations, no demands, just a simple trust that his master would take care of him and see that the right decisions were made for both of them.

Raynard blinked open his eyes and stared at the ceiling. He didn't look at the empty bed beside him before he let his eyes fall closed again and allowed sleep to creep into the corners of his mind.

* * * * *

By the time Raynard stepped through the kitchen doorway the following morning, he'd put all fantasies firmly out of his mind. Ori was his servant; Raynard was his employer, nothing more.

Raynard stopped short on the outskirts of the room and checked his wristwatch. It was indeed early in the morning — at least by his standards. Apparently, ducklings favoured a different brand of timekeeping. Ori had obviously been up and working for several hours.

The scent of freshly brewed coffee floated across to Raynard, as if it had noticed him in the doorway and couldn't wait to make very good friends with his taste buds. Ori was apparently far less aware of his presence.

The boy had found a scrubbing brush somewhere, and was on his hands and knees making good use of it on the far side of the kitchen.

"Good morning."

Ori spun around to face him as he scrambled to his feet. Heat rushed to his cheeks as if Raynard had walked in on him doing something secret and shameful.

The sight of the boy blushing did nothing to help Raynard keep the thoughts that had remained with him through most of the night at bay. He really was a pretty little thing when his submission came to the fore.

Turning his attention pointedly away from Ori, Raynard looked around the room. It was barely recognisable as the shadowy space they'd walked through the previous night.

"What time did you get up?"

Ori glanced at the wall above the countertop. The clock hanging there proclaimed it to be ten past two. No doubt it had been declaring the same time for weeks.

"I'll see if I can fix it, sir."

Raynard turned his attention back to Ori. "It probably only needs to be wound. There should be a key somewhere."

"Yes, sir," Ori murmured.

Raynard ran his eyes over Ori's body again. The clothes he'd worn when he left the nest were already more than a little worse for wear. "You've been working hard."

Ori glanced up at him, his eyes full of confusion, almost as if he thought Raynard was joking.

It wasn't the boy's fault he'd been thrown in the middle of such a mess. Raynard reached out to ruffle Ori's unruly mop of hair in gentle praise as he made his way past him.

Ori tensed, obviously expecting a blow. He blushed

when he received the exact opposite. He soaked up Raynard's approval the way only a true submissive could.

As Raynard approached the coffeemaker, Ori took half a step forward, then hesitated.

"You're allowed to speak," Raynard offered.

"I wasn't sure how you take your coffee, sir. I found some sugar, but…"

But any milk left there would have gone bad weeks ago. "Black's fine. No sugar."

Turning away from the machine once he'd reassured himself that it was in far better order than most of his uncle's possessions, and probably wouldn't explode on Ori any time soon, Raynard sat down at the kitchen table.

"Fetch a cup for yourself too, if you want one."

Having an order to follow seemed to help Ori settle his nerves. His hands were steady as he brought the coffee to the table—just one cup.

"Thank you." Raynard nodded to a chair opposite him.

Ori perched cautiously on the very edge of the seat.

"Tell me what your duties were at the nest."

"To follow whatever orders were issued to me, sir."

Raynard studied Ori carefully. "Did Hamilton speak to you about what you would and wouldn't be expected to do, what orders other men were permitted to give you?"

Ori shook his head. After a second's silence he offered, "Mr. Hamilton said permanent arrangements and specific duties will be discussed when I become a fully-fledged shifter, sir. Until then…"

Raynard took a sip of his coffee. It burned his tongue, but he swallowed it down regardless, eager to wash away the bitter taste the eagle's actions left in his mouth.

Hamilton was responsible for what happened to any *shifter* in the nest. He obviously hadn't stooped to take care of a mere fledgling who didn't have a species to call his own. Tempering his anger as best he could, Raynard pushed the matter aside to deal with at a later date and focused in on more immediate concerns.

"As you've probably noticed — my uncle's house lay empty for some time before I arrived. Even when he was alive, he obviously didn't see that it was properly maintained. It'll take a great deal of work to set the building in order."

Ori nodded very earnestly at the pronouncement. "Yes, sir."

"You don't appear to be afraid of hard work." Raynard let his eyes travel around the kitchen again, allowing Ori to see that he was very pleased with his first impressions of him.

Ori dipped his head a little, obviously unused to even such mild approval.

"Find a pen and some paper. Make a list of the supplies you think you'll need in order to make a start on those tasks that need to be completed most urgently."

"Yes, sir." He sounded confident enough about his ability to do that.

Picking up his coffee, Raynard rose from his chair. Ori stood too.

"When you're done with the list, come up to the study. It's just off the hall — follow the trails in the dust and you shouldn't get too lost."

"Yes, sir."

Raynard walked away, back up to his study. The prospect of sorting through yet more of his uncle's jumbled pieces of paper was hardly appealing, but he couldn't help but be aware that it wasn't just his destination that made him less than inclined to leave the kitchen. There was something curiously fascinating about the man who occupied the servants' quarters which made Raynard eager to study him further.

When he heard a soft knock on his study door an hour later, Raynard was more than ready to put his paperwork aside and resume his observations of the boy. "Enter."

Raynard forced himself to keep his attention on the last page of the document he was reading as Ori stepped into the room and walked across the grubby carpet to stand in front of his desk. When he finally looked up, Ori looked far less happy to see Raynard than Raynard felt to see him.

Raynard bit back the smile that had tried to creep onto his lips. "Ori?"

The boy remained silent for a second, then — "I broke one of the other coffee cups, sir." He rushed the words out so quickly, it took Raynard a few seconds to untangle them and straighten them out into a sentence that made sense.

From the way the duckling's Adam's apple bobbed, Ori seemed to think the breakage was some sort of hanging offense. He stared at the empty coffee cup on Raynard's desk as if worried it might leap up and try to take some sort of caffeine fuelled vengeance on behalf of its fallen brethren.

Raynard leaned back in his chair and studied Ori carefully. "I'm assuming it didn't happen while you were juggling them or pitching them across the room?"

If nothing else, the question convinced Ori to lift his eyes and meet Raynard's gaze.

"No, sir...?" he hazarded.

"Accidents happen — providing they don't occur through carelessness, they won't get you into too much trouble with me."

Ori moved his weight from one foot to another, obviously doubting Raynard's decision would stand the test of time.

"Ducks aren't generally known for their hand-eye coordination," Raynard pointed out, as patiently as he could manage. "Neither are fledglings for that matter. When you're fully fledged, you may well find your limbs far easier to control."

Ori smiled, just a fraction, but Raynard saw real relief rushing through him. There was no need to ask if he'd have been punished at the nest. His expression said it all.

"Did you make out the list?"

"Yes, sir."

Raynard held out his hand for it.

Ori passed it across the desk without a word.

A brief scan down the slightly crumpled piece of paper and Raynard was satisfied that Ori knew what he was doing. Much to Raynard's relief, it appeared his new charge wouldn't need to have his every move mapped out for him.

Opening the top drawer of the desk—the only drawer in the entire house that he'd managed to empty of inherited jumble and refill with his own belongings, Raynard took out a credit card and offered it to the boy.

"The pin number is four-five-four-three."

Ori stared at it as if he'd never seen a piece of plastic before, or perhaps as if it had never occurred to him that anyone would trust a servant with such an item.

"I'm visiting my uncle's lawyers later this morning. I'll drive you into town, and you can pick up enough to get started."

"Yes, sir."

Raynard waved his dismissal to Ori. Turning his attention to the spider's web of jottings that were apparently his uncle's only written record of a business deal that had run into the millions, he nodded to himself.

A servant who was capable of putting the house in order without constant observation would take one thing off his own list of concerns.

Yes, of course, a sarcastic little voice piped up in the back of his mind. *That is the only thing you're interested in using the boy for.* Raynard rubbed at the furrow between his eyebrows. He really would have to find a few hours in which to do more than paperwork...

* * * * *

By the time Ori had been under his protection for a few days, it seemed to Raynard that everything had fallen into a simple but effective routine. It generally centred around

Raynard making sure he remembered the difference between what he was permitted to do to the image of Ori while he lay alone in his own bed, and what he was allowed to require of the actual man the rest of the time.

Still, Raynard was starting to believe he had quite a good read on the boy. When Ori came to stand before his desk and appeared to be even more wary than he usually did when arriving there on his own accord, Raynard had no doubt what brought him there.

"Did you keep the pieces?"

"Sir?"

"From your expression, you don't think whatever's been broken will be easy to replace."

Ori blushed, but he shook his head.

"There's something else you want to speak to me about?" Raynard prompted when Ori failed to speak up of his own volition.

Ori stared silently at Raynard's desk for a few more seconds. His eyes rested on some paperwork, but he seemed to be more interested in getting his thoughts in order than reading a boring business contract upside down. "You said my duties here would be the same as they were at the nest, sir," he finally said.

"Broadly," Raynard allowed, relaxing back in his chair to study Ori more comfortably. He was wearing the clothes that Raynard had selected and purchased for him—black trousers and a white shirt of discreetly good quality. The simplicity suited him well, even if the way he was standing, with his hands in his pockets, didn't show the tailoring to its best advantage.

"At the nest..." Ori faltered. "I mean, some of the other shifters who visited the nest...some of the..." He took a deep breath. "There are other ways I could be serving you, if you wanted me to, sir." He risked a brief glance up.

Raynard caught Ori's gaze and held it. There was no doubt what he was suggesting. The only question Raynard had was whether Ori had picked up on his attraction to him and felt some sort of submissive need to accommodate it, or if he simply assumed that any man who took him into his household would wish to use him as a whore.

"You're not at the nest now," Raynard said, choosing each word with care. "That sort of service isn't required here."

Ori looked down. Fresh colour rushed to his cheeks. "I didn't mean any disrespect, sir. I just thought…"

Raynard nodded. Ori stopped trying to explain himself. He shoved his hands deeper into his pockets, pushing his shoulders up, making him look even younger and less sure of himself than ever.

"You're not in trouble," Raynard reassured, as gently as he could muster — which admittedly wasn't very, right then. "You may go back to your duties."

For the first time since he made his offer, Ori seemed to breathe. "Yes, sir."

He backed away from the desk. He had to take one of his hands out of his pockets to open the door. The front of his trousers didn't settle into place the way Raynard expected. His hands hadn't been the only thing altering the line.

Talking about servicing his master hadn't just made Ori nervous. It had made him hard.

Suddenly, there was one more potential explanation for the offer and it quickly expanded to push all alternatives out of Raynard's mind. It was just possible that Ori's offer hadn't been made for his employer's benefit. Staring at the door Ori had closed neatly behind him on the way out, Raynard soon found his own fly in much the same, tented state.

By the time a few more days had passed quietly between them, Raynard had become used to staring at doors Ori had left through, trying to work out exactly what to think of the boy. He'd also become accustomed to looking forward to seeing Ori when he arrived home after another day doing ever more frustrating battle with his uncle's lawyers and business associates.

He never knew exactly what the little fledgling would have achieved while he was gone, but seeing Ori blush when he was offered even the tiniest scrap of praise inevitably eased Raynard's mood.

As he walked into the house that particular day, a little over two weeks after Ori had come to serve him, Raynard heard a noise emanating from the library. A nudge had the door swinging silently open. Ori had obviously been to work on it, eliminating the squeaks and creaks from the hinges.

Raynard paused in the doorway, staring intently across the room. It wasn't quite what he had come to expect from his rather shy little duckling, but it was one hell of a 'welcome home, sir'.

Chapter Three

Ori made his way slowly down the library ladder. Balancing the heavy box of books awkwardly on one forearm, he kept a firm grip on the mahogany rail with his free hand as he descended. Some of the books he'd collected looked old and valuable. It wouldn't do to fall and drop them.

Stepping off the narrow wooden rungs, Ori flexed his bare feet against the rug that covered the floorboards in that corner of the library. Even as he relished standing on the more comfortable surface, he frowned.

He'd been so sure he'd got the fire established properly this time.

Placing the box of books carefully on the library table, he turned to the fireplace.

A blaze was still flourishing in the huge hearth. It hadn't gone out again. Yet a cold draft still swirled around his ankles. Ori's frown deepened. Raynard would never be able to use the room comfortably while—

"Hello, Ori."

Ori spun around. Raynard stood in the doorway, his expression unreadable as he took in every detail of the scene before him.

"You're back early!"

It sounded like an accusation, as if Ori didn't think the man had the right to walk into his own house whenever he damn well pleased. Ori mentally cursed himself for letting the words slip out, but it was too late to drag them back.

As Raynard continued to stare across the room at him, his reaction became easier to interpret. He looked amused rather than angry. That was good. Raynard's gaze left Ori's face and travelled down. That wasn't good.

There was nothing submissive about the way Raynard lowered his eyes. Ori's brain finally snapped into action. He brought his hands in front of himself to cover his crotch. It didn't feel like enough, especially not when being in the same room as Raynard tended to have a quick and noticeable effect on his cock.

Even as embarrassment rushed to Ori cheeks, blood hurried to his shaft, encouraging it to stiffen and rise for Raynard.

Raynard finished his leisurely inspection of Ori's body. Their eyes met again. Ori quickly looked away. With every moment that passed, he expected to be dismissed so he could fetch his clothes, but no order came.

Finally, Ori cleared his throat. "With your permission, sir?" Incapable of moving his hands in order to make any other sort of gesture toward his escape route, he nodded toward the door. "I'll fetch my clothes."

Raynard leaned against the doorframe, apparently in no mood to let Ori leave. "Where exactly are your clothes?"

"In the butler's quarters, sir."

"And you're not wearing them because…?"

Ori swallowed. After the fool he'd made of himself by offering Raynard the kind of service he obviously wasn't interested in receiving from him, Ori could hardly blame Raynard for thinking that he'd intended him to walk in on a naked man and change his mind. He shuffled his feet as a fresh wave of humiliation coursed through him.

"Ori?" Raynard prompted.

"The dust, sir. It's easier to…"

"Easier to wash the dust off your body than your clothes?" Raynard finished for him. He took a step forward.

Ori managed a jerky nod in response. The clothes Raynard had bought him were all perfect tailoring and expensive material. They had to have cost a small fortune. There was no way he'd have been able to keep them in good condition if he started cleaning in them. His simple solution had seemed so logical until a few seconds ago.

Raynard strolled closer still. Ori forgot how to breathe. Somehow, he found himself holding Raynard's gaze as the hawk closed the gap between them. Raynard stopped, barely a foot away.

Ori had to tilt his head back to keep their eyes locked.

Raynard stroked his thumb down Ori's cheek. It came away smudged with dust.

Ori dropped his gaze to stare down at the digit, completely mesmerised.

"A few days ago, you came to my study."

There could be no doubt which visit he was referring to. "Yes, sir," Ori whispered.

"Because you thought you should, or because it was what you wanted?"

His gaze now fixed on the third button of Raynard's shirt, Ori found himself entirely incapable of making words happen.

Raynard touched his face again. Sliding a knuckle under Ori's chin, he guided him to tilt his head back.

"I guess what they said in the nest was true, sir," Ori blurted out, as he realised there was no way he'd be allowed to walk away from the conversation without answering the question. "Head down, arse up is a natural position for a duck."

Raynard said nothing, but his touch lingered under Ori's chin, trapping him exactly where he wanted him.

"I'm sorry, sir. I shouldn't have...I know none of the men in the nest who...I know none of them have your rank, sir."

"You think that's why I failed to take you up on your offer, because I consider you to be beneath me?"

Ori swallowed. It was hard to think of two avian species that could be farther apart in the hierarchy. It was equally hard not to picture himself physically pinned beneath

Raynard's body when Raynard used that phrase. Ori's cock stiffened further behind his hands, as if desperate to push his fingers out of the way and show off for the hawk.

Glancing up, Ori tried to ready himself to hear the worst, but Raynard still looked vaguely amused. Ori dropped his gaze again. His attention fell on Raynard's fly. The material was pulled taught by a very obvious erection. Ori's eyes snapped back up to Raynard's face.

"You were right when you thought my decision had something to do with rank. Hawks are raised to respect their servants — not to take advantage of those who they take under their protection. I don't order my servants to my bed, Ori."

"Yes —" Before the honorific could leave Ori's lips, Raynard moved his knuckle up to rest against Ori's mouth. Ori's lips had been slightly parted. Raynard's knuckle now settled between them, not allowing him to open his mouth to speak, but not permitting him to bring his lips back together either.

"A submissive, however," Raynard mused, apparently more to himself than anyone else. "That would be a very different matter. Do you know the difference between a servant and a submissive, Ori?"

Ori shook his head, just a fraction. His lips moved against Raynard's knuckle, making him desperate to kiss it properly.

"A submissive doesn't simply offer to obey another man's orders and do his bidding — he truly belongs to his master, and his master may do anything he wants with him, *anything*." His knuckle slid a little farther into Ori's mouth. "His master doesn't just have a right to make use of his submissive's time and his skills. He owns him. Body. Mind. Soul. Everything."

Ori whimpered.

"A servant has rights that a submissive can't lay claim to. A certain degree of freedom. Some level of privacy. The chance to shape his own life and make a great many decisions on his own behalf. Some men find it hard to give up such rights."

Raynard's knuckle seemed to fill Ori's physical world, just as Raynard's words filled his head. The temptation was too great. He ran his tongue over it.

Raynard smiled slightly. Emboldened by that, Ori looked up and met his eyes. There was a light shining in them that Ori had never seen before. Raynard moved his knuckle slightly, seeming to encourage Ori's attentions to it.

Ori sucked cautiously against Raynard's skin. His eyes dropped closed as the taste of Raynard seeped into his mouth.

"There's no shame in being another man's submissive, Ori. But if you're not truly suited to it, if it doesn't call to something deep inside you, I'd imagine it's little better than torture."

Ori whimpered as he tried to suck Raynard's finger deeper into his mouth. Without any warning, the digit was taken away.

Ori blinked open his eyes. Raynard was still studying him very carefully.

Raynard tilted his chin up. His voice changed. It lost it's considering quality and became all brisk and business-like. "Make your choice, fledgling. What are you to be—a servant or a submissive?"

Ori could barely breathe, let alone think. He had to swallow rapidly before he could make his throat let words through. "Whatever—" He stopped short when he saw the look in Raynard's eye.

"Whatever your place in my house, if I ask you to make a decision, I expect you to make it."

Ori took a shaky breath. There was really no choice to be made. There was only one answer he could possibly want to give. "Submissive, sir."

Raynard didn't smile, but the light in his eyes grew brighter. In some way that Ori didn't really understand, he sensed that he'd pleased Raynard, that he had pleased his master. Closing his eyes for a moment, Ori relished the possibility.

"When you've finished your work here, join me in the study."

"Yes, sir."

Raynard took a step back. Ori remained perfectly still as he waited for Raynard to leave the room, but the hawk merely stood there, less than a yard away from him. He raised an eyebrow as if asking what Ori was hanging around for.

Ori hesitated. "Shall I fetch my clothes, sir?"

"No." It was a simple statement of the way things were going to be. No room for argument existed.

Very slowly, Ori nodded his understanding.

In theory, he knew he hadn't been wearing a great deal when he'd served at the nest. The shorts hadn't hidden much. But he'd have given anything to be wearing them at that moment.

Standing before Raynard, with his hands still covering his erection, Ori found himself frozen in place. He couldn't move.

Raynard didn't stir either.

It was one thing to say he wanted to be Raynard's submissive, to say he'd obey any order Raynard issued. It was quite another to do it. And as he stood there, Ori knew this was his first test.

A servant would be permitted to fetch his clothes. A submissive was not. He took a deep breath as the differences between the two titles made themselves felt inside his head for the first time.

Tension poured into Ori's body. Every joint ached. Each muscle cramped. If Raynard had told him to get on his knees, it would have been so easy. It was the idea of calmly returning to his duties while Raynard was clearly able to see how he affected him that made the breath catch in Ori's throat and threaten to choke him.

Looking up, Ori met Raynard's eyes one more time. He

held his gaze as he finally managed to drop his hands to his sides.

"Back to your duties," Raynard ordered again.

Ori turned away from him. His legs threatened to give way as he picked up a box of books and carted it the rest of the way across the room, but he made it.

Raynard's eyes tracked Ori's every action, trailing over his bare skin. His hands shook with the effort it took to keep working rather than stop and cover himself. A few minutes passed before a movement out of the corner of his eye made Ori look over his shoulder.

Raynard nodded to him, just once, turned and left the room.

Resting his hands on the table in front of him, Ori closed his eyes and tried to make his head stop spinning. Relief at pleasing Raynard glowed inside him, but with it came a kind of fear he'd never really felt before, a terror that Raynard's approval wouldn't last forever, that it would be all too easily lost and that once that happened, he'd never be able to get it back.

Taking a deep breath, Ori tried to turn his attention back to his work. He looked around the library, desperately trying to focus in on the task at hand. It was a stunning space, or it would be once it was put in order.

Books had been pushed haphazardly onto the shelves wherever they would fit—and shoved into gaps where they didn't really fit. Dozens still lingered in boxes, while some of the shelves remained empty. There was several weeks' worth of work to be done in there, fitted in around his day-to-day duties, but Ori couldn't help but hope that Raynard might be pleased with the finished result.

Half an hour later, Ori straightened a pile of boxes. Then he straightened them a fraction more, until they couldn't possibly be any straighter. The simple fact was the tasks he had assigned himself for that day were complete. He no longer had any excuse to linger in the safe solitude of the library.

Taking a deep breath, Ori turned toward the door leading out of the library — the one that would take him back to Raynard, to his master. Looking down his body, Ori bit his lip. He was still as hard as ever. He shouldn't really face Raynard as he was. Not just erect, but covered in dust too.

It wouldn't take him long to rush down to the servants' quarters and jump in the shower. A cold shower would solve all his problems. A hot shower and a hand slicked with shower gel would be an even better solution.

Ori stepped into the hallway and looked toward the door leading down to his quarters. His hand tightened into a fist at his side as he fought against the urge to take refuge there. If Raynard had wanted him to shower, that's what he'd have ordered him to do. Raynard didn't forget to mention things like that.

It didn't matter if he'd lived in Raynard's house as a servant or as a submissive. Ori knew him well enough to know that, if he'd wanted him clean and presentable, Raynard would have ordered him to be that way.

Ori's bare feet made no sound on the freshly scrubbed hall tiles as he walked across to Raynard's study door and tapped tentatively on the dark, panelled wood.

"Enter."

Ori opened the door just wide enough to slip inside the room. Raynard's attention remained on his paperwork for a few seconds. Ori closed the door behind him and stood to one side of it, waiting for Raynard, for his master, to recognise his presence.

His master. The term rushed to Ori's cock even as it wrapped around him and made him feel strangely safe.

Finally, Raynard looked up. He ran his eyes over Ori from tip to toe, taking in every detail — dust smears, erection and everything else. It was all Ori could do to keep his hands at his sides.

"Come here."

Ori stepped forward.

Before he could reach the spot where he usually stood, directly in front of the desk, Raynard turned his chair and looked pointedly at the floor just in front of his feet.

Ori altered his course. The next order was obvious. He dropped to his knees in front of his new master. Raynard made no complaint about that, but when Ori reached for his fly, he found Raynard's hand wrapped tightly around his wrist, stopping him short before he even had a chance to unzip him.

He should have waited for permission. All at once, that was obvious. Ori looked down, mentally cursing himself for letting his stupidity ensure Raynard's possession of him would now begin with a whipping rather than a blowjob.

"Don't get ahead of yourself, fledgling."

Ori kept his gaze on Raynard's feet. When Raynard released his wrist, Ori let his arm drop down and hang idly at his side. He stayed very still then, unable to do anything more than exist until his master's next order hit the air. He hadn't stumbled across a whip when he'd been cleaning the house, but he had no doubt there'd be one somewhere. His time at the nest had taught him that much. There was no such thing as a high ranking avian who didn't own a whip—who didn't know how to use one on any lower ranking shifter who was foolish enough to displease him.

"Look up."

It wasn't the command he'd expected, but Ori still obeyed it. His eyes met Raynard's. For a long time, Raynard held Ori's gaze, and Ori found it impossible to look away.

When Raynard finally turned his attention elsewhere, he reached into his desk drawer and picked up a narrow black box. Ori kept his body motionless, but he couldn't stop himself following his master's movements with his eyes. The box was far too small to contain a whip. Raynard opened it. A black leather collar lay against the crisp white lining.

Ori stopped breathing.

It was a simple item—no more than an inch wide and decorated with nothing more flamboyant than a simple silver buckle and a circular tag. It was impossible for Ori to make out the engraving on the tag, but he knew what would be there. He'd seen more than a few collared men come and go at the nest.

One side would declare *Property of Mr. Frederick Raynard*. The other would show his master's rank as a hawk. It would give whoever wore it the protection of that rank.

"You understand what a collar means between avians?" Raynard asked.

Ori opened his mouth, but quickly closed it again, just in time to stop himself from giving the worst possible answer. A second later, he found the right response. "Yes, sir."

"Tell me your first instinct."

Swallowing down his nerves, Ori forced himself to utter his original answer. "Mr. Hamilton said that collars are only for men who knew who they really are, sir—shifters who know what sort of avian they will become when they're fully fledged."

"Do you have any doubts that you'll become the kind of avian whose species makes him suited to wearing another man's collar?" Raynard asked, seriously.

Ori shook his head.

When he looked up, he saw a tiny smile twisting Raynard's lips. "Neither do I."

Ori found himself smiling back. Relief rushed through him as Raynard's acceptance flew through his veins.

"Nevertheless," Raynard said, his expression once more unreadable. "The collar will be removed when you go in front of the elders to complete your first full shift. You'll be given a free choice over if you wish to retain it after everything is certain."

"I will want to, sir," Ori blurted out.

"Then," Raynard corrected. "Not now. For now, all you need to be sure of is that you wish to wear it until then."

"Yes, sir." No answer had ever been easier to give.

Raynard took the collar from the box. The leather slid through his fingers as if he'd been handling the material his entire life. A shiver ran along Ori's spine as the collar encircled his neck for the first time. His master's knuckles brushed against his skin as he fastened it in place and slipped two fingers inside it to check the fit, just the way Ori had seen humans check the size of a new puppy's collar.

A slight colour made its way to Ori's cheeks with the comparison. But the knowledge that he now belonged to Raynard in every way there was, went swiftly to his cock.

Ori hadn't thought it was possible for him to get any harder. He'd been wrong. He could barely hold back a whimper as his cock begged for attention. A few strokes would be all he needed.

He quickly swallowed down the desire for his own pleasure. His new collar moved around his throat, reminding him of Raynard's dominance over him. He had a master now — there was only one man whose enjoyment he should be thinking of.

Lifting his eyes, Ori looked to his master, hoping Raynard might have changed his mind about allowing him to go down on him.

"Go to your quarters. Clean yourself up."

"Yes, sir." Pushing aside his disappointment, Ori rose very slowly to his feet. He kept his hands by his sides through sheer force of will as he felt his master's eyes track his progress across the room.

As he closed the heavy wooden door behind him, Ori let out a breath he hadn't even realised he'd been holding. His hands rushed to his crotch, hiding his erection even though there was no one else in the hallway.

Looking down his body, Ori stared at the back of his dusty hands. Just because Raynard wasn't there to see him, that didn't mean he could forget how his master wanted him to behave.

His limbs fought him every inch of the way, but somehow, Ori managed to bring his hands down to his sides. His cock curved proudly up toward his stomach, begging for attention, the only part of him not embarrassed by his own enthusiasm.

Ori took a deep breath. If Raynard didn't want him to cover himself, the best way he could serve his master was to get used to that fact as quickly as possible. He refused to let his hands creep back to hide his erection.

His fingertips went to his collar instead. It felt good around his neck, a solid reassuring reminder of Raynard's ownership of him. Ori smiled to himself as he turned his attention to Raynard's next order.

Down in the servants' quarters, he quickly made his way into the little bathroom off the butler's bedroom and turned on the shower over the tub. As soon as the spray reached a comfortable temperature, Ori tipped back his head, letting the warm water saturate his hair and cascade down his body.

A shudder ran through him as rivulets caressed his aching shaft. Eyes closed, he stood very still. He wasn't going to come just from the feel of the shower. He wasn't.

Ori took a deep, gasping breath. Water trickled into his mouth as he fought for control. His hand went to his collar again. The leather was wet. His fingers slid over it. Hooking the digits between his neck and the buckle, he tugged gently at it. A whimper escaped from the back of his throat as his imagination turned the sensation into something that could only be produced when his master attached a lead to the collar and called him to heel with it.

Blinking open his eyes, Ori stared down his body. The fingers of one hand still hooked into his collar, he was helpless to stop his other hand going to his cock. There was no thought of hiding his erection now.

From the first moment his hand touched his shaft, his hips refused to stay still.

Ori.

A chiding note crept into Raynard's voice as he said his name. Ori didn't have his master's permission to move that way.

As he closed his eyes once more, a mental picture of Raynard standing next to him, staring down at him, filled his mind. His master's hand replaced reality. Ori bit back a moan as he fought for breath under the pounding water.

Stay still, and I just might let you come.

Pleasure made Ori weak. Releasing his hold on his collar, he reached for the wall in front of him to steady himself. His palm slipped against the wet tiles. He tried to adjust his footing in the bottom of the bath, and almost stumbled. A shiver ran through him despite the heat and steam that swirled around the room.

"That's enough."

For a second, the words seemed no more real than any of the others Ori had 'heard' his master say since he stepped under the shower. Very slowly, reality reasserted itself.

Spinning around, Ori came face to face with his master in the flesh.

Raynard stepped further into the room. All Ori could do was stare as Raynard reached the edge of the bathtub.

"Come here."

Ori's feet took over. He stepped forward, out of range of the shower, out from behind the clear glass partition that separated it from the rest of the room.

Raynard took hold of Ori's wrist. Suddenly, Ori realised that his hand was still wrapped around his cock. Fresh embarrassment rushed to his cheeks. He tried to snatch his hand away more quickly, but Raynard's grip ensured Ori moved at exactly the speed his master chose and no faster.

"As of this moment, only one man's hands touch you."

Ori swallowed.

"Answer me."

"Yes, sir."

"You don't jack off. You don't touch your cock. You don't come without my permission—no exceptions."

Eyes once more fixed somewhere around the third button of Raynard's shirt, Ori nodded. "Yes, sir."

Raynard slid his other hand into Ori's hair. Strong fingers tugged at the wet strands, pulling his head back. Ori lifted his gaze. His eyes met his master's eyes.

Raynard had no reason to be pleased with him, but Ori saw no evidence of annoyance in his expression. The light he'd seen in his eyes earlier was still there.

"I'm sorry, sir," he whispered, fear and uncertainty combining to turn the words throaty and hesitant.

Raynard raised an eyebrow. "For doing something that I've never forbidden you from doing?"

Ori wasn't sure what to say. He tried to lower his gaze, but Raynard tugged his hair again and made him look up.

"Now that I *have* forbidden it, I expect you to follow the order."

"Yes, sir."

Raynard released both Ori's wrist and his hair, and took a step back. Ori once more dropped his arm to hang idly at his side.

He had to fight against the urge to cover himself as Raynard ran his eyes over him from top to toe once more. Ori lowered his gaze. He wasn't attempting an inspection of his own, but it was impossible to miss the fact that, behind his nicely tailored trousers, Raynard was just as hard as he was.

"May I serve you, sir?" Ori whispered.

Raynard looked up from his inspection. When Ori would have spoken again, unable to bare the silence that grew between them, Raynard stopped him short with a shake of the head. "I'm going out."

Ori looked into the adjacent bedroom and his clothes. "Shall I—?"

"Alone," Raynard cut in.

Ori quickly dropped his gaze again, trying not to let

Raynard sense his disappointment. It was silly to think that the collar would have really changed anything between them. He might have become a submissive rather than a servant, but he was still a duck rather than a hawk. Raynard was his master. It wasn't Ori's place to assume an invitation to follow him around wherever he went. It was stupid to think the collaring could be as important to Raynard as it was to him.

"Shall I lay your clothes out for you, sir?" Ori offered, as emotionlessly as he could manage.

"That won't be necessary."

"Yes, sir." Ori mentally fumbled around for something else he might be able to offer Raynard, but found nothing.

Raynard brushed his knuckle against Ori's cheek. When Ori looked up, an amused little smile was twisting Raynard's lips. "There are some places you can't follow me just yet, fledgling." He looked past Ori to the small window in the corner of the bathroom. There was no view as such. All that could be seen was a wall and a patch of sky above it.

Sky.

"Oh..."

Raynard chuckled. He ruffled Ori's sodden hair before he stepped back. "Finish up."

He didn't leave the room. When he'd said that a submissive couldn't assume he would be granted any privacy, Ori hadn't realised that could mean he'd be provided with an audience at such unexpected moments. He turned his attention back to his shower, but his hands didn't seem inclined to cooperate. The soap, the shampoo, everything jumped out of his hands. It took a lifetime of scrabbling around in the bottom of the bath to retrieve all the things he dropped before the last of the dust that had coated his body was washed away and he could turn off the water.

His towel hung on a hook next to the bath. Resisting the temptation to hide his still flourishing hard-on with it, Ori rubbed at his hair.

Within a few minutes, he was as dry as he was going to

get. He glanced across at Raynard.

"Follow me."

Ori hesitated next to his clothes as they walked through his bedroom toward the kitchen.

Raynard glanced over his shoulder. "Move a set of clothes to the coat closet in the hallway so you can dress before answering the door. I expect you to appear dressed in front of everyone except your master."

Ori swallowed. He was going to have a permanent hard on walking around naked in front of Raynard all the time. No, Ori mentally corrected himself, that wasn't quite right. He was going to have a permanent hard on *that he had no chance of hiding*. That would be the only real difference. It wasn't as if he didn't find Raynard as erotic as all hell when he was dressed.

A glance at Raynard and Ori realised he was waiting for a response. "Yes, sir."

Apparently satisfied, Raynard nodded and led the way up the stairs. They reached the hallway and continued up the main staircase and along a corridor on the upper floor. Opening a door that looked no different to any of the bedroom doors, Raynard revealed another corridor, far narrower than those in the servants' section of the house.

The floor was shrouded in an even thicker blanket of dust than the rest of the house had been when Ori first arrived. Cobwebs hung in the corners. As he followed his master, Ori automatically added items to his list of jobs that would have to be attended to when his daily duties allowed.

At the top of yet another set of stairs, the narrow space opened up considerably. A huge dormer window looked out over the garden. Ori stepped toward it. There was a small balcony on the other side of the glass, concealed from the neighbouring houses by the steeply pitched roofs on either side of it.

"Open the window."

Ori did as he was told. It was too big to really be called

a window. It was more like a door — taller than Ori and several feet wide. As Ori opened it, cool evening air poured into the room, caressing his bare skin.

Fabric rustled behind Ori. Tearing his gaze away from the view, he turned around.

Raynard was undoing his shirt. For a second, all Ori could do was gape, until Raynard looked pointedly at the far corner of the attic room. Ori followed his gaze and spotted a rail where several empty coat hangers lingered.

Rushing forward, Ori picked up one. Raynard handed him his shirt. With clumsy movements, his eyes still feasting on the slowly emerging view of his master's body, Ori placed the shirt on the hanger. By the time he'd returned it to the clothes rail and retrieved another hanger, Raynard was already kicking off his shoes.

Ori knelt at his feet to take them away. He was still kneeling there when Raynard began to undo his belt. Ori froze, staring up his master's body, but the hawk's gaze was fixed firmly on the window and the sky beyond it. He obviously had other things on his mind. A blowjob wasn't a priority. Ori carried his shoes away and put them beneath the hanging clothes. Raynard's socks and underwear were soon folded on top of them, and his trousers were on a hanger.

Removing his watch, Raynard handed that to Ori too. Raynard's attention never once wavered from the sky and, while he showed no interest in looking in Ori's direction, Ori found that he was free to run his eyes over his master's body as much as he pleased without any fear of being caught.

Each line of muscle stood out beautifully in the evening half-light. Ori watched, mesmerised, as Raynard stretched.

Arching his back, Raynard lifted his arms and rolled his shoulders. His fingers brushed against the sloping ceiling. Ori bit his bottom lip, desperate to reach out and touch, but lacking the courage.

The tension that was always present in Raynard's movements seemed to fade away before Ori's eyes. The dwindling sunlight flooded over his skin as he stepped toward the window.

"The window stays open until I return."

"Yes, sir," Ori managed to rasp out.

Raynard looked over his shoulder at him then. A slight smile played around his lips, as if he was party to some amusing little joke the rest of the world would never understand.

"Shall I wait here for you, sir?" Ori whispered.

Raynard shook his head. "No. Go back downstairs."

"Yes, sir."

Raynard stepped through the window and onto the balcony. One moment a fully-grown man stood looking down into the garden. A second later, a beautiful goshawk perched on the balcony railing, feathers shimmering in the light.

Ori's mouth dropped open. In some way he didn't understand, it was as if there had always been both a hawk and a man there, but the picture of the man had faded back until the hawk became the only image he could see before him.

Ori stepped forward.

The hawk turned its head toward him. The look in Raynard's amber gaze still had the power to stop Ori in his tracks.

Then, without any warning, Raynard was away — swooping down over the garden. Wings extended, he quickly regained height to soar out over the town. Flinging himself onto the balcony after his master, Ori leaned against the railing, eyes open very wide as he traced the hawk's movements. It circled effortlessly over the city, barely seeming to flap its wings. All too soon, it disappeared from view.

When Ori dropped his gaze, his grip on the balcony turned white knuckled, his stomach turned over as he saw how high up he was. He quickly returned his attention to the sky as he stepped back from the balcony's edge and closer to the security of the house.

Once safely inside, Ori couldn't help but study the sky again. His master was out there.

Ori had his orders; he knew that. He was to go back downstairs. Raynard didn't want him to wait there for his return. Ori absentmindedly ran his fingers over his collar and caressed the silver tag hanging from it. It was what his master wanted that was important now, not his own wishes. Reluctantly, Ori turned away from the sky and did as he was told.

Chapter Four

To a hawk flying high over the city, Raynard Lodge was barely more than a dot—just one speck out of the thousands that littered a landscape that stretched all the way to the edge of the world. Raynard glided in swooping circles through the evening air. With his hawk instincts pulled to the front of his mind, it was impossible for him not to consider everything within his field of vision to be his own personal territory and every man who lived there to be his property.

Yet, even with everything in this domain to admire, Raynard kept finding his attention drifting back toward his uncle's house. Even in flight, it was all too easy for Raynard to conjure up a mental image of his new submissive waiting patiently for his return.

A tiny tilt of the wings and he found himself circling back to the house, for all the world like a damn homing pigeon who couldn't resist racing back to the boy.

The balcony came into view. After so many weeks in human form, Raynard's landing was nothing short of embarrassing. He completed his shift a second too soon. His human feet materialised several inches above the wooden boards.

He landed heavily, only just gaining control of his hands in time to reach out, brace himself against the balcony railing, and stop himself from tumbling into a messy heap on the moss coated surface. The world spun as Raynard glared into the gloomy little room on the other side of the window. Ori, obedient little duckling that he was, hadn't lingered there to see his master make a fool of himself.

Raynard bowed his head for a few minutes, filling his

body with deep lungfuls of air as he fought to push his mind back into an entirely human shape. Hawk or human, he still found his thoughts full of one man.

Stumbling away from the balcony, Raynard headed off in search of his fledgling.

Legs which thought they would be better off pulled up tight against his body while his wings took the strain, were not well suited to stairs. It was more luck than judgment that got him to the ground floor in one piece. When he caught sight of light shining from beneath the library door, Raynard was happy to avoid the awkward little staircase that led down to the servants' area.

He pushed open the library door, his hands still clumsy and uncoordinated after his shift. The heavy wood slammed into the bookcase behind it.

Ori spun around. The book he'd been lost in fell from his hands and landed on the hearth rug. His eyes opened very wide as he saw Raynard standing in the doorway.

Raynard stepped forward. Ori remained frozen in place, not even blinking as Raynard closed the gap between them with slow, deliberate steps. Stopping barely a foot away from Ori, Raynard looked down at the book Ori had been so fascinated by.

"I wasn't reading it, sir," Ori rushed out. He dropped to his knees for a moment and picked up the book. As he rose, he turned to put it on the shelf.

Raynard's reactions were still as fast as a true hawk's. He had his fingers wrapped around Ori's wrist before the duckling had pushed the book halfway into the gap left between its neighbouring volumes.

Ori hesitated, but when Raynard guided his hand away from the shelf, Ori didn't try to leave the book behind. He turned the cover toward Raynard for his inspection.

I wasn't reading it, sir. As if he'd been caught committing some horrible crime.

"Don't lie to your master."

Ori swallowed. "It won't happen again, sir."

Raynard shook his head. That was wrong—Ori was promising to avoid the wrong thing. "When you've completed your duties, you may have free use of the library—unless you're foolish enough to lie to me again."

"Yes, sir." Ori glanced up at him, apparently pleased with the permission, even if he was rather confused by it.

With his head still full of flight and the sensation of air rushing beneath his wings, Raynard knew he was in no condition to make sense of Ori's idiosyncrasies.

Ori looked down. For a moment, it looked like a simple expression of his submission. Then, Raynard followed his gaze. His impatience hadn't allowed time for clothes. Ori wasn't the only avian naked and incapable of hiding his reaction to the man standing before him.

Ori's gaze caressed Raynard's flourishing erection. When he dragged his attention up to Raynard's face, an offering was clear in his eyes. Raynard wanted to come, and Ori was obviously more than ready to serve him in whatever way would please him best.

There was just a hint of nervousness mixed into Ori's expression. "At the nest, they taught me to... I do know what I'm doing, sir," he whispered, as if he thought he might have to beg for the privilege.

Raynard hadn't believed there was anything that would make him stumble before claiming his new submissive that night, but the softly spoken words were a very effective trip wire.

He could easily imagine the kind of lessons Ori received at the nest. The boy was such a gentle soul, and he'd probably never received a single kind touch from any man when he was at the club.

Raynard released his grip on Ori's arm. Stepping forward he rested his fingers gently on Ori's jaw line. Tilting Ori's head back, Raynard brushed their lips together in a kiss as tender as any hawk could ever bestow upon another man.

Ori gasped against his mouth. His lips parted. Raynard ran his tongue against them, tracing a line along the sensitive skin. When he pulled back, Ori's eyes were closed, looking for all the world as if it was his first kiss.

It couldn't have truly been that, but Raynard's possessive side still bayed its joy at the idea. Ori opened his eyes. He stared up at Raynard, wide-eyed and impossibly innocent.

It took every scrap of self-control Raynard possessed to step away from him, to get his instincts under control and have his inner avian tethered, hooded, and perched on a mental gauntlet.

Another few steps back. Raynard sat on one of the overstuffed leather armchairs that Ori had unearthed from beneath the dust covers.

"Bring the book with you," he bit out.

Ori did as he was told, a slight frown marring his normally smooth brow as Raynard lost all ability to mellow his voice.

A cushion rested on the neighbouring chair. Raynard snatched it up and dropped it on the floor by his feet. "Sit."

Ori lowered himself onto the cushion and crossed his legs beneath him. He didn't look away from Raynard once.

"Start reading where you left off," Raynard ordered.

"Sir?"

Raynard looked impatiently at the book on Ori's lap. Ori followed his gaze. Opening the book, he looked up at Raynard again, before cautiously starting to read aloud.

The words were tentative, but that didn't matter. The most confident rhetoric in the world wouldn't have registered with Raynard right then. Closing his eyes, he forced himself to concentrate on each meaningless syllable, to push his human side to the fore and try to understand what was being said. It was important to be able to understand human words and ideas when dealing with a man like Ori.

Raynard knew he'd been right to stretch his wings

before doing anything with the boy. His mind, as it slowly regained its humanity, was clearer than it had been for months. Opening his eyes, Raynard found Ori peering up at him.

The words were still flowing. Every few seconds, Ori dropped his gaze to scan another sentence, but he quickly lifted his eyes again to stare damn near worshipfully up at his new master. The syllables faltered as their eyes met. Ori parted his lips and flicked his tongue out to moisten them. No further words emerged.

Raynard knew that his mind was as human as it was going to get that night. There was only so much that words could do to push a hawk's instincts away, and they did nothing at all to temper a dominant man's predilections. Seconds ticked past. Raynard continued to stare down at Ori, unable to hide his fascination with him.

Ori swallowed and Raynard sensed the nerves building rapidly inside him.

"Scared, fledgling?" he asked.

Ori dropped his eyes to the book. He nodded, just one jerky little movement. "But only because I think you might send me away without allowing me to serve you, sir," he whispered after a moment. He nibbled at his bottom lip as if he immediately regretted his moment of daring.

Raynard quickly caught the sensitive bit of skin between his thumb and forefinger and took it out of range of Ori's teeth. Ori's tongue brushed against his fingertip.

Raynard didn't pull away. Ori wrapped his lips cautiously around the top knuckle of Raynard's finger. A moment passed. Neither of them moved. The world hung in the moment, wings spread, riding the air currents.

Ori looked up at Raynard, his eyes full of need — to be accepted, to be owned, to be allowed to serve and please his master. It seemed to come so naturally to him. Raynard supposed that was because it actually did.

It was as hard to imagine a dominant duckling as it

would be to picture a submissive hawk. Raynard smiled slightly at the idea. Ori caught the expression and immediately reflected it back, his lips caressing his fingers with the movement.

Raynard took his hand away from Ori's mouth. Winding his fingers into Ori's hair, he pulled him forward a little. Ori's eyes sparkled with relief as he moved onto his knees and leaned closer of his own volition.

Raynard tightened his hold on the fledgling's messy hair. Ori stilled, surrendering all control of his movements to Raynard as he gradually guided him nearer.

Ori opened his mouth in expectation. Raynard brushed the head of his cock against Ori's lips and feasted on the sight of him, so willing, so eager.

Raynard rocked his hips. The tip of his cock disappeared into Ori's mouth, and Ori quickly formed his lips into a firm seal around the girth of his shaft. Ori's eyes dropped closed, and he made no attempt to hide how he savoured his first true taste of his master's cock.

Raynard could almost believe the little fledgling was imprinting on him—creating a mental vision of him inside his head which went beyond simple thoughts and senses and cut right down to the very instincts that made a submissive what he was.

Ori whimpered gently around Raynard's cock.

There was no guile in him. Whatever he might have done or what he may have been taught in the nest, Raynard had no doubt that, as Ori knelt at his feet, every reaction he offered him was the simple truth. There could be no doubt Ori was exactly where he wanted to be.

Ori dipped his head and tried to take more of Raynard's shaft between his lips. Tightening his grip on Ori's hair, Raynard stopped him short.

There was only one man who could ever be in control of what happened between them. Ori couldn't be allowed to think that task fell to the duckling in the relationship. Ori opened his eyes. He seemed to understand. Raynard relaxed his hold a little as he guided Ori closer – at the pace Raynard chose.

Ori moved easily with his hand, tenderly working Raynard's shaft as more of the length slid between his lips. As Raynard pulled him back a few inches, a touch of uncertainty made it into Ori's eyes. He was obviously afraid his treat was going to be taken away.

Raynard said nothing. He just tugged Ori closer again, feeding his cock back into his mouth. A moan of pure pleasure surrounded Raynard's shaft. No words were necessary.

Ori placed his hands on Raynard's sides in an effort to balance himself. They were nothing like the soft, fluttering hands of the humming birds that had knelt before Raynard in recent years. These were a working man's hands, a service sub's hands – strong and calloused by enthusiastic servitude.

Raynard guided Ori's head up and away from him again. No fear now, Ori's expression was all eager anticipation at being dragged back in toward his master. Perfect, wet heat caressed Raynard's cock with each movement, sending waves of pleasure racing through his veins. He let even more of his shaft slide between Ori's lips, until the tip touched the back of his throat.

No panic, no hesitation, Ori accepted everything Raynard was willing to offer him as if it was a gift he was truly blessed to receive.

A dexterous tongue laved the head as Raynard let Ori move far enough away from him to fawn over the very tip of his cock for a little while, but Raynard soon tired of the teasing. He pulled Ori lower over his lap, quickening his movements, letting the friction of a hot willing mouth slide against his cock from tip to base. For just a little while, Raynard stopped worrying too much about Ori and simply let his body take its pleasure from him.

"That's right," he whispered.

The snippet of praise pulled a murmur from Ori. He

tugged at Raynard's hold on his hair and dipped his head lower. Raynard's cock slipped into his throat for the first time.

Raynard held him there, permitting no retreat. Ori looked up at him, wide-eyed and glorious. There was no way he could breathe with Raynard's shaft filling his throat, but there was no sign of panic in his eyes. He stared up at Raynard, trusting and perfect, and he didn't pull back until Raynard tugged gently at his hair. For a moment, Raynard's cock slipped from between Ori's lips.

Panic flashed, sudden and frantic, in Ori's eyes. He immediately bobbed his head back down toward Raynard's erection. A tightened grip on the messy, mottled strands stopped him short once more.

Unable to reach Raynard with his lips, Ori extended his tongue and licked the pre-cum leaking from Raynard's cock-head. Perfect. Unable to wait another second, Raynard finally released his grip. Ori sucked his way back down his shaft as if he had been born to serve another man that way.

Ori's fingers dug into Raynard's sides as he held onto him more tightly. He seemed to be trying to encourage Raynard to move.

Raynard resisted Ori's attempts to coax him into thrusting forward, but it was impossible to ignore the bliss Ori's mouth offered. Left to his own devices now, Ori worked him fast and feverish, whimpering with need as he seemed to try to beg an orgasm out of him.

Raynard tipped his head back as blistering pleasure rushed through him. He couldn't help but thrust forward. His cock slid even farther into Ori's mouth as his climax stole all the oxygen from the world. Ori's reactions were quick. He pulled back, just far enough to catch the full taste on his tongue, as Raynard came into his mouth for the first time.

Ori swallowed, his throat working rapidly as he took everything Raynard was willing to feed to him. Pleasure flew through Raynard like the rush of air beneath his wing feathers as he twirled and danced high in the evening sky. Every muscle, every fibre in his body gave up all objectives bar the simple processing of bliss.

As Raynard finally collapsed back against the seat, his mind went blank. Eyes closed, it was easy to believe the entire world had ceased to exist, until the sensation of someone gently suckling on his softening cock tenderly called him back to reality.

Raynard opened his eyes, but Ori's remained closed. His lips were thinned into a narrow pink line as he cradled his master's cock in his mouth and caressed it with his tongue. Ori didn't protest when Raynard, too sensitive to really appreciate his continued service, nudged him away.

The little fledgling knelt on the cushion at Raynard's feet with his eyes closed and his breathing ragged. One last time, Raynard threaded his fingers into Ori's hair. Pulling him forward, Raynard prompted him to rest his forehead against his leg while he got his breath back. The invitation earned Raynard another pleased little murmur from Ori.

Taking a deep breath, Raynard dropped his head back to rest against the high cushioned support of the chair. Everything he'd told himself about remembering to let his hawk side fly more often was pushed aside by the knowledge that there were even more important needs a man couldn't fail to ignore. A master couldn't ignore his submissive.

When Raynard lifted his hand from the back of Ori's head, Ori hesitatingly looked up at him. His own needs were written plainly in his expression. Raynard didn't doubt that, if he looked farther down Ori's body, he'd see hard evidence of the fact. Ori would be just as turned on as he had been most of the day, and more desperate to come than ever.

Raynard smiled slightly to himself. *Not yet.*

Standing up, Raynard stretched to his full height. His body was all sleepy satisfaction now, content to rest easy after sating its desires for both flight and everything else.

Ori stayed on his knees, staring up at him.

"Stand."

Ori obeyed. His movements were more than a little clumsy, which Raynard expected. But there was also a stiffness in his actions, which betrayed that all wasn't well in Ori's world.

Raynard ran his hands over Ori's shoulders, working his fingers into the deep layers of muscle. They were knotted with far more than frustrated desire.

"Sore?" Raynard asked.

Ori swallowed. "I'm fine, sir."

Raynard frowned. Perhaps it was time to think of adding another servant to the household. "Your work has been—"

"It's not that, sir!"

Raynard raised an eyebrow at the unexpected interruption.

Ori hesitated, but pushed on. "It just happens sometimes, sir."

Raynard ran his hands over Ori's shoulders again, testing the muscles as they moved beneath his fingers.

Ori was right about one thing, it wasn't his work that was the problem. Ori was merely going through the same process as every other shifter who was approaching his full avian maturity. Resting hadn't helped ease Raynard's growing pains when he was Ori's age. It was unlikely to help Ori now.

Raynard nodded to himself and added a new item onto his mental to-do list, but he was surprised just how relieved he was to be able to hold off on getting another servant and keep the boy to himself a while longer.

He was about to turn away from Ori and make his way up to his bed when he remembered just how inexperienced a submissive his little duckling was. Tucking a knuckle under Ori's chin, Raynard made him look up. "You remember the orders I gave you earlier?"

"Yes, sir." Ori's voice was hoarse and roughened by desire for his own release. A touch of colour rose to his cheeks, but there was no lack of understanding there.

Raynard nodded, satisfied that in spite of his obvious need, Ori would follow the command not to come by his own hand.

"Good boy." Raynard offered him an approving nod before leaving him to switch off the lights, damp down the fires and retire to his own bed below stairs.

* * * * *

Raynard glanced to his side as he stopped the car at a set of traffic lights. Ori sat next to him, calmly watching the world go by through the passenger side window. If he was at all curious or concerned about where they might be going, he hid it well. Raynard smiled slightly to himself. There might be some things his fledgling needed to work on in the future, but giving up control of any and all decisions to his master wasn't one of them.

Ori chose that moment to glance in his direction. He immediately echoed Raynard's smile, apparently delighted by the simple fact his master was pleased about something.

About ten minutes later, Raynard pulled up outside a leisure centre. Ori glanced at the sign above the door, but made no comment. He got out of the car when Raynard nodded for him to do so, and followed Raynard into the building without a word. Ori only hesitated when they reached the changing rooms and Raynard handed him a towel, along with a pair of swimming trunks.

"Sir?"

"You know how to swim?"

Ori nodded.

"Get changed."

Ori did as he was told, quickly stripping out of the clothes he'd put on just before leaving the house and squirmed into the tight black swimsuit.

Soon, the only thing Ori wore, apart from the speedos,

was his leather collar. Raynard reached out to remove it. Ori jerked away from him. For a second, Raynard thought that Ori was worried that his raised hand meant a blow. But no, the look on Ori's face made it clear that had he realised exactly what Raynard had been about to do. His instinctive aversion to the idea of losing his collar had apparently got the better of his manners.

Ori peered up at Raynard, his eyes full of pleading. Raynard held his gaze, offering no response. Ori swallowed rapidly. Dropping his gaze, he finally stilled and accepted Raynard's decision. Within seconds, the buckle was undone and the leather gone. Ori's neck was only bare for a moment before Raynard had a thick silver chain fastened in its place.

Ori looked up, his expression full of both relief and confusion.

"Chlorine and leather don't mix," Raynard explained. And public displays of Ori's submission wouldn't mix well with humans who couldn't be trusted to understand what a collar really meant between avians either.

Ori nodded. He ran his fingers over the silver chain as if to reassure himself it was just as substantial as his usual leather collar. He found the tag and nodded again. "Yes, sir." Ori put his clothes neatly in one of the lockers, along with his towel. When Raynard indicated he had no inclination to take it from him, Ori fastened the elastic band holding the locker key around his ankle.

Raynard nodded toward the door leading through to the pool. "Go on."

Ori didn't go so far as to speak up and question Raynard's order, but he did look at Raynard's clothes as if wondering when Raynard intended to change.

"Hawks aren't known for their love of water, duckling. I'll be up on the balcony," Raynard informed him, only just resisting the temptation to usher him on his way with a sharp tap on the arse. But, no, it wouldn't do to send him out there with an erection testing the elastic on his speedos.

Once Ori had left his sight, Raynard made his way out of the changing rooms and up the stairs. A wide gallery ran the whole length of the pool, with tables and chairs set up at regular intervals so spectators could watch the swimmers in comfort.

There weren't many people venturing into the water at that early hour of the day, and there were even fewer people watching them. Raynard took a seat at the table with the best vantage point. He was just in time to see Ori approach the pool and lay claim to a lane no one else was using.

Settling his toes on the tiled edge, Ori took a slow breath and peered into the deep water as if it contained the answer to every question in the universe. Then he looked up. Raynard saw Ori's gaze travel along the length of the balcony rail as he looked for his master. When Ori found him, one nod was all the encouragement he required. Ori no longer needed to ask anything of the sparkling blue depths.

Ori's dive was the most graceful movement Raynard had seen him make. He cut through the water as if he'd been born there and was merely returning home. Long, powerful strokes took him to the far end of the pool. Disappearing beneath the water, he tucked himself into a tight ball, spun around and pushed away. He glided for several yards before his head broke the surface and he raced down the length of the pool again.

Raynard relaxed in his seat. There was no sign of all the tension that had been building in Ori's muscles now. It wasn't flight, but for an avian who was destined to be as at home on the water as he was in the air, it seemed to be as close an approximation as Raynard had hoped it would be.

Another length, then another, and Raynard watched as Ori seemed to lose himself in the simple pleasure of feeling his body turn weightless in the water.

As he stared down at Ori's lithe, muscular frame cutting through the water, Raynard let his mind wander back toward his own recent flight. Did it feel the same for Ori as it had for him, when he'd eventually made it back into the air after so long trapped on the ground?

By the time Ori finally stopped at the edge of the pool, over an hour had passed. From his vantage point, Raynard watched Ori pull deep lungfuls of air into his body. He'd pushed himself hard. It took him a few minutes to catch his breath while his head remained bowed over the edge of the pool.

Suddenly, he looked up. A hawk's vision let Raynard easily spot the question in his eyes. Some of Ori's recently discovered peace left him. He was obviously concerned his master would be angry with him for spending so long there.

Raynard let Ori see his approval shining down on him. As quick as ever to echo his emotions, Ori's expression morphed into a stunning smile—more carefree then than Raynard had ever seen him.

He gave Ori another hour to soothe his muscles in the pool before he finally beckoned him away from the water to join him upstairs.

Ori was out of breath when he arrived at Raynard's table, his hair more than a little damp and his cheeks flushed. He obviously hadn't dawdled on his way back to Raynard's side.

Tapping the leg of the opposite chair with his toe, Raynard pushed it away from the table. Ori took the hint and sat down.

"Feel better?"

"Yes, sir." He looked down for a moment, as if not sure what to make of the question now that he'd uttered his automatic response. It seemed as if he had been so busy enjoying himself he hadn't noticed the pain slip from his joints.

"The aches will start to fade away once you achieve a full shift," Raynard promised.

Ori looked up at him through his lashes.

"You're allowed to speak," Raynard reminded him,

when Ori failed to say a single word of his own volition.

"Most of my foster parents said they were just growing pains, sir."

Raynard considered the statement. "Broadly speaking, they were right—the avian version. Your body is preparing itself to be able to shift properly in a few months' time."

Ori nodded.

Raynard pushed the tea he'd bought for the fledgling a little closer to him.

"Thank you, sir." Ori wrapped his hands around the mug.

"Did any of your foster families know you're a shifter?"

Ori stared at his tea. "The Greens were the last family I stayed with, sir. Mrs Green encouraged me to find out one way or another."

"And you did that by?" Raynard asked, as he suddenly realised that he had no idea how an avian raised among humans would do that.

"I went to a doctor. She did blood tests. They showed I'm an avian, but they can't distinguish between species."

Raynard remained silent.

"Once I knew, I started trying to research things." He frowned at his tea. "Humans don't know much about..." He sighed. "I found out there were nests, but that was about it. I approached a few of the nests, but most of them are..." He rubbed the back of his neck.

"Species specific?" Raynard suggested, guessing that he'd landed in breeding colonies.

Ori nodded. "Finally, a woman at one of the nests that didn't want me, directed me to the Anderson Nest. She said it catered to all avian men, regardless of species." He sipped his tea. "It sounded perfect. I guess it was. I mean, they let me stay."

Raynard tightened his grip on his own cup of coffee. The less he thought about Ori's treatment at the nest the less likely it was that he'd want to kill someone. He cast around for another topic.

"You said you had foster families plural?"

Ori nodded. "Seven altogether, sir. I...I wasn't very good at fitting in." He blew gently on the surface of his tea before taking another sip. "I don't know if it's because I'm not really... Maybe it was just me..." He forced a smile. "The clumsiness didn't help... There was always something that would break, then I knew it wouldn't be long before the social workers would be sent for to take me back."

There was a wistful tone in his voice that clawed at something inside Raynard. As changes of topic went, his choice had been bloody awful. Ori didn't say anything else as they finished their drinks. Raynard wasn't sure what to say either. Finally, he stood up and it was impossible to let the silence linger any longer between them. "Come on, fledgling. Time to go home."

Ori smiled up at him, as if Raynard had somehow chanced to say the perfect thing. Raynard ruffled Ori's hair as he stepped past him. For the first time, Ori didn't flinch at all at the sight of a raised hand.

As he made his way out to the car, Raynard found himself feeling rather pleased with himself as well as his submissive.

Chapter Five

Ori stepped reluctantly away from the huge window. He'd already lingered in the attic room for far too long as it was. Raynard had given him permission to go down to the main part of the house, and Ori had been living under his roof for more than long enough to know that permissions and orders were merely the two sides of the same coin.

He should have gone back to the library an hour or more ago, but somehow, he hadn't quite been able to bring himself to leave the shadowy, little attic space. Even now, Ori couldn't drag his gaze away from the sky. Every so often, he saw a brown dot that just might have been his master, circling high above the house.

Stretching his wings, Raynard called it. Ori took a deep breath and let it out very slowly. He knew what kind of mood "stretching his wings" put his master in. He'd be inclined to tease when he finally returned and came to the library in search of him.

When he stormed into the room, Raynard would call him to sit at his feet and read to him. And with every word he said, Ori would get more and more nervous, more and more desperate for Raynard to want them to do more than merely sit. But Raynard would still make him wait until he was given permission to set the book aside and find a better use for his mouth than reading aloud.

For a moment, Ori managed to turn away from the window, but a second later, he looked helplessly back through it. It had been several lifetimes since Raynard had decided Ori didn't have permission to come via his own hand, and in that moment, Ori felt every second of that time pressing down on him.

Part of him was aware that it had probably been far less than a month since his last climax, but it was impossible for him to be certain.

He wasn't sure what date he'd been brought to his master's house, when he'd been given his collar, or even what day it was right then. Living with Raynard had a simple rhythm to it. Dates weren't important when everything could revolve seamlessly around Raynard leaving the house and coming home, when everything could be decided by what Ori's master was doing and how Ori might best please him at any given moment.

Ori smiled joyously into the evening air as his hand crept up to stroke his collar. It was a good way to live a life. Pulling himself away from the window, he finally forced himself to leave the room.

Down in the library, he'd barely picked up a book and lowered himself to his favourite place on the hearth rug when he heard a footfall on the stairs. As usual, after his flight, Raynard hadn't bothered with inconvenient human things like clothes. He strode into the room, as naked as Ori—or maybe even more so, since he didn't have a collar.

Ori stared across at him, as mesmerised as ever.

"Good book, fledgling?"

Ori swallowed, but he couldn't even tear his eyes away from Raynard for long enough to glance at the title.

Raynard's usually immaculate hair was disordered, windblown and wild after his flight. But what caught Ori's attention was the look in the hawk's eyes—something truly feral flashed there in a way it never had before.

Instead of moving to his usual chair, Raynard flung himself carelessly onto one end of the leather sofa opposite the fire, all long limbs and perfect lines of muscle. "Answer the question," he snapped.

The book... Ori managed to look down at it. "It's one I've read before, sir," he stuttered out.

Raynard's eyes narrowed, his attention focused on Ori the same way a true bird of prey might stare down at some small, furry animal scurrying around in the undergrowth — or perhaps at some scared little duckling, sitting vulnerable on the edge of the lakeside.

"Come here."

Ori stood up.

"Leave the book."

Crouching down, Ori set the volume carefully on the rug before stepping forward.

A cushion rested on the floor by the side of his master's usual chair. No similar level of comfort existed next to the sofa. Ori lowered himself to the bare floorboards, but his knees had barely touched the well-polished wood before Raynard spoke again.

"No, up here."

Ori looked up. Raynard's expression was still unreadable. All Ori could do was obey and hope his obedience pleased Raynard in some small way. He sat on the edge of the sofa, not sure what to do with himself, not sure why his master had suddenly invited him to share the same piece of furniture.

Raynard slid his fingers into Ori's hair and pulled him forward. All of Ori's confusion vanished as Raynard guided his head down toward his lap. Ori licked his lips, as eager as ever to wrap them around Raynard's shaft.

The grip Raynard had on his hair wasn't painful, but it was firm. He was definitely going wherever his master took him, and suddenly Ori found his face turned toward Raynard's stomach rather than his cock.

Bent over in an awkward position, Ori hesitated. Putting his hands out, he attempted to steady himself. He tried to look up and gauge what Raynard wanted him to do, but the angle made it impossible to see Raynard's expression properly.

"Pull your feet up."

Ori clumsily obeyed and found himself lying on the sofa, his head resting chastely against his master's body as Raynard sat upright. Raynard took his hand out of Ori's hair. When Ori would have tried to sit up, a sharp little tap on his backside stopped him short.

Shock enabled Ori to twist his head just far enough to be able to look up. Raynard stared back down at him.

Lack of permission to move was the same as an order to stay still. Ori understood that now. He froze, not even moving his eyes, until Raynard looked away and silently freed him to drop his gaze.

Ori's mouth was barely an inch away from his master's abs. Raynard had to feel his every breath. As he stroked down Ori's back, Raynard had to sense the tension in him, too.

"I asked you about your book."

Ori swallowed. "Yes, sir."

"Tell me about the part you read while I stretched my wings," he demanded.

Ori closed his eyes. "I…"

Raynard slid his palm back up Ori's spine. His hand was strong, his touch unyielding. It seemed to creep under Ori's skin and possess parts of him that he'd never even known about until he met Raynard.

Raynard's fingers caressed their way down to Ori's arse again. No tap fell against his skin, but Ori tensed in expectation of one. Desire to feel his master's hand fall on his backside warred with the need to have Raynard pleased with him until he found he had no idea what he really wanted.

"I only read a few lines, sir. I only stepped into the library a moment before you." He looked up, fearing the worse.

Raynard smiled his approval. "The word hawkeye exists for a reason. Did you really think I wouldn't spot you lurking by the window?"

Ori scraped up a shallow breath, forcing air into lungs that didn't seem to remember how to work on their own.

Raynard's smile didn't fade as he looked down Ori's body again. He stroked the curve of Ori's arse, back and forth, again and again, making his skin tingle, until Ori had to fight with himself in an effort not to arch his back and push his arse more firmly against Raynard's hand.

Raynard's smile broadened, as if he knew what his teasing was doing to Ori, as if he liked knowing just how well he held him in the palm of his hand — not just physically, but mentally.

Raynard slid his fingers between Ori's thighs. One fingertip brushed against Ori's hole, pulling a gasp out of him.

Raynard replied with a chuckle, a warm rich sound Ori had hardly ever heard in all the time he'd spent with Raynard. Heat rushed to his cheeks.

Raynard brushed the knuckles of his other hand across the flushed skin. "I'm right to call you a fledgling, aren't I, Ori?"

Ori dropped his gaze, not sure what the right answer should be. For a horrible moment, he thought Raynard was going to pull away from him, that he'd regret inviting him so close, that he'd send him away thinking him too foolish and inexperienced to serve him.

Turning his head, Ori pressed a desperate kiss against Raynard's skin. Raynard stroked Ori's hair in a brief moment of praise before he turned his attention back to the rest of Ori's body.

Cheeks still warm, Ori helplessly rubbed his face against Raynard's torso. Wriggling forward, Ori instinctively tried to get even closer to him. More of his bare skin brushed against Raynard's, and he found himself surrounded by Raynard's presence. The feel of his flesh, his scent, everything about Raynard called to him, wrapping around him, like a hundred different collars embracing every part of his skin, every part of his being.

And he needed to come so badly...

Ori was sure that shouldn't have been his main

concern. Whatever his master desired was far more important than anything he wanted could ever be. He knew that in a way he'd never really understood anything else. He knew it in the same way he'd known he didn't really fit into any of the human families that had fostered him.

He hadn't belonged there—he belonged here, with Raynard—with his master. It was stupid to think about his own petty concerns when he was finally home, safe with his master. But he needed to come so badly…

A frustrated little whimper escaped from the back of Ori's throat. He lifted his hand to cover his mouth, but Raynard's fist wrapped around Ori's wrist before his hand was halfway there.

Ori looked up, his eyes opening very wide in sheer disappointment with himself. "I'm sorry, sir. I…"

Raynard placed Ori's hand back on the sofa, precisely where it had rested before. He wanted Ori to stay still. Ori closed his eyes and concentrated on obeying that order, but movements kept creeping past his self-control. Raynard's corrections weren't harsh. He simply rearranged Ori, putting him back where he wanted him to be. Ori still felt pain rush through him each time his position needed to be adjusted, knowing he had let Raynard down.

Any sounds he was unable to hold back were received rather differently. Raynard never tried to discourage them. If anything, he seemed to repeat those actions that caused Ori to moan and whimper all the more often.

Raynard played him like a virtuoso, coaxing sounds out of Ori that Ori would have never believed existed inside him until he heard them. He squirmed helplessly under Raynard's touch, feeling even more of his master's skin move against his body until he finally felt his cock brush against Raynard's leg. Ori's eyes snapped open. He gawped at his master, and at the position he now lay in.

Without ever intending it, Ori had somehow travelled farther and farther up the sofa with every minute of teasing

Raynard had layered upon his skin. His torso now rested over Raynard's lap, and his arse was tilted up—offered to Raynard to tease, to spank, to do with as he pleased.

Ori saw the amusement in Raynard's eyes. He saw the desire in them too and had no idea if he should retreat or not. Raynard had corrected any movement that displeased him—that much Ori was sure of. Seconds ticked past. Ori relaxed slightly as he realised that he *couldn't* actually be where he was without his master's approval. Permission was just another word for a command. He was exactly where he should be.

Raynard ran his hand over Ori's backside again, palming the firm, round muscle. His touch disappeared for a moment, before falling back against his skin. The spank was light and sent tingles and warmth through Ori's skin rather than pain. Every tendril of heat rushed straight to Ori's cock as he helplessly rocked his hips, shamelessly rubbing his erection against Raynard's leg.

Raynard's hand fell again, still light and more of a tease than a real spank. Then again, no harder than before. Slowly, methodically, his hand made contact with every square inch of Ori's arse, coating the skin with layer upon layer of heat and frustration.

Whimpering and squirming, Ori prayed for more. When Raynard lifted his hand away from his backside and didn't immediately bring it back down, Ori held his breath waiting for the first real blow.

Raynard's hand came down, but it was gentler than ever. Resting his palm against Ori's arse, Raynard used his fingertips to tap out an unfamiliar rhythm on the fullest part of the muscle. It was as if Ori was nothing more to him than a convenient place to rest his hand while he was deep in thought. But it didn't matter if that was all the touch represented. Pleasure danced in Ori's veins. He whimpered again.

The tapping fingers slowly moved down between his

cheeks.

Ori squirmed and spread his legs in offering. Raynard's tapping fingertips found Ori's hole, making him rock his hips even more frantically. His cock rubbed against his master's leg with every twitch of his hips, sending wave after wave of pleasure crashing through him.

Raynard's fingers ceased their tapping and slid farther down between Ori's legs to cup his balls. He palmed Ori's testicles, pulling them away from his body as he examined them. Ori's grip on the edge of the sofa cushion turned white knuckled as he fought to stay still.

His cock nudged Raynard's leg once more. Raynard wasn't unaffected. His erection rubbed against Ori's stomach as he wriggled across his lap, but there was nothing Ori could do for Raynard right then. He was trapped in a world full of sensations, unable to think, let alone serve.

Raynard pressed his thumb against Ori's hole, massaging the tight ring of muscle and the sensitive strip of skin leading down toward his sac.

Ori bit his bottom lip as he scrabbled for control. It had been so long since he'd been allowed to come, since he'd started spending what felt like every hour of the day hard and aching under his master's gaze.

Doing whatever Raynard wanted and not coming without permission became impossible. He felt the pressure building inside him, doubling over and over until...

"Come for me, fledgling."

Ever since his master had placed a collar around his neck, Ori had done whatever he was told to the very best of his ability. He didn't fail Raynard then. Arching his spine, he pushed his arse back against Raynard's hand as he came. His cum spilled on Raynard's legs as Ori writhed across his lap, his grip biting into the edge of the sofa.

Raynard continued to manipulate Ori's balls and his hole, drawing his orgasm out further and further, until Ori's frozen lungs felt like they would explode, and he was sure his heart would burst from the sheer force of pleasure pounding through his veins.

A sound escaped him as he shuddered against Raynard. Even Ori wasn't sure if it was a cry or a scream. He just knew the room sounded impossibly quiet when the noise had faded from the air. Ori slumped forward and collapsed in a broken heap over his master's lap.

Raynard removed his hand from between Ori's legs and rested it gently on his buttocks. He stroked the skin there, almost tenderly.

Ori fought for breath, control, thoughts, for anything at all. He didn't know what to say. He wasn't sure if he had permission to move or if he was to remain exactly where he was until given leave to do otherwise. So, he simply lay there in silence, more raw, more vulnerable, and more content than he'd ever believed possible.

When Raynard moved his hand off his arse some minutes later, Ori tentatively took that as an order to rise. He pulled himself awkwardly off Raynard's lap. He'd been turned half upside down for far too long. The head rush almost toppled him. Unable to lift his eyes and risk meeting Raynard's gaze, Ori dropped his eyes to Raynard's lap instead.

He'd come all over his master. Ori didn't want to believe it, but the evidence was right there on Raynard's legs. Worse still, Raynard was still as hard as he had ever been. Unsatisfied and cum-splattered, he had to regret ever bringing Ori to his home, let alone allowing him to wear his collar.

Barely holding back a mew of horror, Ori leaned forward and dipped his head, hoping to make amends in some small way.

Raynard slid his hand into Ori's hair and took a tight grip on the ruffled strands. For a moment, it felt as if he intended to drag him away but, as Ori lapped rapidly at the mess he'd made, Raynard's hold in his hair eased. His touch changed to one of acceptance or even encouragement. He allowed Ori to linger and lick up each and every drop of stickiness.

Working his way meticulously over his master's skin, Ori gave his task his full concentration, only glancing up when he'd completed it. A faint smile graced Raynard's lips, as if he was pleased with Ori for some reason.

Once the last smudge had been licked away, Ori tried to turn his attention toward his master's cock.

Before Ori's mouth could touch the hard shaft, Raynard's attitude changed. His hand dropped down to Ori's collar and he tugged him away.

Ori kept his eyes down as he waited fearfully for Raynard's verdict.

"I have other plans for you tonight."

Ori's gaze snapped up. Raynard's grip on Ori's collar kept his head tilted partially down, but it didn't stop him staring up through his lashes. The desire hadn't faded from Raynard's eyes, if anything it burned even brighter.

Ori swallowed. "Yes, sir."

Raynard let go of Ori's collar. He stood up, stepping past him and toward the door. "Come along, fledgling."

Scrambling off the sofa, Ori followed Raynard out of the library and up the main staircase. Ori had walked along the same route several times a day for weeks now. There were still rooms on the upper floor to be cleared of dustsheets and put in order, landings to be cleaned.

Even Raynard's bedroom, where dustcovers hadn't lingered for weeks, wasn't uncharted territory. The bed needed to be made every morning, the en-suite tended to. Clothes had to be collected, then returned after they had been washed and ironed. Ori had visited the master bedroom almost every day since he'd first been brought into Raynard's house. Until that moment, he'd never been in the room at the same time as Raynard.

Ori found himself hesitating on the threshold, one foot still lingering on the hallway carpet.

Already alongside the bed, Raynard glanced over his shoulder. A moment later, he turned to face Ori properly, but he didn't issue a single command. Ori had the distinct feeling he could wait forever, and no order would ever be issued.

If Ori wanted to step forward, he'd have to do it unaided. If he wanted to run away, he'd have to make that decision on his own too. The whole world hung in the balance, and he didn't even have his own physical need to help him along.

Ori lifted his eyes and met Raynard's gaze. If he went to his master's bed, it would be because he wanted to please his master and not because he wanted, or expected, to get any pleasure for himself. In that moment, Ori realised that the timing of the invitation was no accident, neither was his having been given permission to come while they were in the library.

Something settled inside Ori with the realisations. He stepped into the bedroom and closed the door softly behind him. Turning to face Raynard, he took up the post he'd been taught in the nest, standing neatly to one side of the door, out of the way, but ready to obey when called upon.

"Come here."

Ori moved forward, his bare feet silent on the thick carpet. Raynard stood perfectly still as he waited for Ori to reach both him and the bed.

Swallowing rapidly, Ori stopped, less than a foot away from his master.

Raynard slid his hand into Ori's hair, making him tilt his head back and expose his throat. Raynard's eyes had travelled over his naked skin hundreds of times before. Ori had never felt as naked as he did then.

Taking half a step forward, Raynard brought their bodies together. His erection rubbed against Ori's skin, pulling a gasp from him. With his head still held tilted back, he found his gaze caught by Raynard's eyes. He couldn't look away.

"Please." The word left Ori's lips without his permission. He wasn't even sure what he was asking for. Anything. Everything.

Raynard's lips covered his.

They'd only shared one kiss before, a brief touch of their lips that took place a lifetime ago. This was nothing like that chaste little salute.

Raynard took instant possession of Ori's mouth. There was no pretty request for Ori to invite him in. Raynard's tongue thrust past his lips as if he already had all the permission he needed to do whatever he wanted with him, and he was no longer interested in pretending otherwise.

He tightened his grip on Ori's hair even further, tugging his head back, demanding that he somehow make his body adapt to Raynard's demands, and adopt the position he wanted.

In that moment, the only thing that was important, the only thing that really existed, was what his master wanted. Ori whimpered into the kiss as he felt Raynard's dominance wrap around him more securely than ever.

Raynard moved his body against Ori's smaller frame, teasing his senses and overpowering his mind. Ori's cock tried to rise to the occasion, but it was too soon. The attempt produced more pain than pleasure, but even that rushed through his blood, feeding instincts deeper than Ori had ever been aware of possessing.

His hands scrabbled at Raynard's skin, trying to hold on to him and steady himself as he lost sight of all familiar landmarks. His brain refused to care that his master's touch felt different from other men's careless caresses. All it wanted to do was follow wherever he led.

As Raynard's hands travelled over Ori's body, rough and demanding, it was impossible for Ori to fight the confusion that filled his mind. Raynard was all strength and certainty. Ori simply gave himself up to Raynard's control and moaned his pleasure into the kiss.

When Raynard broke the kiss, his grip on Ori's hair stayed strong. He pulled Ori forward, placing Ori's ear just an inch from his lips. "In the future, when I return to the window, you'll be there waiting for me. You don't leave that room until I return. No excuses will be tolerated."

"Yes, sir," Ori managed to whisper. His grip on Raynard's arms tightened as he tried to balance himself on his tiptoes.

Raynard ran his hands down Ori's back and settled them on his arse. The taps he'd laid against Ori's skin downstairs had turned his buttocks into a mass of sensitised nerve endings. Ori squirmed under the caress, helplessly pushing his arse back against Raynard's hands.

Raynard chuckled. "Do you like being played with that way, fledgling?"

Ori nodded.

"Speak up properly when I ask you a question."

Ori glanced up and met Raynard's eyes. "I guess the men in the nest were right about that too, sir."

Raynard tensed.

Ori pushed on. "Ducks are pain sluts as well as the regular type of…" He managed a smile, but it quickly faded when Raynard failed to return it.

"You're not at the nest any more. You belong to me — no one else." His expression damn near dared Ori to try to disagree with him on the point.

Ori managed to speak on his second attempt. "Yes, sir."

Raynard hooked his fingers into Ori's collar and tugged at the leather as if he thought Ori needed to be reminded of its presence. "What other men think is irrelevant."

"Yes, sir," Ori repeated quickly.

Raynard slid his other hand down Ori's arm and wrapped his fingers tightly around Ori's wrist. "Mine."

The word was little more than a growled whisper. It still sent shockwaves through Ori's spine, rushing to his cock, which remained rather less than ready to receive all the adrenaline that flooded through him.

Raynard stepped forward. Ori stepped away in clumsy retreat. The back of his knees hit the edge of the bed. At the same moment, Raynard's support disappeared. Ori toppled onto the neatly made sheets, his hands slipping against them as he tried to steady himself.

Raynard stared down at him.

Ori pulled his feet up onto the bed and pushed himself back a little farther onto the mattress, but he made no effort to entice his master to join him. Any attempt at seduction would have been ludicrous. He belonged to Raynard. Raynard either wanted him or he didn't. All Ori could do was hope.

Raynard set his knee on the bed between Ori's feet. Ori quickly shuffled his legs farther apart.

Raynard leaned forward, his hands found Ori's wrists and pinned them to the blanket on either side of Ori's head as his body covered Ori's smaller frame.

His cock rubbed against Ori's limp shaft, teasing him with his inability to respond as the weight of Raynard's torso pinned him down. Ori whimpered his pleasure, but as suddenly as Raynard had pushed him back onto the bed, Raynard pulled away.

They remained apart just long enough for Raynard to unceremoniously roll Ori over onto his stomach. Before the room had stopped spinning, Raynard's knee was back between Ori's legs. Ori spread his thighs wide apart as he sensed his master lean away from him.

Again, their parting was brief. Raynard soon slid his hand between Ori's buttocks, his fingers slicked with lube. For all the strength Ori felt in his master's fingers, the first contact was gentle—a test, to see what Ori could take.

Ori pushed back against Raynard's fingers, consciously relaxing his body so he'd be ready to accept Raynard as soon as possible. Raynard obviously sensed his willingness. He soon had three fingers inside him, stretching him open and preparing him to take his master.

Scrabbling at the sheet beneath him, Ori did his best to trust Raynard's judgment. His master would decide what happened between them—including when Ori was permitted to consider himself ready. It wasn't Ori's place to scream that he'd been ready forever, any more than it would have been his place to complain if Raynard wanted to rush him.

Ori's cheek slid against the blankets as he squirmed. A whimper escaped. He closed his eyes and fought for control. Raynard's hands left him.

Opening his eyes, Ori looked over his shoulder. He was more than willing to apologise, to beg, to do whatever it took to regain Raynard's touch. There was no need. Raynard's body moved over his. For just one second, their eyes met. Ori quickly dropped his gaze, suddenly afraid how much his expression might reveal.

Raynard's torso slid against Ori's, layer upon layer of muscle pinning him to the bed. He caught Ori's wrists again, holding them down against the sheet.

Ori murmured his pleasure. He turned his face into the mattress and tried to silence himself as his forehead rubbed against the bed. Raynard's cock nudged against his hole, and Ori froze, held in place as much by his own instincts as by his master's grip upon him.

Raynard pushed steadily forward, slowly stretching Ori open as he slid into him. Ori gasped. His eyes fell closed. He'd taken Raynard into his mouth often enough to know how large he was, but he still found himself biting his bottom lip as his master stilled inside him, seeming to fill him more completely than any man at the nest ever could have.

With glacial speed, the painful stretch morphed into a pleasure-filled ache that made Ori desperate to feel Raynard move inside him. Still frozen in place, there was nothing Ori could do.

Raynard made the decision for him. After slowly pulling back, he thrust forward again. Trapped beneath him, Ori had no chance of gaining enough purchase on the mattress to move in a way that might complement Raynard's rhythm. All he could do was take him.

Robbed of his ability to do anything but accept, every detail of what Raynard offered him was magnified a hundredfold. Ori felt the pleasure rushing through Raynard's body; he sensed the barely controlled strength in his every movement.

Adrenaline and endorphins pounded through Ori's veins. His brain scrambled to process everything, to memorise every detail.

Arching his back as much as he could, Ori gave everything up to his master. Raynard's breaths came faster, his heart raced almost as rapidly as Ori's. His shaft seemed to swell inside Ori. Each thrust hit against his prostate, sending shockwaves to his cock and pre-cum leaking onto the sheet below him as he finally started to stiffen.

Another thrust—harder now. Raynard's grip tightened around Ori's wrists until Ori was sure there would be marks there when he woke the next morning. Raynard's body pressed him more harshly into the mattress.

A yell split the air as his master pounded into Ori with a series of sharp thrusts and spilled inside him. The room fell perfectly still then, perfectly silent—perfectly perfect.

Ori let his eyes drift closed as Raynard moved just far enough away to collapse onto the sheet next to him. The whole world seemed to shimmer with a glorious rightness that Ori had never known existed.

He had to get up and go back down to the servants' quarters, Ori knew that. But still... Just a few seconds, Ori thought to himself. He'd just rest for a few seconds...

* * * * *

Ori blinked open his eyes. Sunlight streamed into the room. For a minute, he didn't fully register what that meant. The warmth from the morning rays caressed his skin as they fell across the bed. Arching his back, he felt the soreness in his muscles, and all his memories from the previous night came rushing back to the forefront of his mind.

His master's hands on his skin, Raynard's body pinning his down against the bed. Ori squirmed against the softness of the sheet as he remembered every single sensation and relished every moment that he'd locked into his memories.

Ori looked at his wrists. Just as he expected, there were faint marks there. He blinked again and peered at the sheet his arms rested on. His sheets were blue. This one was white. He opened his eyes wider. Details of the room he lay in flooded his mind. Tension poured into him.

He turned his head. His master lay stretched out on the other side of the bed, his eyes closed, his face turned away from the morning sun's invasion of the room. He was glorious, more relaxed than Ori had ever seen him—his hair falling across his temple and his lips slightly parted.

Curse after curse scrolled through Ori's mind. Gritting his teeth, he tried to extract himself silently from the tangle of sheets. The mattress wobbled underneath him. Raynard's eyes sprang open. No trace of sleepiness lingered in his gaze. He immediately fixed in on Ori.

"I'm sorry, sir."

Raynard raised an eyebrow.

"It won't happen again..." Ori offered.

Raynard frowned, obviously far from impressed.

Ori let out a few more mental curses.

"What are you talking about?"

"I know I shouldn't have fallen asleep here, sir." Ori wasn't sure if admitting that he was well aware of that fact would make his behaviour better or worse in a hawk's eyes, but he couldn't have lied either way—not to his master.

Raynard's expression remained blank for a moment. Then a slight smile touched his lips before disappearing again. "You were asleep long before me. If I'd had a problem with you being here, I'd have woken you up and ordered you back to your room."

Ori met his master's eyes.

Even without a smile to soften his expression, Raynard looked more than a little amused. "As and when I choose to bring you to my bed, you may assume you have permission to stay here until I tell you otherwise."

Ori hesitated for a moment, before shyly smiling his understanding.

Raynard ruffled his fingers through Ori's hair, in that teasing way Ori was quickly falling in love with. "Go on."

"Yes, sir." Ori slipped from the bed and made his way down the stairs, but even when he reached the kitchen, he wasn't quite able to wipe the glowing smile off his face.

As and when... The words swirled around and around inside his head. He was going to be invited back to his master's bed again. Even another broken saucer having to be added to the increasingly long list of casualties to his clumsiness couldn't dent his joy that day or for several days after.

Chapter Six

Ori hadn't set himself a task that required him to lurk in the hallway so he could greet Raynard the moment he walked through the front door, the way he so often had over the previous weeks.

Raynard was sure that merely remembering those welcomes shouldn't have been enough to make him smile, especially after a long day filled with more badly organised paperwork than should ever be allowed to exist in the world. If his uncle hadn't already died a very natural, peaceful death at a ripe, old age, Raynard would have been inclined to think up some cruel and unusual way to kill off the cantankerous old sod — if only because he harboured a vague suspicion that the murderer wouldn't inherit the victim's bloody paperwork.

Leaving his briefcase and coat in the hallway, Raynard pushed all thoughts of his uncle aside and went to find out what task his fledgling had found so engrossing that he'd failed to notice the hours pass.

The library was the obvious place to start. The duckling's pet project, cataloguing all the books in there, seemed to be coming along well. Raynard took care and made no sound when he nudged the door open. He fully expected to catch Ori with his head buried in an ancient volume he'd unearthed from one of the crammed shelves.

No such luck. The room lay deserted. The fire wasn't even lit.

The study proved to be equally cold and empty.

Raynard stopped in the middle of the hallway, wondering if his next course of action should be to go up the stairs to those rooms that still harboured dustsheets or down to the servants' quarters.

The bell pull called to him. Ori would hurry quickly to his master's side when summoned. But then Raynard would miss the startled look and all the blushing that would ensue when he caught Ori doing whatever it was that he'd become so distracted by. A door on the other side of the hallway led, if Raynard remembered correctly, to a formal dining room that hadn't yet received Ori's attention. The door was slightly ajar.

Raynard strode across the hall. The last time he'd set foot in the room it had still been shrouded in dustsheets, but a day's hard work from Ori would have transformed it. The yards of moth-eaten fabric would be gone and the dust cleared away. The furniture would be shining, the scent of furniture polish hanging in the air. And Ori would be standing in the middle of it all, dirt clinging to his skin, his body exhausted, but his eyes shining with achievement.

Raynard had seen Ori look that way so many times now, but he doubted he'd ever get tired of seeing Ori turn toward him, tentatively hoping for some hint of approval or praise.

Raynard pushed the door leading into the dining room. It swung open on beautifully well-oiled hinges.

Blood.

The thick, metallic smell hit Raynard, even before the scene before him registered in his mind. He stopped short, his breath catching in his throat. A mahogany table filled the centre of the space. A matching cabinet stood beyond it, set between the windows on the far side of the room.

The cabinet doors hung open. The glass in one was cracked.

The floor at the cabinet's base was hidden from Raynard's line of sight by the oversized table.

Raynard's hand convulsed around the door handle. He couldn't release it, couldn't take a step forward. His whole body remained locked in place as eons passed and horrors rushed through his imagination. Finally, his lungs kicked into action. He managed to both breathe and release the door handle. He stepped forward, circling around the table.

Shards of glass led his eye to a broken footstool. A chair lay toppled over next to it. Then blood. So much blood—it pooled on the expensive carpet, so dark it looked almost black. As Raynard stared at it, the blood became his only solid point of reference.

Eventually, he managed to take another step forward. With glacial speed, the part of the floor that had been blocked from his view came into sight. The side of the blood pool was smeared, but there was no broken body laying at the edge of it, still bleeding—or worse, no longer able to bleed.

Ori was gone.

Raynard backed toward the door. A drop of blood on the richly patterned carpet caught his eye. Raynard spun around. His eyes scanned the carpet. Another drop of blood. Then another. He raced out of the room. Droplets of deep red led toward a larger smudge of blood on the door leading down to the kitchen. Raynard raced down the stairs, almost tripping in the darkness—far too frantic to think about the light switch until the door at the top of the stairs had swung closed behind him.

The bright sunlight flooding into the kitchen dazzled him. He lifted a hand to shield his eyes.

More blood. That was the first thing he saw as he turned toward the kitchen table. More blood.

Raynard focused on pushing the sickening scent out of his head, praying that would enable his brain to work. A bowl of blood-stained water rested on top of the pine boards. Lengths of bandage littered the well-scrubbed surface, some stained with red, others still pristine.

A sound on the other side of the room pulled Raynard's attention away from the carnage before him.

Ori stepped into the kitchen from the corridor leading toward his bedroom. He obviously hadn't heard a maniac race down the stairs. He stopped short when he saw Raynard.

"What the hell did you do?"

Ori's eyes opened very wide, but Raynard couldn't have kept the words serene if his life had depended on it.

"I'm sorry, sir," Ori whispered. "I'm on my way to clean it up now."

He hurried forward, his face deathly pale. When he reached out to pick up the bowl of blood-stained water, his hands were shaking.

Raynard caught Ori's shoulder and pushed him roughly toward one of the kitchen chairs before he collapsed all over his nicely mopped floor. One of Ori's arms was heavily bandaged. Raynard couldn't take his eyes off the lengths of white material binding the limb, couldn't force the image of glass cutting into Ori's skin out of his head.

He could have been killed.

For a long time, silence reigned over the room. Several minutes passed before Raynard dragged his gaze up to Ori's face.

"What happened?" Even to his own ears, he sounded completely calm now — in the way a man only could manage if he'd gone straight through panic and emerged on the other side.

"I was cleaning the cabinet in the dining room, sir. I slipped and…"

Raynard's mind flashed back to the view in the upstairs room. He'd been standing on top of the stool, which he'd balanced on top of the chair, and he probably still hadn't been tall enough to reach the top of the ancient monstrosity. He'd have had to have gone up on his toes, leaning and stretching to reach the corners of the cabinet.

"What possessed you to be so…?" Raynard shook his head as he spun away from Ori and paced toward the other side of the room.

He could have been killed.

Raynard reached the far wall and swung back around to face Ori. The bandage on his arm extended all the way down to his wrist. How close had the shards of glass come to his veins? How close had he come to bleeding out before he'd managed to stem the flow? Questions ricocheted around in Raynard's head. For the first time he could remember, true terror swirled inside him, and it was all about what could have happened, at the scene he could have walked in on when he came home.

His gaze snapped up. He met Ori's eyes.

He could have lost him. Raynard had never known fear like it.

"I..." Ori's words faded away. He dropped his gaze. "I'll clean up the mess, sir."

"You think that will fix everything?" Raynard demanded, striving to keep the volume down, but once more unable to make the words gentle.

Ori stared mutely at the table.

"Your behaviour today has been entirely unacceptable," Raynard threw at him. "Clearing away the evidence will change nothing."

Ori's gaze dropped even lower, until it was impossible to tell if his eyes were open or closed.

Raynard parted his lips to make his views on the risks Ori had taken completely clear, but the harsh clang of a bell rang through the air before he even got started.

Ori's attention went to the line of bells displayed next to the door leading up to the main house. Raynard followed his gaze to the label indicating that this particular summons came from the front door.

Ori rose unsteadily to his feet and stepped forward.

"Stay where you are." Raynard's words cracked like a whip, echoing off every hard surface in the kitchen.

Ori fell still.

Raynard looked to the bandaged arm, trying to push his anger aside to deal with the most pressing matters first. "The bleeding has stopped?"

"Yes, sir."

"Completely?" he demanded.

"Yes, sir."

Raynard nodded as he tried to force his mind back into some sort of working order. The doorbell rang again. Ori tensed as he barely resisted the urge to fulfil his duties.

"Go to your room."

For the first time Raynard could remember, Ori hesitated to follow one of his commands. The moment was brief, but after so much instant obedience, it was a vivid and unmistakable deviation from normality. Another moment passed when Ori did nothing but stare at the floor in front of Raynard's feet.

"Yes, sir." He turned and went, his bare feet moving rapidly across the tiles as he scurried for cover.

Raynard stood in the kitchen for several long seconds, until the doorbell rang out for a third time and snapped him from his thoughts. Making his way upstairs, he answered the door and signed for the parcel the postman was so intent on delivering to him.

Back in his office, Raynard tossed the package onto his desk and sank into his chair. Resting his elbows on the table, he let his head fall forward into his hands as he took a deep breath and let it out very slowly.

What had happened that day couldn't be changed. But it was never going to happen again. He could see to that. Raynard straightened his back. Several more deep breaths and some semblance of thought indicated the best way for him to ensure that it never happened again.

The idea of going down to the kitchen and seeing Ori's blood turned Raynard's stomach. Far better to call Ori upstairs and deal with the situation with what calm he'd been able to muster in those few quiet moments, than to go through the bloody kitchen and feel the anger pour back into his veins, hot and more uncontrollable than he'd ever believed possible.

He tugged the bell pull hanging down the wall behind his desk, knowing the sound would echo through to the butler's room. It didn't take Ori long to respond to the new summons. A gentle tap fell on the study door.

"Enter."

Ori pushed open the door and slipped through the gap he'd created. Raynard directed him to stand before the desk with a glance.

He hadn't thought it possible for Ori to become any paler than he had been in the kitchen. The fledgling looked terrified. Raynard couldn't bring himself to believe that was entirely inappropriate.

The scene Raynard had arrived home to was never going to be repeated. He wanted that knowledge to have an important place inside Ori's mind. If he ever thought of doing something so reckless again, Raynard wanted him to remember how it had felt to stand in front of his master, and he wanted him to think better of it.

For the first time in what felt like years, Ori wasn't even vaguely hard in Raynard's presence. Pushing aside his desire to run his hands all over Ori and ensure that he was truly fine, Raynard forced himself to remain in his seat and be content with merely scanning Ori's body in as thorough a visual inspection as possible.

"Do you have any questions?" he bit out, making no attempt to gentle his voice.

Ori's Adam's apple bobbed as he seemed to struggle to get his words past his emotions.

Raynard waited.

"May I know if I'm permitted to return to the nest, sir?"

For a moment, Raynard thought he'd misheard the whispered words—or maybe he simply *wanted* to believe that he'd misheard them. Eventually, he had to admit, to himself at least, the syllables were what they were.

Ori was probably still in shock. It was silly to think that a fledgling could stand firm in the face of his master's anger after everything he had gone through that day. Raynard still couldn't help but be just a little disappointed with the realisation his little duckling would turn tail and fly away from his master so easily.

"Is there an explanation to go with that request?" Raynard asked, his voice somehow remaining level.

Ori swallowed again. His hands clenched into fists at his sides. The bandage moved around his left arm with the motion, but no red seeped through. He hadn't opened the wound with his fidgeting.

"I..." Ori closed his eyes briefly, before trying again. "I only overheard part of your conversation with Mr. Hamilton, sir. But, I thought, perhaps even if I'm found unacceptable to serve you here, I might still be considered an acceptable servant at the nest."

He thought he was being dismissed.

As Raynard stared across the desk at him, there wasn't room for another thought inside his head. Ori thought he was being dismissed.

He wasn't running away, he was...Raynard's eyes narrowed as he studied Ori's expression more carefully. He was...holding himself together by the skin of his teeth, fighting against his instincts and somehow forcing himself to accept his master's desertion of him.

"Upon what grounds do you think you're being dismissed?" The words were even harsher than all those that had gone before.

Ori frowned slightly. His whole body trembled as he took a shaky breath. "The cabinet, sir. I know it's not the... I..."

Raynard stared at Ori, completely speechless. It obviously didn't occur to the boy that his master could be worried about the damage to something far more important to him than any bit of furniture.

Some of Raynard's anger drained away—or at least found a new direction. If that's what Ori believed, it was because that's what he'd been taught to believe—at the nest, at those foster homes. A fledgling couldn't be blamed for that.

Raynard turned his chair to the side. "Come here."

From the look on Ori's face, anyone would have thought Raynard had asked his submissive to crawl over broken glass to reach him. Yet, Ori still obeyed the command. He walked very slowly around to stand before Raynard.

At any other time, Raynard had no doubt that Ori would have immediately dropped to his knees, the way he always did when Raynard called him to that side of the desk. Right then, he didn't. Raynard had to look pointedly at the floor by his feet before Ori finally lowered himself.

The moment his knees hit the floor, Ori's hand went to his collar. He turned it around so the buckle faced Raynard. Even now, he was trying to serve—even if it meant helping Raynard take back the mark he'd given him.

Raynard tucked his knuckle under Ori's chin as he realised exactly why he had struggled to circle the desk. "Is that really what you've been taught to expect from me, fledgling?"

Ori frowned as if he didn't understand the question. "I know you've been very tolerant of my clumsiness, sir. I can't blame you for finally losing patience and—"

Raynard covered Ori's lips with his palm. "That's enough." He caught hold of the tag on Ori's collar with his free hand. "When I gave you this what did I tell you it means?" He took away his hand to permit an answer.

"That I belonged to you, sir."

"You're still wearing it. Correct your tenses," Raynard snapped.

The collar moved around Ori's throat as he swallowed. "That I *belong* to you, sir."

"And do you think a good master would disown a man on a whim?"

Ori shook his head.

"Do you really think I'd disown you over an accident?"

"You said..." Ori frowned and looked away as if the memory of the words was too painful for him to echo.

"That your behaviour today was unacceptable," Raynard finished for him, refusing to flinch away from the statement. "It was. That doesn't mean you'll be disowned — it means your behaviour will be corrected."

Ori looked up at him. Raynard watched as Ori's expression turned from uncertainty, to hope, to relief. He nodded, a jerky little motion that promised acceptance of anything and everything that might entail.

"What do you think that means?" Raynard asked, not about to take anything for granted right then.

"A punishment, sir."

Raynard leaned back in his chair, taking his touch away from Ori. The duckling didn't falter without his master's hand under his chin to steady him. The strength seemed to have poured back into him with the simple knowledge that his collar wasn't under threat.

"You've been punished before?"

Ori nodded again, a far more certain gesture now.

"At the nest?"

"Yes, sir."

"How?"

Ori looked down for a moment, then back up to him. "The whip, sir."

"Anything else?"

"Sometimes they spoke about extra duties as a punishment, sir."

"You disagreed?"

"I was there to work, sir," Ori said, an uncertain frown lurking around his eyes.

And they both knew he wasn't afraid of hard work. "Anything else?" Raynard prompted.

Ori seemed to think carefully about the subject. "It wasn't always a whip, sir — sometimes it was a crop or a paddle."

"But always a physical punishment?" Raynard pushed.

Ori nodded. "Yes, sir." As if he had no idea there could

be any other sort.

Raynard knew then what had to happen next. It was time Ori learnt exactly how different a punishment could be when it was delivered by an avian who truly understood what dominance and submission meant.

Taking a thick pad of lined paper out of his desk drawer, Raynard set it on the desktop. Pen in hand, he stared at the blank page.

He could sense Ori's eyes on him, feel the confusion pouring off Ori as he tried to work out what was going on. The boy still had so much to learn about the difference between serving at the nest and serving one man — between being a servant and a submissive.

Raynard tapped the end of his pen against the desk. No doubt he had a lot to learn himself — about how to care for a submissive who he had no intention of ever releasing from his protection — a man he cared about as well as one he owned.

It only took Raynard a few seconds to scrawl the words across the top of the page once he'd decided what they were to be. Turning in his seat, he handed the pad to Ori.

"One thousand."

Ori took the pad from him. His right hand appeared uninjured by his fall. Raynard offered him the pen. He took that as well.

"Lines...?"

Raynard didn't bother to agree with a statement of the obvious. Ori looked from the paper, to him, and back again.

"I..."

Their eyes met. Raynard raised an eyebrow.

"Yes, sir." Ori just sounded more confused than ever. He was silent for a few seconds.

"You may use that table." Raynard pointed to the other side of the study.

"Yes, sir." Ori continued to kneel there, staring at the papers in his hand.

"Start now."

"Yes, sir." He still didn't move. A full minute passed before he rose to his feet. He took a few steps away before turning back to Raynard. "Just this, sir?"

"Just that," he agreed, somehow still managing to sound insanely calm.

"Yes, sir."

Ori sat down at the table on the other side of the room. Raynard looked back to his own desk. There seemed very little for him to do but get on with some work. There was certainly enough of it crammed into his briefcase. He automatically reached for it.

The briefcase wasn't in its usual place at the side of his desk. For a few seconds, Raynard stared at the empty patch of floor, with just as much confusion as Ori had stared at his stack of lined paper.

Of course, his briefcase would be in the hallway where he'd left it. Shaking his head at himself, Raynard went to retrieve it.

Ori looked up as he walked past, but he didn't speak. When he saw Raynard carry the briefcase back into the room, he bowed his head guiltily over his work, as if there had been some occasion between Raynard arriving home and that moment when he should have found time to move it for him.

Settling himself at his desk, Raynard calmly worked his way through the first file — mostly. There were just a couple of occasions when he found his attention wandering across to the big mahogany table on the other side of the room.

If Ori found Raynard's presence as distracting as Raynard found the fledgling's, Raynard never caught him at it. Whenever his gaze strayed toward Ori, the boy's head was bowed industriously over his work, his hand making steady progress across, and gradually down, the page.

Ori held his injured arm absentmindedly cradled to his chest as he wrote. He was still pale, his skin barely distinguishable from the bandage, but Raynard doubted he'd remain that way for long. After the tumble he'd taken, he'd probably be black, blue, and lots of other interesting colours by the next morning.

He could have been killed.

Raynard swallowed down the bitter taste the thought left in the back of his throat.

He could have been killed.

Raynard mentally rolled his eyes at himself. Ori was right there, and he was fine. He was being kept right there, making a start on his punishment, when it would have been far more logical for him to finish clearing up after the accident, principally because it allowed Raynard to keep him safe and within sight while he gave his own panic time to fade.

Ori was fine.

Except, he could have been killed.

Pushing his first file into one of the trays on his desk, Raynard reached for his mobile phone. Ori had obviously had a very eventful day. There were certain routine duties that hadn't been performed as a result. It was lucky then, that Raynard still remembered all the take-away numbers that had been his very good friends before the duckling joined his household.

Order placed, Raynard looked across the room. Ori's head was still bowed over the papers, but his hand wasn't moving. Raynard watched him for a few moments, but Ori remained frozen in place.

"Do you have something to say, Ori?"

He licked his lips before he attempted to speak. "Shall I get dressed so I'll be ready to answer the door, sir?"

"No." The idea of Ori's body being covered up, of Raynard not being able to see with his own eyes that there weren't any truly serious injuries on him, sent a chill down Raynard's spine and lent a snap to the word.

Ori made no comment as he resumed his lines.

The doorbell rang some twenty minutes later. Raynard left the room. When he came back, take away bag in hand, Ori glanced up.

"Shall I fetch...?" He trailed off and closed his eyes as if he couldn't force himself to go on.

Stopping next to the table, Raynard held out his hand.

Ori looked down at the lines he'd written. The first page was full, as was a second. A third page had just been started. "I haven't finished the thousand, sir."

"Hardly surprising in this length of time." Raynard continued to hold out his hand.

Ori eventually surrendered the pages to him.

"Fetch a tray from the kitchen."

Relief poured off Ori. He scurried from the room as if afraid his master might change his mind. Raynard set the bag down on the coffee table and took a seat on the little sofa that occupied one corner of the room. He'd barely had time to set the take away cartons on the table before Ori had returned with his tray.

Either his arm wasn't hurting him, or he was used to working through pain. Whichever it was, being allowed to provide Raynard with some kind of service seemed to have settled his nerves somewhat.

The tray was set for one. Raynard watched Ori kneel down and lay everything neatly on the coffee table before him. He was curious to see what his fledgling might do next. With the last item set in place, Ori rose. He looked toward the table where he'd been writing out his lines.

Raynard pointedly dropped a cushion where Ori had knelt on the carpet a moment before. Ori hesitated but lowered himself without needing Raynard to issue a verbal command.

Even then, Ori didn't think he was going to be fed. Raynard could see it in his eyes.

Opening one of the boxes, Raynard ate a forkful of food. Ori made no comment. Raynard stabbed the fork back into the box and speared another mouthful. This time, Raynard offered the fork to Ori's lips.

Ori pulled back slightly. He looked toward the table

where he'd worked. "I haven't finished, sir."

"The lines will keep you busy for several days. I don't intend to starve you in the meantime." He nudged the fork against Ori's lips.

Slowly, Ori opened his mouth and took the food from his master's fork. A blush rose to his cheeks as he looked down at the things he'd brought up from the kitchen and seemed to realise he'd miscalculated.

"Shall I—?"

"Stay where you are."

Raynard offered him another forkful. There was something curiously pleasing about watching the fledgling practically eat out of his hand. Raynard picked up the next mouthful of food with his bare fingers. That made an even more pleasing picture, and Ori blushing over it was hardly going to put him off—especially not when it suited Ori so well.

The colour didn't fade from Ori cheeks as the meal continued. Not when Raynard held his glass to Ori's lips for him to share his drink, or when he offered him his dessert, every mouthful of it lapped from the palm of Raynard's hand. It made him look wonderfully healthy and alive. And how much of his embarrassment was down to the fact Raynard fed him by hand, and how much was due to the realisation that he was getting turned on by his master feeding him that way, was debatable anyway. As naked as he was, there was little Ori could do to conceal his cock as it stiffened and rose.

Raynard had always had a vague awareness that Ori would probably like being fussed over a little. It had never occurred to him that Ori would be turned on by it. Raynard hadn't realised that he'd find it so pleasant a way to pass the time either.

As the food gradually disappeared from the coffee table, Raynard felt himself relax. Ori was fine. If he was in danger of anything at all, it was spontaneous submissive combustion due to Raynard's teasing.

Reaching out to him, for once with no food on his fingertips, Raynard stroked his thumb across a heated cheek. Ori's eyes dropped closed as he seemed to glory in his brief caress.

It was late. Ori was in no condition to be taken to his master's bed. Still, when Raynard rose to his feet he couldn't bring himself to send Ori back to the servants' quarters.

Ori wasn't a servant, he was a submissive, and a submissive slept wherever the hell his master wanted him to sleep. Raynard had every right to take the boy up to his room.

"Follow me."

Ori had already started to collect up the empty take-away cartons, but he stopped what he was doing and clambered to his feet as soon as Raynard spoke. He followed Raynard out of the study and up the stairs without a word. Within a minute, they both stood in Raynard's bedroom.

Tentative pleasure shone in Ori's eyes, screaming his relief at being wanted there. Raynard looked across the room. As much as part of him would have loved to push Ori down on the bed and bury himself inside his body, to feel the life pounding through Ori and prove to the whole world beyond any doubt that Ori was fine, Raynard held back.

Ori's ribcage rose and fell as he took a deep breath. He could easily have cracked a few ribs when he'd fallen.

Ducks were said to be hardy creatures, but Raynard didn't have enough experience with them to know how quickly marks would show on a duckling's skin to reflect any damage that lay beneath it.

Raynard stepped forward. Ori smiled cautiously up at him. Raynard caressed his cheek first, just as he had in the study. The same delight at his touch spread across Ori's face.

Keeping his examination light and careful, Raynard began to explore the rest of Ori's body, looking for hidden wounds as he gloried in the health and vitality that pulsed through Ori's veins.

Ori stood very still, a touch of confusion creeping into

his eyes as he registered that he wasn't receiving the kind of caresses he'd come to expect from his master when he invited him to his bedroom.

Raynard ignored that. The inspection was too important for him to allow himself to get distracted. Gradually, his hands mapped out every inch of Ori. No complaint was uttered, but Raynard had a good enough read on Ori to notice the tension that crept into his muscles as Raynard moved his hands over his body.

There were a few shallow scratches that had already stopped bleeding. By the end of the examination, Raynard had a good idea where the bruises would be by morning too.

The only place he hadn't examined for himself was the forearm beneath the bandage. No blood seeped through the crisp white fabric. Raynard was loath to unwind the material unnecessarily. He ran his fingers lightly over it. "Painful?" he asked.

Ori shook his head.

"The truth," Raynard demanded.

"It was at first, sir. It's not so bad now."

Raynard continued to glare at the binding. "If the pain gets worse, you're to tell me immediately — the same if it starts bleeding again."

"Yes, sir."

Raynard tucked his knuckles under Ori's chin and made him meet his eyes for several long seconds, so he could see how important the matter was to him. "I'm serious, Ori."

Ori's jaw twitched under Raynard's touch as he swallowed. "Yes, sir."

Raynard made him hold his eyes for a few seconds longer, before he was finally satisfied with what Ori understood.

"Into bed."

Ori turned away from him. He didn't seem to know quite what to do with himself. By the time Raynard had tossed aside his clothes and was ready to slide between the sheets next to him, Ori was still sitting on top of the blankets, apparently awaiting further instruction.

Raynard tugged the covers as far back as they could go while Ori sat there. The duckling shuffled around until they were freed from beneath him. Raynard lay down next to him and pulled the blanket up over them both.

Ori frowned slightly as he stared across the bed at him. There was little point in Raynard pretending that all he wanted to do was sleep. If there had been fewer injuries hidden just beneath Ori's skin, there would be no question of what they would do next. Raynard couldn't be the only man in the room who knew that.

As things stood, Raynard merely lay under the blankets on the other side of the bed and tried to push his pillow into some position that might allow him to sleep. Switching off the light, he stared up into the darkness.

For a long time the room was silent enough that he was almost willing to swear he could hear the wheels turning around in Ori's head.

"Speak," he ordered, when the tension in the room built up to a level he wasn't willing to tolerate.

"If you've changed your mind, sir…" Ori whispered.

"You sleep where your master wants you to sleep," Raynard said, leaving no room for argument in his tone.

Silence seeped back into the room. Then, finally—"Yes, sir." He sounded thoroughly obedient, but as Raynard lay listening to his breathing, it was obvious his fledgling wasn't making the least attempt to sleep.

Reaching across the bed, Raynard caught Ori around the waist and pulled him back along the sheet until Ori was curled in front of him, while Raynard spooned behind him.

Every muscle in Ori's body tensed, yet it only took him a second to alter his position, and offer his body for his master to take whatever he wanted.

"Sleep," Raynard reminded—himself just as much as Ori.

"I…" Ori hesitated. "Yes, sir."

Knowing he was curled up safe in his master's arms seemed to reassure Ori that he truly was welcome in his bed that night. If the knowledge didn't sink in to his mind, it at least registered with his physical self. Within a few minutes, the heat from Raynard's larger body mass seemed to have soothed him into a deep, contented slumber.

Moving carefully, so as not to wake him, Raynard rested his temple on the back of Ori's head. That was right. Their positions were solely for his fledgling's benefit, so Ori would be able to sleep knowing he was safe.

Ori was safe. Raynard repeated that fact just one more time inside his head, and it was impossible to believe that anything was entirely for Ori's benefit.

Raynard would just take one night to reassure himself that Ori was fine, and that would be the end of it, Raynard told himself firmly. Tomorrow everything would be back to normal, and Ori would mean no more to him than any of the other avians who'd submitted to him in the past.

And Raynard almost believed everything he told himself. Almost.

Chapter Seven

"Busy day, Ori?"

Ori spun around.

Raynard stood in the kitchen doorway. Today, of all days, he'd come home early. All of Ori's plans to have everything perfect for Raynard as he stepped through the door were ruined, but he still couldn't help but be pleased to see his master. The house was different when Raynard was home. The world was a very different — much better — place.

Raynard walked slowly across the kitchen toward him. "Don't you have anything to say?"

"Hello, sir," Ori offered.

"I asked if you've had a busy day," Raynard reminded him, as he stepped past and around Ori.

"I couldn't find the lines, sir," Ori blurted out. And he'd wanted so badly to have them finished for his master when he came home.

"I locked them in my desk drawer."

Not sure what to say, Ori studied the kitchen floor just in front of his feet.

"Punishments are always supervised — you don't have permission to work on them unless I'm here."

"Yes, sir."

Raynard was standing right behind him by that point. He settled his hand on Ori's waist and stroked his thumb back and forth over a rare patch of unbruised skin. Ori closed his eyes.

Raynard had already thoroughly inspected the injuries that had become visible overnight. It had been a torturous, teasing process that had left Ori with an erection that had lingered long after Raynard had left the house that morning.

"Were you good while I was out?"

Ori nodded. Raynard leaned forward and pressed his body against Ori's back. Ori whimpered helplessly with need as Raynard moved against him. But he couldn't completely give himself up to the embrace. His master had asked him a question. Had he been good?

Ori took a deep breath. Raynard had provided him with a long and detailed description of what being good entailed on that particular day. It principally involved not clambering about on unsteady bits of furniture, and resting if his injuries made his chores too painful to complete.

"Yes, sir." He'd been good.

"Did you rest?"

"I...I didn't need to, sir." Ori's voice faltered as Raynard wrapped his hand around his hardening cock. It was, much to Ori's relief, one of those rare parts of his body that didn't bear any marks from his fall. There was no need for Raynard to let his fingers play there unless it was for the pure joy of seeing his submissive squirm while he teased.

"You've been cooking."

"Yes, sir," Ori managed to whisper.

"What?"

"Sir?"

"What have you been cooking?" Raynard clarified, more than a little amusement creeping into his voice as he rubbed his thumb across the head of Ori's cock, smearing the pre-cum that leaked from the slit all over the glans.

"I..." Ori couldn't make his mind work. Food. He'd been making something. He knew that. After failing to prepare anything the previous day and Raynard having to order a take-away when he might not have wanted to, Ori had been determined not to fail at the same task two days in a row. There was food on the cooker top. He just couldn't remember what the hell it was.

Raynard chuckled as he turned Ori around. He brushed his lips against Ori's mouth very lightly. It was just as much a tease as his fingers were against Ori's skin.

Ori's eyes dropped closed. He savoured Raynard's acceptance until he felt him step away and leave him standing alone by the kitchen table, not entirely steady on his feet.

Raynard turned and walked away. As he reached the door leading back up to the main part of the house, he looked over his shoulder. "Ori?"

"Yes, sir?"

"Spaghetti."

Ori blinked at him.

"Dinner tonight—it's spaghetti." He tilted his head toward the pans on the cooker. Ori followed his gaze. The scent of the sauce made its way back into his senses. Spaghetti. That was right. He heard Raynard chuckle as he left the kitchen.

Ori remembered how to breathe. Shaking his head at himself, he turned his attention back to his duties, but his mind didn't seem to be willing to come back under his control.

Raynard had been angry with him. He remembered the feeling well. Raynard had been furious with him. And he'd also fussed over him, and let him sleep upstairs in his bed for no reason at all and...Ori shook his head again. Replaying it all over and over inside his mind wasn't making his mind work, it was just starving his brain of blood supply as it all rushed to his cock instead.

Raynard was pleased with him now. He even seemed to have gone out of his way to tell him so. Lifting his hand to his collar, Ori just reminded himself, one more time, of the things that were really important. He belonged to his master, and Raynard wasn't going to send him away. Everything else could be worried about later — or maybe never at all.

He didn't let any doubts creep back into his head until the last of the dinner things were put neatly away, the kitchen cleaned and he was free to go in search of his master once more.

Slipping into the library, Ori found Raynard already there, sitting in his usual chair by the fireside. Ori was halfway across the room, heading for the cushion by his master's feet, when Raynard looked up.

A nod from Raynard directed Ori's attention to the table on the other side of the room. The pad of paper Ori had started to write his lines upon rested on the polished mahogany surface. A pen lay next to it.

Ori looked toward Raynard. Their dinner had passed very nicely, almost companionably, while Raynard patiently tried to explain to him exactly why it was so important to keep proper business records and just how much of a fool his uncle had been.

There was no hint of the man who'd sat opposite Ori at the kitchen table now. It was as if the simple act of taking the pen and paper from his desk drawer had reminded Raynard just how angry he had every right to be.

Not knowing what else to do, Ori retreated to the table and sat down.

The lines weren't a problem. They weren't even a real punishment. There was no harm they could do him, except give him a slightly sore wrist. Part of him understood that.

Being banished from his master's side was a different matter. Ori hadn't really realised how much he loved that quiet part of the evening when he was allowed to simply sit with Raynard and feel both his presence and his approval wrap around him after a hard day's work.

Ori stared down at the lined paper for several long seconds before he could bring himself to pick up the pen. Raynard had said it would take him days to finish the lines. If the only time he'd be permitted to work on them was during this part of the evening, he was right. Ori could easily believe it would be weeks before he was allowed to crawl back to his master, before he could know if he would truly be welcomed back at the end of it all.

Finally, Ori put the pen to the paper and set about

copying the same words out again and again. The ink slowly filled the page. Forming each letter as neatly as he was able, Ori concentrated all his energy on completing the task to the best of his ability in spite of the way his hand wanted to shake and tremble.

His other arm burned beneath its bandage. Scrapes and bruises that hadn't bothered him through the day started to complain loudly. It was as if Raynard's disapproval made them worse than they could ever be while Raynard was pleased with him. With every moment that passed, more and more pain rushed through Ori, until he was lightheaded with it.

"That's enough."

Ori jumped as Raynard's words cut through the silence of the room. He had no idea how long he'd been working away at the lines. A few of the pages were full now, but he wasn't anywhere near the total that had been prescribed.

He stared as Raynard rose from his chair by the fire. He crossed the room, took the pen and the paper from Ori, and locked them away in his desk drawer again.

Ori stayed in his seat by the table, waiting for an order, for some indication of what might happen next. Turning the key in the lock on the drawer seemed to change Raynard's mood.

When he turned his attention back to Ori, a slight smile graced his lips. Wary of returning it, just in case he was somehow misinterpreting the situation, Ori stayed serious. Raynard crossed the room to him. He slid his fingers through Ori's hair, tightened his grip on the strands and guided Ori to tilt his head back and look up at him properly.

"Tired, fledgling?" Raynard asked.

Ori shook his head, tugging roughly at his own hair in the process.

Raynard raised an eyebrow. "Oh?"

"Not too tired to…" Ori blushed. Ever since his master first allowed him to go down on him, not a day had passed when they hadn't had sex—when Ori hadn't either tasted Raynard on his tongue or felt him thrust deep inside him as he came.

Ori might not have been allowed to find his own pleasure every day, but he'd always served and serviced his master. Except for yesterday. Ori's hand clenched into a fist at his side. He wasn't at all inclined to lose that time with his master as well as their chaste little moments in front of the fire.

Raynard traced a fingertip gently down Ori's cheek, but he shook his head. "No."

Ori looked up, just in time to see Raynard's eyes wander across his battered skin.

Heat raced to Ori's cheeks. He couldn't blame his master for thinking he looked like hell. He was right.

Rising to his feet, Ori's only thought was to retreat to the servants' quarters as quickly as possible. He'd leave his master in peace, and perhaps he'd find some way of getting over his embarrassment before he had to face Raynard again in the morning.

With all the speed of a true hawk, Raynard caught hold of Ori's good arm before Ori had a chance to scurry from his sight.

"Do you really think I could be put off so easily?" Raynard asked, pulling Ori back until their bodies were pressed tightly together.

Raynard's erection rubbed against Ori's backside through Raynard's trousers. Ori hesitated. He tried to look over his shoulder, but Raynard's grip on him wouldn't allow it.

"I told you before that you're not a servant in some stupid gentlemen's club any more, Ori. You belong to me. I'm your master. I'm responsible for you. Do you understand that?" Impatience made each word harsh.

Ori would have nodded, but Raynard slid a hand underneath Ori's chin and held his head back so it rested against his shoulder, preventing the gesture.

"Yes, sir," Ori managed to whisper.

"And that means you'll be taught to behave in the way I expect. It means you'll be punished when you make mistakes. And it means I'll think with my brain and not my cock when I decide what should happen between us. Is that clear?"

"Yes, sir."

"Don't expect me to fawn over you while you're receiving a punishment. And don't expect me to cling to any anger I may feel when the lines are locked away."

Ori closed his eyes as relief rushed through him. "I understand, sir."

"Good. You can stop thinking you can screw your way back into my good graces while you're still paying for your mistakes, too."

Ori swallowed, his throat working rapidly beneath his master's hand. "Yes, sir."

"Bed, now." Raynard sent him on his way with a sharp tap on his backside, catching him neatly between the bruises from his fall.

In the hallway, Ori hesitated.

"Upstairs, until you're told otherwise," Raynard shouted after him.

He was still earning his forgiveness, there was no way in hell his master was going to do anything more than tease him until he'd finished every last line. Ori wouldn't even get a healthy dose of second-hand pleasure when he was allowed to go down on Raynard. But Ori was still glad his master had decided that he'd be allowed to sleep next to him.

* * * * *

"Ori?"

Ori closed his eyes. He'd never thought he could hate anything about Raynard, but he loathed knowing his master was displeased with him far more than he could ever have detested any punishment the men in the nest had been able to come up with.

A whipping would have been so much kinder than this. The flesh on his back was far less important to him than Raynard's good opinion of him. Ori understood that now.

"Is there a reason why you've stopped?" Raynard asked. Even his tone of voice was different when the lines were on the table.

Ori swallowed down his nerves. "One thousand, sir."

He'd neatly numbered every line, all the way down the side of each page. After checking them twice, he no longer harboured any doubts. He had written out exactly one thousand lines, and he'd never been more petrified in his life.

"Come here."

Somehow, Ori forced himself to stand up and carry the pages he'd filled with words across to his master. When he reached him, Ori wasn't sure if he was permitted to kneel for him or not. He stood uselessly before the fire, shuffling his feet against the hearth rug.

Raynard held out a hand. Ori offered him the lines. Raynard slowly looked through each page, seeming to read each often repeated word one at a time.

Without any way to release his nerves, all Ori could do was get more and more anxious. He folded his arms across his chest, cradling the sore wrist against his body. The bandage around his other arm had been dispensed with a day or two before. The dining room was cleaned and polished to within an inch of its life.

The only evidence of Ori's mistakes lingered in his master's hand.

When he looked up, Ori realised that Raynard's attention had moved away from the paper. He was staring straight at Ori now. When Raynard stood up, Ori remained frozen in place, unable to even step back and get out of his way.

Raynard handed him the lines. "Burn them."

"Sir?"

Raynard looked toward the fireplace. Ori followed his gaze. He stared into the flames for a long time. The order was very simple. There was no excuse for failing to obey it instantly, but his hand didn't want to cooperate.

The lines were supposed to fix something. In some way that he hadn't quite been sure of, they were supposed to make everything better. That was what had kept him going through each evening while he'd been banished to the other side of the room in disgrace. When he finished the lines, somehow everything would be okay.

The most valuable possession my master owns is his submissive. I will take great care that no harm comes to my master's submissive whenever he is not there to watch over me himself.

Ori briefly closed his eyes before sacrificing the papers to the flames. The dry sheets caught quickly. In what felt like seconds, every word had been consumed, and Ori's hopes of them healing the rift between his master and himself along with them.

The most valuable possession my master owns is his submissive. I will take great care that no harm comes to my master's submissive whenever he is not there to watch over me himself.

Raynard placed his hand on Ori's shoulder as he moved to stand directly behind him. With the heat of the fire in front of him, and the warmth of his master's body against his back, it would have been so easy for Ori to fall into the trap of believing that the comfort that surrounded him made everything okay, but nothing was okay. As Ori stared into the fire, he was overwhelmed by the deep and inescapable knowledge that nothing would ever be okay again.

The most valuable possession my master owns is his submissive. I will take great care that no harm comes to my master's submissive whenever he is not there to watch over me himself.

"You took your punishment well."

Ori swallowed down his emotions and closed his eyes.

"Speak up, fledgling."

"I hated it, sir." There was no excuse for the words, but there was no way he could keep them back either. If the punishment had fixed something, it might have been worth it, but as things still stood between them...

The most valuable possession my master owns is his submissive. I will take great care that no harm comes to my master's submissive whenever he is not there to watch over me himself.

Raynard's fingers stroked through Ori's hair, tugging him back to lean against a larger, stronger body. "It wouldn't be a very effective punishment if you didn't hate it, would it?"

Raynard had barely finished the sentence before he stepped away, leaving Ori alone and unsupported on the hearth rug.

Ori watched Raynard re-take his seat. He settled himself comfortably, then, against all of Ori's fears, he glanced at the cushion on the floor at his feet. Ori rushed to kneel there, hope hastening back as quickly as it had deserted him.

Raynard smiled and stroked one knuckle down Ori's cheek. "You're expected to learn from your mistakes, but not to dwell on them after they've been dealt with. Understand?"

Ori nodded, very quickly, and turned his head into his master's touch. Raynard chuckled as Ori leaned so far he almost lost his balance. The sound was rich and perfect. Even as Ori ducked his head in embarrassment, he found himself smiling cautiously up at Raynard.

Ori was back with the version of his master that existed when there was no penance in force and, with the lines consigned to the flames, there was no way they could sneak back out of the desk drawer and ruin things between them again.

The most valuable possession my master owns is his submissive. I will take great care that no harm comes to my master's submissive whenever he is not there to watch over me himself.

Gathering up his courage, Ori placed his hand on the inside of his master's knee. Raynard seemed to consider the suggestion very carefully before shaking his head. Ori snatched his hand back, not sure how he could have misread the situation so appallingly. Raynard had his fingers wrapped around Ori's wrist before he had a chance to retreat too far.

"I think we can do better than that, can't we, fledgling?"

"Sir?"

Raynard brushed the thumb of his other hand across Ori's lips before rising to his feet, pulling Ori up alongside him. "Let's see if we can't find a better way to celebrate you being properly back in my good graces, shall we?"

Ori nodded rapidly, making Raynard chuckle again.

Raynard glanced at the fire. "Put everything in order before you join me upstairs."

"Yes, sir."

There wasn't much to do except damp down the fire and switch off the lights. All trace of the aches and pains that had filled Ori's body while he was being punished were a distant memory now. He raced through his evening chores, eager to go to his master as quickly as possible.

The most valuable possession my master owns is his submissive. I will take great care that no harm comes to my master's submissive whenever he is not there to watch over me himself.

When he reached Raynard's bedroom door, Ori found it closed. Unable to raise enough daring to push it open without an invitation, he knocked politely against one of the dark wooden panels.

"Enter."

Nudging the door ajar, Ori slipped inside. His master stood on the far side of the room by a big oak coffer. Once upon a time, it had contained old blankets. Raynard had ordered Ori to empty it weeks ago, but Ori had never seen what Raynard had refilled it with. As Ori watched, Raynard pulled a set of leather cuffs out of the coffer and placed them on the top of the chest of drawers to his right.

Minutes ticked past. Raynard brought more and more

leather out of the coffer and scattered it on top of the chest of drawers.

Ori had seen some of the toys that the higher-ranking shifters liked to play with while he was serving at the nest. Some of the more middling ranks had even brought him into their experiments with them. He swallowed rapidly as the memory of the leather moving around his limbs rushed back and entwined itself with the knowledge he already had of his master.

Raynard's words in the library had Ori's cock hard and aching long before he reached the bedroom, but the idea of Raynard and the leather together raced to his shaft, making him stiffen and rise even further, until he could almost believe he'd come right there, while everything he longed for was still on the other side of the room.

Raynard finally glanced over his shoulder. Setting down a blindfold next to the cuffs, he beckoned him across the room.

Ori rushed to Raynard's side, but Raynard shook his head when he would have lowered himself to his knees. Stepping around him, Raynard ran his hands down Ori's arms, tugging his hands behind him.

He guided him to wrap his right hand around his left wrist. A moment later, Raynard nudged his shoe against the inside of Ori's ankles, prompting him to spread his legs a little farther apart.

Moving to stand in front of Ori once more, Raynard tapped the back of his fingers under Ori's chin. "In the future, whenever you're waiting for an order, you're to stand exactly like this."

"Yes, sir."

"There's no reason to keep your eyes on the floor unless you think there's something there that you might trip over."

Ori was about to say the wrong thing. Just in time, he changed the answer to — "Yes, sir".

Somehow, Raynard still seemed to know that it hadn't been his first, instinctive response. From the hawkish look in his eyes, Ori was sure Raynard would stare at him for as long as it took to get the answer he wanted.

"In the nest, some of the men said that the lower orders shouldn't look their betters in the eye," Ori whispered. He'd never been very good at following that directive when it came to Raynard. Standing there and admitting he'd known the rule but hadn't obeyed it was just about the hardest thing he'd ever done.

"They were wrong."

"Yes, sir."

"It's not about that." The words were slow, as if Raynard was thinking about the matter carefully and choosing his words very deliberately.

Ori glanced up at him through his lashes.

Raynard's knuckles fell away from Ori's chin, and stroked down the centre of his chest in an idle caress.

"It's about each man finding a place in the world that suits his nature. Do you think you'd enjoy being in charge of a gentleman's club like the nest, giving out orders and taking responsibility for all the men under your control every time they stepped into the building?"

Ori shook his head.

"Do you think you'd like to be responsible for putting an estate like my uncle's in order, taking over all his business interests and managing all those things a man needs to control when he takes up the reins of one of the leading avian families in the city?"

Ori shook his head even more forcefully.

Raynard smiled. He continued to stroke his fingertips over Ori's skin, almost absentmindedly—the way a man might stroke a favoured pet—one that he liked to fuss over, but that was still a pet for all that. "That's not because you're not good enough to do it, it's because it's not in your nature to want those things. There's nothing wrong with men who prefer to follow rather than lead. They have their strengths, too."

Their eyes met. Ori couldn't look away. He'd never seen his master more serious, not even during his punishment. The whole concept was important to him. Ori nodded his understanding, even if he wasn't really sure he did comprehend everything Raynard wanted to explain to him.

Raynard's expression gradually changed as he seemed to set aside serious things, perhaps to be revisited at a later date. "There's nothing wrong with a man who prefers to be bound rather than to bind other people, either," he whispered in Ori's ear, his tone quickly turning teasing.

Ori took a deep breath as Raynard picked up the leather cuffs. Holding the restraints between them so Ori could see them clearly, Raynard ran his fingers over the leather.

"Have you ever been bound, Ori?"

He nodded. "At the nest, sir. Some of the other shifters liked to practice on me."

"Did you like it?"

"I'll like it when you do it, sir," Ori promised.

Raynard raised an eyebrow. "Answer the original question properly, fledgling."

"Sometimes, sir."

"But not at other times?"

"I don't think I was supposed to enjoy it those times, sir," Ori observed, trying to make the words sound as neutral as possible.

Raynard nodded. He seemed to be aware of everything Ori *didn't* say as well as what he did.

"Now that you're with me, you're always supposed to enjoy your leather."

Ori nodded.

"Over time, you'll learn that these cuffs will keep you exactly where I want you. They mean you belong to me, and that'll always be a good thing, won't it?"

Ori nodded again. "Yes, sir."

Dipping his head, Raynard brushed their lips together. Ori tried to open his mouth in invitation, but Raynard had no need of one. He kissed him like he owned him, as if he wanted to remind Ori that he knew he owned him, and that would never change.

A moan escaped from the back of Ori's throat. His right hand tightened around his opposite wrist behind his back as he leaned into the kiss. Raynard pulled him closer, so their bodies were pressed tightly together.

Ori rose up on his toes as he tried to bring them nearer still. Raynard smiled into the kiss, easily keeping them both balanced when Ori would have toppled them.

When Raynard finally pulled back, Ori leaned up and tried to bring their mouths back together. He was desperate to cling to the moment forever, but Raynard wouldn't permit it, not even when Ori let out a pathetic little whimper.

Raynard considered the cuffs for a second before dropping them back onto the pile of toys and selecting the blindfold instead.

He smiled as he placed it over Ori's eyes, not a half smile or a little twist of the lips, a real, full smile. It was a rare sight, and the last thing Ori saw before the world went black around him. He could still sense Raynard's presence in front of him, but suddenly that was the only thing he could be sure of.

"I'm going to tie you up now."

Ori gasped as the words caressed his ear. His master's hands were strong as they settled against his arms. Guiding Ori's hands around in front of his body, Raynard led him blindly forward.

Ori had walked across the bedroom a hundred times and more, sometimes in the halflight of dawn and occasionally in the real darkness of night. He'd have thought he could stride confidently across the space with his eyes closed, but stepping forward wearing the blindfold was harder than he'd ever imagined it could be.

He knew full well how easily things had materialised to trip him up whenever the shifters at the nest had covered his eyes. Objects that hadn't existed the last time he'd been permitted to see, had a way of popping into existence right in front of him for the amusement of the crows.

Sliding his toes along the carpet, Ori desperately tried not to make a fool of himself in front of his master and ruin everything between them with his clumsiness.

Raynard kept his hands around Ori's wrists as he led him forward. At some point after he put the blindfold on Ori, Raynard had picked up the cuffs again. Ori could feel them hanging from Raynard's fingers, swinging gently with each movement.

"Trust your master, fledgling."

The most valuable possession my master owns is his submissive. I will take great care that no harm comes to my master's submissive whenever he is not there to watch over me himself.

Except, his master was there. Ori didn't need to look after himself when Raynard was there to do it on his own behalf, did he? Ori swallowed. He took another step forward lifting his foot from the floor, moving more quickly, feigning a confidence he really didn't feel.

"Better," Raynard praised.

Ori smiled slightly as he took another step forward. Nothing jumped in front of his feet as his master guided him forward. It wasn't easy to trust Raynard when other men's laughter at his blind clumsiness rushed back into his mind and his nerves increased, but Ori called up every scrap of strength he possessed and gave everything he had to the endeavour. When Raynard turned him around and nudged him backward with a push against his shoulders, Ori let himself fall as if he had no doubt the bed would be there to catch him.

He bounced as he hit the mattress.

He smiled his relief as he slid his hands out across the sheet to steady himself. Sitting up, Ori lowered his feet to the carpet by the side of the bed. Raynard nudged the inside of Ori's foot with his shoe once again. As Ori obediently spread his legs farther apart, he sensed Raynard move closer and stand between his thighs.

Tilting his body forward, Ori sought out his master. His forehead came to rest against Raynard's shirt, and Ori instinctively leaned into him, rubbing his face against his torso.

Raynard's hand came to rest on the back of his head, encouraging Ori to believe he was welcome there. When Raynard stepped back, there was no sense of rejection. When he pushed against Ori's shoulders, his touch wasn't harsh.

Ori toppled willingly backward onto the mattress. Before he even had a chance to try to right himself, one of the leather cuffs was wrapped around his left wrist. He had a fair idea how it would look against his skin, but he had no idea if his master would be pleased with the sight or not.

"Sir?" Ori bit his tongue, but it was too late. The plea for reassurance had already escaped.

Raynard didn't say anything, he just tugged Ori's wrist up toward the headboard. As Ori blindly scrambled to please him, the mattress dipped, letting him know that Raynard had joined him on the bed. Raynard's clothes brushed against Ori's bare skin as he leaned over him to cuff his right hand in place alongside the left. Ori wriggled beneath him, blindly glorying in a world that was suddenly full of wonderful sensations.

Then, Raynard disappeared.

Ori strained his hearing, trying to get some sense of where Raynard was. His heart raced faster, filling his world, making it even harder to distinguish any clue as to where Raynard might be.

A hand grabbed Ori's erection, catching him by surprise. He automatically thrust up into the very welcome touch. Raynard chuckled, but it was nothing like the laughter Ori had heard so often at the nest. There was a warmth to it, as if his master was pleased with him as well as amused by his enthusiasm.

Ori nibbled at his bottom lip as Raynard began to stroke his cock, his every movement strong and confident. A lifetime had passed since Ori had been allowed to touch himself. He tried to remain still, but it was impossible to do that. As Raynard's fingers set off wave after wave of pure pleasure cascading through his veins, Ori pushed up into each stroke.

Raynard's hand disappeared. Ori kept thrusting blindly up into the empty air above him until Raynard's hand returned to Ori's world—this time to rest over his hipbone. Raynard soon settled his other hand over Ori's other hip. He pressed him down against the mattress, forcing him to still himself when he tried to continue humping nothingness.

Ori scrambled for control and panted for breath, but his body was no longer his to command. The cuffs kept his hands in place more securely than he would ever have been able to keep them there himself. The hands on his hips were stronger than his own willpower. Raynard owned every scrap of him.

Ori was his master's submissive, and there was only one man making any decisions.

Hot wetness closed over the tip of Ori's cock. He let out a cry as his hips redoubled their efforts to thrust forward. For a moment, Ori's erection slid even deeper into his master's mouth.

The air rushed out of the room. The ensuing vacuum pulled each molecule of oxygen from Ori's lungs. His head spun as every drop of blood in his body rushed to his cock, leaving nothing for the rest of him. Raynard pulled back. His tongue swirled around Ori's cockhead, teasing his foreskin, making him squirm.

Raynard tightened his grip on Ori's hips as he dipped his head again. Ori opened his eyes behind his blindfold and tried to stare down his body at Raynard. The darkness behind the blindfold remained. His imagination took over.

A mental image of his master's head bobbing over his cock flooded his mind. He saw his shaft disappearing between Raynard's lips as Raynard sucked around him and dragged him closer and closer to the edge by the moment.

He wasn't allowed to come without permission. From those times when he had gone down on other men, Ori was reasonably sure he shouldn't want to come without permission—not after just a few seconds. But he did. He wanted to come. He *needed* to come so badly.

"Sir, please…"

Raynard murmured around his shaft, as if he loved listening to him beg—maybe even as if he intended to draw out the blowjob simply because he wanted to keep hearing him pleading for his release. Vibrations shot through Ori's body, making him arch up. He pulled at the cuffs and kicked against the bed sheet. Raynard's fingers bit into his sides as he held Ori still, forcing him down against the mattress as he toyed with him in his mouth.

The marks from Ori's tumble had faded away. Ori was sure that, by the following morning, he'd have new marks from where his master had held him so tightly. They'd be marks he'd never want to lose.

Ori whimpered as, once more, his master's hands left him without any warning. When one rematerialized, it slid between Ori's thighs, slick with lube. Ori instinctively spread his legs wide apart on the mattress.

Raynard rubbed two fingers against his hole. Within moments, they were buried deep in Ori's arse, pounding against his prostate. Raynard wrapped his lips around Ori's shaft again. His mouth worked around his cock in time with the fingers thrusting inside Ori's arse until the pleasure was so intense it became pain.

"Please…" Ori bit down on his bottom lip, hard enough to draw blood, but there was no way he could keep back the stream of breathless begging.

His head thrashed against the pillow, his hands clenched and unclenched into fists above his head as he strove for control and failed. Just when he thought there was nothing he could do, that he'd come with or without permission, his master's mouth left him. Raynard's fingers vanished from his world.

Ori parted his lips to resume begging but he didn't get a chance to say a word. Raynard's mouth came down on Ori's lips, stealing the words from him. A movement against the mattress and Raynard's body covered Ori's. His slicked erection nudged against Ori's hole as his tongue stroked across the cut on his lip.

Raynard sucked against the broken bit of skin, just as he'd suckled around Ori's cock. Ori whimpered into the kiss as Raynard pressed his cock against his hole again, teasing him, then denying him until, with one deep thrust, Raynard was sheathed inside him to the hilt.

The kiss ended as Ori tossed back his head. He was so close. "Please..."

"Come."

He did as his master commanded. The permission left Raynard's lips and rushed straight to Ori's cock without bothering to check in with his brain en route. He came, clawing at his cuffs as crescendos of pure bliss rolled through him, and his cum spilled between them, landing on his stomach to be smeared against their bodies every time his master ploughed forward.

Raynard thrust into him again and again, drawing Ori's pleasure out until it was impossible for him to remember a time when he hadn't been in the grip of a kind of ecstasy he'd never guessed existed before that night.

As Ori slumped back on the bed, too exhausted to move, Raynard yelled out. He came, pounding into Ori harder than ever as he lost himself in his own pleasure.

Ori blinked in the darkness behind the blindfold,

wishing he could see the look on his master's face. When Raynard pulled away from him and rolled onto the mattress beside him, the cuffs were the only things that kept Ori from trying to follow him across the bed.

Raynard wasn't far away. Ori could feel his presence right there. But there was no such thing as being close enough to his master right then. He wanted to feel his master's cock buried inside him forever, anything else was a paltry second best.

Raynard didn't leave him bound and trapped on the other side of the bed for too long. The cuffs and the blindfold were soon tossed aside.

Raynard stroked Ori's cheek as he turned his head to face him. Ori slowly lifted his gaze. Success shone in Raynard's expression, and Ori knew his master had realised that he was the first man who'd ever actually gone down on Ori; he was the first person who'd ever thought he was worthy of receiving that sort of pleasure.

Raynard curled his lips into an approving little smile. Ori echoed Raynard's expression as his master's satisfaction with the discovery seeped into his mind.

Turning his head, Ori kissed his master's fingers in a way he would never dared to have done with any other man — tentatively hoping that Raynard would understand what he was trying to tell him.

Raynard chuckled at his silliness, but it was a gentle sound, as if he really did understand, and didn't mind that Ori didn't know a better way to show it.

He ruffled Ori's hair before he took his hand away. "Good boy."

Ori felt heat race to his cheeks.

"Put these away before you settle," Raynard said, handing him the cuffs and blindfold.

Ori carried them over to the oak coffer, his knees still not quite steady under him. He put those items his master had tossed on top of the dresser away as well. They were all simple bindings, but he couldn't fail to notice that some of the toys still left in the chest had nothing to do with keeping someone bound where his master wanted. Carrying the key back to the bed, he offered it to his master.

He could feel Raynard studying him carefully as he took the key, but Ori couldn't bring himself to meet his gaze. He'd seen the whip in there, and he knew that his master would realise that the moment their gazes met.

"You said you've been whipped before?"

That he'd realised it even *before* their gazes met...

Ori nodded. Raynard patted the bed next to him, guiding Ori to lie down on his stomach alongside him. He stroked his palm up and down Ori's back. There weren't any marks there right then, but there often had been, during the time he'd spent at the nest.

"Always a punishment?" Raynard asked.

Ori was about to give an automatic answer, when he stopped himself short. "Sometimes, I think they made up an excuse, just because they wanted to whip me, sir," he admitted.

"And did those whippings feel different?" Raynard asked.

Ori thought about it for a little while, as he savoured the feel of his master's touch sliding over his skin. He nodded, his cheek rubbing against the sheet beneath his head.

"Did you like it?"

Ori bit his lip as he realised the truth, as he let the truth come to the front of his mind and really make itself known for the first time. He nodded again. "I never liked knowing I deserved to be punished, sir," he added, a few seconds later, unable to stand the idea of Raynard thinking he didn't care whether or not he pleased those he served.

Raynard's hand continued to stroke Ori's back, along the lines where the lash had landed so many times. The memory of the whip tingled along his skin. His imagination rushed forward, wondering what it would have felt like if his master had been the one holding the whip, and if Ori had known that he was only whipping him because he wanted to.

If he hadn't already been so completely filled with satisfaction, Ori knew he'd have stiffened against the sheet.

"Shall I fetch the whip for you, sir?" he asked.

Raynard shook his head. "Sleep now. You're going to need your energy. Tomorrow, I'll be starting your formal training."

Ori nodded. He didn't really understand what that might mean, but his master sounded pleased with the prospect. Right then, that was enough to please Ori too.

As he closed his eyes, the same words that had gradually been seeping into his mind every time he wrote them down, replayed themselves once more inside his head.

The most valuable possession my master owns is his submissive. I will take great care that no harm comes to my master's submissive whenever he is not there to watch over me himself.

Chapter Eight

Raynard ran a critical eye over the dining table. It was set to perfection. If Ori hadn't actually pulled out a ruler and measured the gaps between each item, no one would have ever guessed it. Every piece of silverware shone, every glass sparkled.

If his first forays into it were anything to go by, the more formal rituals of high service were going to suit Ori very well. More than a few times over the last few days, Raynard had caught sight of a quietly satisfied smile on the duckling's face. After all the grunt work he'd put in while making the house fit for habitation, getting to play with a bit of sparkle was obviously doing him a world of good.

A smile crept to Raynard's lips too. The simple fact that Ori had managed to do it all without adding to the list of things he'd broken, seemed to have done wonders for his confidence as well.

Raynard looked over his shoulder. Ori stood by the dining room door, his hands folded neatly behind his back and his chin up—his stance as perfect as everything else he'd laid out for his master's inspection.

The table was set for two, just as Raynard had ordered.

Raynard nodded to Ori, signalling that he was ready for the food to be served.

Ori reappeared three minutes later, ornate silver tray in hand. He'd followed Raynard's orders when he'd prepared the food and hadn't panicked about producing something that fitted the elaborate trimmings that graced the table.

The scent of the meal called to Raynard. Not as much as the sight of the naked man carrying it, but still, it promised him a plate piled high with the kind of simple food Ori had quite a knack for.

Raynard took his seat. Ori served the meal, just as he'd been taught to over the previous few weeks, as the kitchen table had found itself set a little more elaborately every day.

He served the empty chair next to Raynard in much the same way before stepping back to receive his master's criticisms.

Raynard didn't have any to give.

"Leave the tray by the door, and take your seat," Raynard ordered, as they reached the end of those sections of a dinner party's proceedings in which he'd instructed Ori so far.

"Sir?"

Raynard raised an eyebrow at him. "Did you think I'd be eating alone?"

Ori hesitated for another second before slipping into the seat to Raynard's right. Just because Raynard had been content to eat with him in the kitchen until that evening, it obviously hadn't occurred to the fledgling that they would *both* migrate to the formal dining room now it was fit for purpose.

"There will be times when the table will be full of guests," Raynard told him. "The Raynards have been a leading family in the area for generations. I'll be expected to entertain."

"Yes, sir."

"In which case, you'll be required to dress for dinner," Raynard added, a little rush of jealousy coursing through him at the very idea of anyone else seeing Ori wearing nothing but his collar.

Ori glanced up at him. He smiled hesitantly, as if not sure his master really meant he'd be allowed to take a seat at the table when there were others there.

"Different occasions require different forms and protocol," Raynard expanded, as the dinner progressed. "If the gathering is specifically for hawks, only hawks will attend."

"Yes, sir."

"But there will be other times when a greater variety of avian species are present. Then you'll be expected to take your place at my side and eat the same meal you serve to our guests."

"Yes, sir."

Raynard studied him out of the corner of his eye, wondering just how much complex thought went on in Ori's head while such simple answers left his mouth. The more time Raynard spent with him, the more determined he was to find out.

Happily, Raynard was confident that he'd have time to learn everything there was to know about the boy, principally, because he had no intention of allowing Ori to wander away from his protection at any point in the future.

Raynard might have been aware that he needed to wait until Ori was a fully-fledged shifter before he could make his intentions toward him a matter of record, but he saw no reason why that should dictate when he actually made his decisions.

He glanced across at Ori again. For once, he didn't find Ori sneaking a return peek at him.

Ori's attention was all on the cabinet at the other end of the table. The glass had been replaced just the previous day. The rest of the monstrous piece of furniture had been cleaned via a sturdy stepladder while Raynard was present to supervise. Earlier that day, Ori had carefully refilled it with all the delicate antique porcelain that had, luckily enough, been removed before his tumble.

The cabinet looked as good as it ever had. But there was still a frown on Ori's forehead when he glared at it.

Raynard reached out and picked up his wine glass. It was filled with water that evening. When he placed it back on the table, Ori glanced at it. Picking up the water jug, he refilled Raynard's glass.

"Thank you."

Ori smiled at him, almost absentmindedly, before turning his gaze back to the cabinet.

Raynard felt his hackles rise. "Ori?"

"Yes, sir?"

"Who do you believe is the master in this relationship?"

Suddenly, Raynard knew he had his fledgling's full attention.

"You, sir," Ori said, very seriously.

"And, that being the case, who do you believe should be the judge when deciding the standard of behaviour you're expected to attain?"

"You, sir," Ori repeated.

Raynard could practically sense Ori's pulse race faster and faster as he tried to work out where the conversation was heading and what the hell he'd done wrong.

"When I punish you for a failure, that's the end of the matter. Acting as if you believe otherwise could easily be interpreted as an insult."

Ori held his gaze, apparently still none the wiser.

"You took your punishment," Raynard told him. "You were forgiven. Unless you have some reason to believe the cabinet is about to launch itself across the room at us, stop staring at it."

Ori looked down for a second, then back up, careful not to even glance toward the cabinet in the process.

Raynard tucked a knuckle under Ori's chin, encouraging him to lift it up a little and not look quite so heartbroken over the rather gentle criticism.

"Do you have any reason to cling to your guilt?" he asked.

"No, sir."

Raynard smiled his approval. As the meal progressed, for the first time since that disastrous day some six weeks earlier, he felt Ori start to relax while in the dining room. By the end of the meal, Ori almost seemed to have reached a point where the cabinet was just another piece of furniture. Almost.

Finally, the companionable dinner had to come to an end. Ori had just brought the tray across to clear the table, when he hesitated. "Shall I light the fire in the library first, sir?"

Raynard shook his head. "Not tonight."

Ori didn't question his decision. He simply went back to clearing the table.

Raynard stood up. "When you've finished here, come up to the bedroom."

"Yes, sir!"

Ori's enthusiasm at the possibility they'd go to bed early had Raynard smiling to himself as he left the room. The marks he'd left on Ori's skin might have faded, but the impression he'd left on Ori's mind when he brought out the cuffs obviously hadn't dimmed in the least. If he was unable to face the china cabinet without feeling guilty, he was equally incapable of walking past the toy chest without blushing.

Raynard made his way up the stairs and into their bedroom. As he automatically set about his self-assigned tasks, he turned that thought over inside his head. *Their* bedroom.

He supposed it was, in a way. Technically, Ori might still have his own room in the servants' quarters, but it had been weeks since Raynard wanted him to sleep anywhere but at his side. It was hard to believe that would change as more time passed. Raynard shook his head at himself, wondering how the hell a supposedly ugly little ducking had managed to burrow his way so deeply into his affections in such a short space of time.

A click from the door caught Raynard's attention. He turned just in time to see Ori's expression drop when he realised that Raynard was getting dressed to go out.

The protocols Raynard had taught Ori came to his rescue. He settled into his at rest position, hands folded behind his back.

"Come here."

He stepped forward. Raynard nudged him in the direction of the shower with a tap on the backside.

"Get dressed when you're done," he ordered.

When Ori came back into the bedroom a few minutes later, he'd already dried himself. His hair stuck up at all different angles after being towelled off.

Raynard ruffled Ori's hair even further as Ori walked past him, making him smile. There was no longer any hint of the flinch Raynard had noticed the first few times he'd raised his hand to offer that kind of affection.

There weren't many choices for Ori to make as he stood in front of the wardrobe Raynard had set aside for his use. All the clothing Raynard had bought for him was very simple. Black trousers. White shirts. Black boots and belts. Ori was ready in minutes.

Raynard watched as Ori turned to the mirror over the chest of drawers. He combed his fingers through his hair a few times, but it made very little difference. He caught Raynard's eyes in the glass and looked quickly down, a slight blush rising to his cheeks at being caught trying to style himself up.

Stepping up behind him, Raynard stared over Ori's shoulder and met his eyes in the reflection. He slipped his fingers into Ori's hair, tugging his head back to rest against his shoulder for a few moments.

"It's always kind of done whatever it wants, sir," Ori admitted.

"That will probably change after you've completed your first full shift."

Confusion flickered through Ori's expression as Raynard ran his fingers through the unruly strands of hair again. The position probably wasn't entirely comfortable, but

Ori made no attempt to lift his head from his master's shoulder.

"Your adult plumage should be easier to manage, a little less like a fluffy little duckling's. The colour can change like that too." Raynard snapped his fingers with the word "that", keeping his tone light, but he couldn't avoid wishing his fledgling would remain exactly as he was, forever.

"It won't turn green, will it, sir?" Ori's eyes opened wide in horror, but it didn't seem to be about vanity, just a disinclination to draw attention to himself in that manner.

Raynard managed to keep a straight face as he pretended to consider the matter very carefully. He gave in then and chuckled. "Unlikely. I've yet to see a mallard's colouring have that effect. Most ducks keep a brown plumage in their human form."

Ori laughed at Raynard's teasing and shook his head at his own gullibility. As they moved away from the mirror, Raynard adjusted Ori's shirt neck, to make sure his leather collar was clearly visible in a way he'd rarely encouraged Ori to display it when going out into the wider world.

Stepping away for a moment, Raynard picked up the leather jacket he'd laid out on the bed and held it up behind Ori. Ori's coordination deserted him. It took him a few attempts to work out how to get his arms into the sleeves so Raynard could settle the jacket neatly around his shoulders.

It was a perfect finish to the outfit.

"But you've already bought me..." *A coat.* Raynard put his finger over Ori's lips before he could finish the sentence.

He did have a very nice coat, a winter one.

"Spring's on its way," Raynard said. And promptly labelled himself a fool for feeling as if he had to make excuses for the purchase. Ori was his submissive, Raynard was free to dress him any way he chose, and he was perfectly free to fuss over him a little if he wanted to.

"Thank you, sir."

Raynard turned away and picked up his own jacket,

not sure he wanted to meet Ori's eyes right then. Quickly leading the way down the stairs, he soon had them both in his car, retracing the route they'd taken when Raynard first drove Ori away from the nest.

The atmosphere in the car slowly changed. Ori grew more and more tense as he realised where they were going. The easiness that existed between them in their bedroom was a distant memory by the time they pulled up outside the nest.

Ori quickly exited the car. Raynard glared after him until he realised that Ori wasn't rushing away, just hurrying around the car to open his door for him. Ori opened the main door into the nest for him too.

Raynard stepped inside, his eyes scanning the men in the large entry hall. On the far side of the room, he spotted another collared submissive opening a door for his master. Raynard relaxed as he realised where Ori had acquired the idea, and that it wasn't directly from another dominant.

Ori looked up as Raynard stepped through one of the doors held open for him, obviously hopeful that his service pleased his master in some way. Clearly, there was no other man, dominant or otherwise, infringing on his thoughts.

In one of the large communal lounges on the main floor, Raynard dropped a cushion onto the floor at the base of a leather armchair before taking the chair himself. He nodded to the cushion, but Ori didn't immediately accept his invitation to kneel there.

"A drink, sir?" he asked, softly.

Raynard nodded his approval.

Ori had waited on him for long enough to know what to fetch without it being spelled out to him. "For us both," Raynard mentioned, just in case Ori still didn't know him well enough to guess that, too.

Ori made his way to the bar on the far side of the room. Raynard was willing to bet every penny he had that he was the only man there who could see just how nervous Ori was about being back there. He didn't relax at all until he was kneeling safely at Raynard's feet, sipping his lemonade.

Raynard stroked his fingers through Ori's hair, certain that he had made the right decision in bringing him back to the nest at least once before Ori found himself standing in front the elders for his first shifting ceremony. That would be a stressful enough occasion for him without anything else added to the mixture.

Ori leaned into Raynard's touch, resting his head on his bent knee, just the way he did in the library at home. It was quite possible to believe that they were alone in the old gothic monstrosity until a shadow fell over Ori.

Raynard glanced up at the men who'd paused by the little group of chairs they occupied.

Two peregrine falcons stood there, waiting to be recognised. Harry and...Harry's brother, whose blasted name Raynard never could remember. He had a vague recollection of them from before he'd moved away from the area. They didn't appear to have changed much, even if their fledgling jeans had been exchanged for overly fashionable suits.

"We wish to pay our respects—we were both very sorry to hear about your uncle's passing," Harry said, sombrely.

Raynard nodded his acceptance and indicated to the sofa opposite him.

As the two men sat down, Raynard sensed Ori looking up at him. A question shone in his eyes. Raynard nodded permission for him to ask it.

"May I serve either of you a drink, sirs?"

"Two beers." Harry didn't even look at him as he said it—ignorant little pillock.

Ori returned with their drinks just as all the bland pleasantries that the situation demanded were concluded.

Neither falcon said anything when Ori set their drinks before them, but Charles, as Raynard had discovered the younger brother was called, glanced at Ori as he once more knelt at Raynard's feet. "Didn't he used to serve here?"

"He did," Raynard agreed.

"Not a bad fuck, if he's the one I'm thinking of."

Raynard felt himself tense at the statement. He looked down but Ori just kept staring at Raynard's knee, his expression unreadable. Raynard stroked his fingers from where they rested in Ori's hair, down to his collar, subtly reminding Ori of the leather's presence around his throat.

"He's belonged to me for several months. He's no longer available to serve other members of the nest."

Charles seemed to sense something in his tone of voice. He quickly dropped the subject, but Raynard wasn't in the mood to lighten the frigid atmosphere. He wasn't overly surprised when the brothers made their excuses and retreated within a few minutes.

Tugging gently at his messy strands of hair, Raynard pulled Ori's attention up to his face.

"You don't belong to the nest anymore, fledgling. You belong to me. No one has the right to lay a hand on you without my permission, and no one has my permission. Understand?"

"Yes, sir."

Raynard held his fledgling's gaze, wanting to make sure that knowledge settled deep into Ori's mind. There was no longer any reason for him to put up with any kind of mistreatment from anyone.

Ori was physically strong enough to defend himself; Raynard had no doubt about that. He just needed someone to give him permission to stand up for himself—to make sure he knew he was worth that.

Finally, Raynard let Ori look down. Ori sipped his drink. His expression was still unreadable, but Raynard found it hard to believe that Ori wasn't remembering all those times when he'd needed someone's protection before and hadn't received it.

Understanding that he was safe now wasn't the same as being able to forget a time when it had been very different.

Ori would always have those memories. Raynard couldn't fix that.

Raynard took a deep breath and pushed down his anger. Thinking about the way the fools at the nest had used Ori had been distasteful enough when Ori was a stranger to him. Now that Raynard knew Ori, and knew how deep his fledgling's instinct for submission went, it was obvious that Ori could never have fought back against the demands they made on him unless he'd had someone there to care about him and prompt him to do so.

"Do you remember Charles?" Raynard asked, as calmly as he could.

Ori shook his head. Raynard guessed there would be more than a few men there that night who Ori wouldn't remember half as well as they remembered him. It was hard to remember the faces of men who didn't think a duckling was good enough to look them in the eye.

"He always was a forgettable little sod," Raynard observed.

Ori smiled slightly, as if it really was that easy for his master to make all right with his world.

A few minutes later, Raynard glanced in the general direction of the kitchens, guessing there would be a few of the servants that Ori might appreciate the chance to visit. When Raynard spotted Hamilton making his way across the room, he decided there could be far worse times to have Ori out of earshot.

"Go and see if there's anything you can do to help your former colleagues for a few minutes," Raynard ordered, with a nod to the kitchens.

"Yes, sir."

Hamilton arrived just as Ori rose to leave. Ori hesitated, but only until he saw a drink already in the eagle's hand. By the time Hamilton had taken his seat, Ori was already on his way down the corridor leading to the kitchens. There was a little more confidence in his stride now than when he'd approached the bar less than an hour before.

"The collar looks good on him," Hamilton said.

Raynard nodded his agreement.

"A little premature though, wouldn't you say?"

"I thought you were a better judge of men than that," Raynard said, taking a sip of his drink.

"Oh?" Hamilton asked, as he leaned comfortably back in his chair.

"Do you really have any doubt that submission is in his nature?"

Hamilton shrugged. "I've no idea what he is. He's not even a true shifter until he —"

"Bollocks."

Hamilton's lips twitched. His accent deepened as his amusement seeped through. "Succinct and to the point — just like your uncle. The boy really has made an impression on you, hasn't he?"

Raynard studied his drink for a second. "He's a good submissive."

"And is that all it is?" Hamilton asked.

Raynard raised an eyebrow at his uncle's old friend.

"You wouldn't be the first man of rank to go giddy over a boy who is, as you've already said, so naturally inclined to want to please his betters."

Raynard had his mouth open and a curt answer on the tip of his tongue, when a crash from the general direction of the kitchens caught his attention. If Ori had all the natural inclination to service that every duck seemed to possess, then he had all the coordination of a true duckling as well.

A face appeared around the corner. It wasn't Ori. Raynard didn't recognise the man but, whoever he was, he looked straight toward Raynard and caught his eye.

Rising from his chair, Raynard strode rapidly across the room, only half-aware of Hamilton trailing curiously along after him. Raynard's heart rate doubled as the image of the dining room sprung back into his mind.

Swearing reached his ears as he turned the corner. Ori stood to one side of the narrow hallway, halfway between the main kitchen and the dining room. Raynard ran his eyes over the scene. Ori stood next to one of the nest's servants. Pots and pans littered the floor around their feet, but they both appeared to be unhurt.

The same couldn't be said for the crow crumpled on the floor with his hands clamped down over his crotch. A knee had obviously made recent acquaintance with his balls.

Another of the crows from the flock that lived at the nest approached Ori, his trainers squeaking against the tiled floor. Ori held his ground far better than Raynard expected, even tilting his chin back and looking the crow straight in the eye.

"And what do you think your master will say when we tell him—"

"His master will tell Ori that he's obeyed his orders very well," Raynard cut in.

Ori jerked around to face Raynard.

"He doesn't have permission to allow any other man to lay a hand on him," Raynard added, catching Ori's gaze and holding it. "I assume you mentioned that fact to them?"

"Yes, sir."

Raynard nodded his approval. "Good boy."

Raynard forced himself to look away so he could meet the gaze of every other man lurking in the narrow corridor. He had a feeling that any man in the nest who was tempted to try to treat Ori as public property, would soon take note. Word like that flew around the nest quickly. *Raynard's sub can defend himself—and his master likes that fact.*

Raynard took a pace back. Without so much as a glance at the other men present, Ori stepped over the prone crow and hurried across to join Raynard. They made their way out of the corridor, stopping only for Raynard to mention to one of the nest's security flock that an eye should be kept on the servant who'd been at Ori's side, just in case the crows took exception to him.

Finding their seats again, Raynard settled himself in his chair.

"You did well," he told Ori, nodding to the cushion at his feet once more.

"Do you really think so?" Hamilton asked, as he took a seat on the sofa opposite Raynard.

"He followed my orders perfectly," Raynard snapped.

"You ordered him to strike out at a higher ranking avian?"

"I ordered him to defend himself if he needed to," Raynard corrected. He barely managed to stop himself pointing out that it was the same order Hamilton should have given Ori when he first came to the nest.

Ori dipped his head to lean his temple against Raynard's knee as he instinctively sought his reassurance. A shudder ran through him. Raynard settled his hand in Ori's hair, encouraging him to stay there and rest until he got himself back together.

Hamilton seemed to linger for a long time, purely to be annoying. Raynard gave the leader of the nest less than half his attention. His focus was on his fledgling. Ori really had come a long way since they were last at the nest. He would never have had the confidence to floor the crow back then. Raynard smiled to himself with the knowledge. Pride rushed through him.

Finally, Hamilton got bored and moved away to bother someone else.

"Where did all that courage come from?" Raynard whispered to Ori.

Ori looked up at him through his lashes as he lifted his hand to his collar. It didn't seem to be an intentional answer as much as an instinctive gesture, but it was still remarkably eloquent.

When Raynard rose, Ori did the same. He fell into step beside Raynard as if it was the most natural thing in the world. If he was anxious about remaining in the nest, he showed no sign of it.

By the time they'd made their way into the maze of playrooms that existed on one of the upper floors of the club, no one who saw them could have doubted exactly who Ori belonged to. Every shifter who had looked consideringly at Ori had also met Raynard's eye — and every one of them had lowered his gaze before a hawk. Raynard was gradually starting to feel a little bit better about the world.

The main exhibition station in the centre of the most overtly leather-clad part of the nest was set up for a whipping. Raynard heard Ori's steps falter when the arched wooden frame came into view. Raynard glanced toward him. Tension ran through every bit of Ori's body, half fear and half something far more interesting.

Raynard walked confidently up to the whipping post as if that had been his intended destination all along. Ori didn't hang back. He didn't speak either.

Raynard carefully examined the cuffs that hung down from the top of the arch. They looked harsh, but they were actually well padded. They would do nicely.

Raynard looked over his shoulder. Their eyes met.

"Take off your coat and shirt."

Ori maintained eye contact as he obeyed. Garments removed, he folded each one and knelt down to place them neatly on the floor just outside the whipping area. And he did it all without looking away from Raynard for a second.

Ori got up off his knees, but he didn't approach the arch. Settling himself into his rest position, he remained on the edge of the whipping area, waiting for his master to invite him closer.

Raynard didn't make him wait too long. He soon had the cuffs wrapped around Ori's wrists, securing his hands above his head. The arch was high and Ori was far from the tallest of avians. Every inch of his body was stretched out taut, creating a perfect canvas for Raynard to decorate in any way he chose.

Ori had healed well after his fall, only a slight scar still lingering on his left forearm. Raynard ran a knuckle along it. Ori swallowed rapidly. He'd expected to be whipped as a punishment for that tumble. He'd have taken whatever Raynard had dished out and thanked him for beating him senseless over an accident. Raynard remembered the look in his fledgling's eyes so well, the pure desperation.

Time for his next lesson in the difference between submitting to a club full of fools and one good master...

"Just because I want to," Raynard whispered into Ori's ear. "Because you belong to me and tonight you've earned the right to have a few extra marks to show it."

As easily as the words left his lips, Raynard sensed any lingering fear leave Ori. He hadn't been lying when he'd told his master that the knowledge it was a punishment was the only thing he'd hated about being whipped.

Ori took a slow, deep breath and looked up at Raynard. The same desperation to please was in his eyes again, but now it was mitigated by the knowledge that Raynard was already pleased with him, and tempered with the realisation that from that moment on, a whipping would be a sign of that and nothing else.

Satisfied they understood each other, Raynard turned away. He picked up a whip from a table where a selection had been laid out for the use of any avian with a high enough rank. Raynard didn't look around the room, but he knew full well that there were already a dozen or more men watching them, waiting to see exactly what the new hawk intended to do with his submissive.

Raynard ran the leather through his fingers as he turned his complete attention to the fledgling's back. Ori's shoulders were a little broader than they'd been when Raynard had first met him — the product of all the work he'd done setting the house in order, combined with frequent visits to the swimming pool. His collar formed a stark black line around his neck, screaming Raynard's possession of him to anyone who was interested.

Raynard ran the whip over Ori's skin as he stepped closer. A shiver raced through Ori, but it had nothing to do with fear. As Raynard looked down Ori's body, the effect the prospect of a whipping had on him was obvious. Ori's trousers weren't tented in front of him because he was afraid.

Far more used to seeing Ori undressed than covered, Raynard itched to reach for Ori's belt, to peel the fabric off and leave him standing naked at the whipping station. Raynard stepped away before he forgot all about the other men in the room and gave in to that temptation.

They might have seen Ori naked before, but that had been prior to Raynard collaring him. It wouldn't happen again without a bloody good reason.

Raynard lifted his arm and flicked the leather against Ori's back. Ori gasped as it connected for the first time. Raynard stepped forward and ran his hand across the mark the lash had left in its wake.

The whip had forced some heat into Ori's skin. A pale red line appeared as blood rushed to transport sensations around his body as quickly as it could.

Ori said nothing as Raynard stepped back, raised his hand and let the whip fall against him once more. No need for an inspection this time. Another flick of Raynard's wrist, and the whip kissed Ori's back a third time.

The whip Raynard had chosen was far from the harshest implement that had rested on the table, and he knew how to make it dance against a man's back in just the way he wanted. Each lash landed perfectly, decorating Ori's skin according to Raynard's exact wishes.

The rest of the club ceased to exist. Other men might have flooded into the space to observe, but they were irrelevant. Ori's ragged breaths filled Raynard's world. He watched, enchanted, as Ori dropped his head back a little on each stroke, as if he was already struggling to keep his reactions in check.

Each touch of leather, each touch from his master, appeared to push more and more pleasure into Ori until he didn't know how to contain it. His hands clenched into fists above his head. One hand fumbled at the opposite wrist.

Raynard let the whip drop to his side as he watched the fingers of Ori's right hand wrapped around his left wrist. It was as close to his rest position as his bondage would allow. He was doing exactly what he was supposed to do when he didn't know what to do with himself. Even then, Raynard sensed that his words were in Ori's head, guiding everything he did.

Raynard moved closer to stand at Ori's side. He rested his hand gently on Ori's back, below all the whip marks.

"Look at me. Look at your master."

Ori blinked open his eyes as he turned his head, his expression unfocused, clouded with pleasure.

Raynard held Ori's gaze as he lifted his hand and stroked his fingers tenderly across the whip marks. They were still light, even after the repeated contact of the leather. Ori arched into his touch as far as he could. His eyes fell helplessly closed as more and more ecstasy seemed to rush into his body with each mark Raynard's fingers passed over.

"Ten more," Raynard said. "Count them out for me."

He waited at Ori's side until his fledgling found his voice.

"Yes, sir."

The words were barely whispered, but the only person who needed to be able to hear them was easily close enough to catch each syllable.

Raynard stepped back. The whip cracked more loudly against Ori's skin as Raynard let a little more of his strength fall against him.

"One, sir."

A darker red line flourished over the lighter ones.

Raynard brought the lash down again.

"Two, sir."

He only gave Ori just enough time to make his responses before he brought the whip down on him again and again. Each time, Ori counted it out for him. Three...four...five...six...

"Seven, sir."

Another kiss of the leather. A little cry as the whip cracked against Ori's skin, harder than before.

"Eight, sir."

Every line of muscle in Ori's body was taut and perfect. His head was tipped back toward the ceiling, but his voice was strong. He was breathless with pleasure, not pain.

Raynard snapped the leather again.

Ori whimpered. His head dropped forward. "Nine, sir."

If he'd been a step farther away, Raynard wouldn't have been able to make out the words.

One more. Raynard raised his arm higher, the whip cracked against Ori's back, crossing several of the other dark lines he'd already painted on his skin.

A scream filled the air as Ori's body jerked. He seemed to rise into the air, hanging from the cuffs. Then the world snapped back into focus. The yell faded away. Ori collapsed, limp within his bonds.

Tossing the whip aside, Raynard strode forward. Ori managed to drag his head up to look at him, even while he wasn't quite capable of supporting himself on his own feet. He licked his lips and swallowed rapidly as he tried to find his words. "Ten, sir."

Raynard slid his hand into Ori's hair as he tugged him forward, just far enough to lean his head on his master's shoulder. "Good boy."

Ori dragged a satisfied breath into his body as he heard the whispered praise.

He trembled slightly as Raynard slid another hand around his waist and encouraged him to rest more of his weight against his master's body. Despite Raynard's coaxing, Ori he stayed stiff, holding himself slightly away from Raynard in a way he hadn't done since he'd first come to Raynard's bed.

"Hush," Raynard whispered to him. He pressed a kiss against the top of his head. "I've got you." Even if they did have an audience...

Another second of hesitation, and Ori relaxed against him. He rubbed his head tenderly against Raynard's shoulder, nuzzling against him in an effort to get even closer than was physically possible.

"That's right," Raynard whispered to him.

As he stroked his fingers through Ori's hair, part of Raynard wanted to look up, to meet the eyes of all the men around them and stare them down one by one, to mark his territory and scream his ownership of the man in his arms.

He resisted the urge. They could be dealt with at any time. Raynard kept his attention firmly on Ori. Some things were too important to be put off until a later date. Ori needed his master right then, and Raynard was no more able to deny his submissive whatever he needed, than Ori was capable of disobeying his master.

Raynard smiled softly against the top of his fledgling's head. "Good boy."

Chapter Nine

Ori arched lazily against the lumpy mattress. With his eyes closed and his mind lost in memories, he was almost willing to swear that he could feel the soft cotton sheet beneath him rubbing against the whip marks on his back.

Of course, the marks were actually long gone. They'd faded slowly, but they hadn't been able to last forever. Ori sighed sleepily to himself as he turned onto his side. The breeze from the open balcony window caressed his bare skin as he lifted his hand to his neck and traced the line of his collar — a mark that would never fade.

It was getting darker. Raynard would be home soon. Ori rolled his shoulders, stretching his aching muscles, before snuggling back into the little nest his blankets had formed around him. His eyes dropped closed, only to snap open when he heard the fluttering of wings on the balcony. Ori barely had time to blink before Raynard was in his human form and striding through the big open windows.

Ori tried to scramble off the mattress and onto his feet; he failed. He didn't even have time to sit up before Raynard was there, his lips on Ori's mouth, his body covering Ori's smaller frame as he pushed him down onto the mattress.

Wrapping his hands tightly around Ori's wrists, Raynard pinned his arms down on either side of his head.

Ori managed a brief "I..." before his words were swallowed by the kiss. He smiled against his master's mouth. Words were wasted when Raynard had just finished stretching his wings; far better to simply part his lips and offer himself freely to his master.

Raynard was already hard. His erection slid against Ori's skin as he pressed him down more firmly against the sheet. Ori squirmed and tried to pull his legs back. It wasn't easy when Raynard didn't seem capable of understanding what he was trying to do.

For the first time, Raynard didn't appear to be holding anything back. There was no attempt to gentle his hold on Ori, no checking to see if Ori was able to keep up with his demands.

Raynard's teeth nipped at Ori's lips, harsh and demanding, pulling a whimper from him as he finally managed to draw his knees back. Raynard's shaft nudged against his already slicked hole. He immediately pushed into him. No hesitation, no doubt of his absolute right to thrust his cock deep inside Ori whenever he wanted.

The lube Ori had applied while Raynard was out stretching his wings only eased Raynard's way so much. Ori arched against the sheet, his hands clenching into fists above Raynard's grip on him, even as he tilted his hips back and tried to spread himself wider and offer himself to his master more readily.

Raynard barely stilled inside him before he pulled away, and thrust back into his hole. Ori's prostate sung out as Raynard pounded into him again and again. The sudden stretch started to ease, and soon, there was nothing to take away the pleasure Raynard pushed into him with every movement.

Hard ever since Raynard had taken flight, Ori desperately tried to hold back. In the half-light, he saw Raynard staring down at him, naked possession flashing in his gaze.

Ori did his best to rock in time with Raynard's movements, to clench around him, to do anything he could to make it perfect for his master. But part of him knew that wasn't really required. All Ori had to do was be there, waiting and willing, when his master came back. All he had to do in order for Raynard to be pleased with him was to be the kind of avian who loved it when his master let the hawk side of himself loose and forgot his human manners.

All Ori had to do was love being owned, and marked, and possessed by his master. Nothing Raynard could ask of him would ever be easier.

Pure bliss shone in Raynard's gaze as he stared down at him. And that was the moment when Ori realised that Raynard truly felt free to be who he was with him, just as Ori felt safe to be himself with his master.

Raynard thrust into him again, rough and seemingly determined to claim a bit of Ori's soul with every movement.

Ori gasped. He pulled at Raynard's hold on him, just for the joy of feeling Raynard's grip tighten around his skin. Somehow, he knew Raynard would understand, that he wouldn't think he truly wanted to get away from him. He was safe in the knowledge that Raynard would never actually release him no matter how hard he struggled. There was no room for begging when his master was in this mood. No room for disobedience either.

Another hard thrust. Raynard dropped Ori's wrist and pushed his hand down between their bodies. He jacked Ori's cock hard, fast and unrelenting, his eyes daring Ori to come without permission. Ori bit down on his bottom lip as he scrambled for control, his free hand clawing at Raynard's shoulder.

"Come."

Ori tossed his head back, his nails biting into Raynard's skin as he came, spilling between them. Gasping for breath, Ori struggled to keep his eyes open, not wanting to miss the sight of his master coming just a moment after him.

Raynard jerked, throwing his head back. Then each muscle froze as he lost himself in the pleasure racing through his veins. The whole world seemed to stop as Raynard came, as if the sight of him distracted the entire universe, and it had to pause to admire the sheer perfection of him.

As the last of his ecstasy drained from his expression, Raynard's strength seemed to leave him. All his weight came to rest on Ori, pinning him to the blanket from tip to toe.

No pretence, no politeness. Ori was Raynard's to do with as he pleased. If Raynard wanted to sleep like that all night, Ori knew he'd love every minute he spent trapped underneath him, barely even able to draw breath as his muscles cramped and his joints turned numb.

All too soon, Raynard came sufficiently back to his usual self to roll away and lie next to Ori. It wasn't a large mattress. A double would never have made it up the stairs into the little attic room.

On the tiny single, they had no choice but to snuggle as they rested. As much as Ori wanted to lie motionless and not disturb Raynard, he couldn't help but try to rearrange himself a little more comfortably as the minutes passed.

"Still sore, fledgling?" Raynard stroked his hands down Ori's arm as he guided him nearer.

Ori helplessly leaned into Raynard's touch, letting it soothe the muscles it passed over. "It's fine, sir."

Raynard gathered him close, cradling him against the heat of his body. "You'll feel better once you complete your full shift."

Ori burrowed a little deeper into Raynard's embrace.

"Nervous?"

Ori shrugged.

"You'll be fine," Raynard promised.

"Yes, sir."

It would be fine. Ori knew that. He rubbed his cheek against Raynard's chest, taking strength from his strength.

A sneaky little voice in the back of his mind reminded him that he'd thought it would be fine last time too. But everyone's attitude toward him had changed once he'd completed his half shift and... Ori held back a sigh.

Everything would be fine. Raynard's right hand rested idly on his chest, just next to Ori's head. Reaching up, Ori stroked his fingers over the tattoo on the inside of Raynard's wrist.

Raynard lifted his head to see what he was doing. Ori was about to pull his hand back and apologise for overstepping some sort of invisible line, but Raynard merely bent his hand back, offering the species mark to be inspected more easily.

Ori cautiously ran his fingers over the mark, tracing the jagged lines of it with his fingertip.

"What does it feel like, sir? Shifting, I mean," he asked.

Raynard seemed to think about it for a long time. "It's as if a part of you that can't flourish when you're in human form is being freed," he offered eventually. "The first few times can be difficult. It can be painful until you get used to it. But it's worth it. So very worth it…"

Ori smiled as he stared up at the expression of pure peace on Raynard's face. Then his smile faltered. "Do you wish…?" His courage deserted him, the rest of the question died, unspoken.

"Ori?" Raynard prompted.

Ori frowned across at the window. "Do you wish I was a hawk instead, sir?"

Raynard chuckled. "Two male hawks seldom lie comfortably together. I doubt even a male and female would make a good pairing if it wasn't for some shifters' innate desire to breed."

Ori glanced up at him.

"I'm very happy with the man I have, fledgling. Don't let all that nonsense a few fools spout about your supposed *betters* turn you into as much of an idiot as them. All species have their strengths and weaknesses, the things they are known for."

"What are ducks known for, sir?" Ori whispered, his fingers still tracing Raynard's tattoo.

"Most find their way into the service of others for good reason. They're hard workers. Strong. Resilient. They enjoy pleasing other people. They're loyal, dedicated and affectionate. Ducks have always made fantastic submissives,"

Raynard recounted, almost matter-of-factly.

Ori dipped his head as a pleased little blush stole its way to his cheeks.

"And there are a couple of lesser known traits," Raynard went on, his tone of voice changing slightly. "Some of them have a way of sneaking under a hawk's skin so that when he least expects it, he finds himself with a servant who becomes a submissive, with a submissive who somehow becomes much more to him than even that."

Ori couldn't bring himself to lift his gaze and see what might be in Raynard's eyes. Instead, he kept his head on Raynard's chest and listened to his master's heart beat out a slow, steady and reassuring rhythm, while his own pulse raced faster and faster.

Raynard took hold of Ori's hand and held it up so his wrist was clearly visible to them both. As Ori watched, Raynard painted a symbol on the skin with his fingertip— mapping out where the mark stating his species would rest, just over the vein.

"A copy of it will need to be added here too," Raynard said, transferring his attention to the tag hanging from Ori's collar.

"I'd like that, sir," he whispered.

Raynard pressed a kiss to the top of his head and relaxed back against the mattress.

As the room turned cooler and the breeze continued to swirl through the open window, Ori curled closer still to his master's warmth and strength.

I love you too, sir.

He couldn't make himself say the words right then, any more than his master seemed inclined to say them out loud before Ori had a mark on his wrist stating who he was.

Ori smiled slightly as he started to doze. Maybe completing his first full shift was something to look forward to after all…

"Sir?" Ori looked up as Raynard reached for the buckle on his collar.

"The tradition of each avian appearing bare before the leaders of his nest the first time he completes a full shift exists for a reason," Raynard informed Ori, in the same serious tone that seemed to have lurked in his voice all day.

Ori swallowed. His clothes lay on a chair to his right. It was easy not to care about them, but his collar...

The leather moved around his throat as Raynard hooked his fingers through it. "As much as I'd like to leave it on, it's best that you don't accidently throttle yourself the first time you shift."

It was a risk Ori would far rather have taken than feel his collar being removed, but he forced himself to accept Raynard's decision. He stood meek and silent as his neck was bared, and left bare for the first time in so many months, without even a silver chain to take its place.

Ori ran his hand over his neck. His eyes met Raynard's. He moved both his hands behind his back and took up his usual waiting position.

Raynard brushed their lips together. Ori tightened his grip around his opposite wrist as he cherished the brief moment of reassurance. Everything would be fine. Raynard had told him that several times, and he believed his master.

"Go on, fledgling," Raynard ordered, nodding toward the curtains lining one wall of the shadowy little space.

Nudging the thick velvet folds apart, Ori slipped reluctantly through the gap and onto the stage. A dozen of the elders sat in a semi-circle, every one of them fully clad in a perfectly tailored suit. Between them, they represented almost all the leading avian species.

Taking a deep breath, Ori moved to the middle of the shifting stage and settled himself in his familiar rest position to wait for an order. He felt the gazes of all twelve men running over his naked body, assessing him, some of them with more appreciation than others.

More than a few of them were familiar in that he suspected they were men who had issued orders to him before he had been taken under Raynard's protection. They hadn't all been pleasant orders to follow. They weren't all pleasant men.

Ori closed his eyes for a moment as more and more tension rushed into his body. As he looked up again, a movement at the back of the room caught his attention. Raynard stepped through the door in the far corner and found a vantage point along the back wall. Ori's nerves settled when he saw him. He noticed a flash of silver in Raynard's hand and recognised the tag on his collar.

His master was waiting for him. All he had to do was get this over with, and he could go back to Raynard, and to his collar, and everything really would be fine. Ori looked to the highest backed chair in the middle of the semi-circle, to the leader of the nest.

Mr. Hamilton nodded for him to begin.

Ori took another deep breath. Releasing his hands from behind his back, he let them hang idly at his sides, just as Raynard had told him he should. Closing his eyes, he searched for that place in his mind where he'd come so close to finding another side of himself once before.

A frown crept to his brow as he pushed his way into unexplored areas of his psyche. As he delved deeper, it became far easier not to care about the men watching him, about the nest, about almost anything.

Some part of him was vaguely aware of his physical body lowering itself so he crouched on the stage, his hands steadying him on the floorboards in front of him. As his senses started to spin, Ori dropped onto his knees.

His mind raced faster, spiralling uncontrollably along paths he hadn't even been sure existed a few minutes earlier.

His partial shift had been all about scrabbling for something out of his reach. It was nothing like this. He gasped. A small cry escaped him as he felt his body being pulled in a million different directions all at once. His mind rebelled against the idea, panicking and trying to pull away.

Like gravity and destiny rolled into one, something relentlessly dragged him forward, down into a place he didn't understand; a place he didn't even know if he wanted to understand.

The stage boards seemed to bow and sway under him, threatening to toss him down into his audience at any moment. Ori shook his head. Pain flashed through his body. And, all at once, it wasn't his body. He had no control, no say over what happened to it.

For the first time in so many months, fear rushed into the space left behind after his control was ripped from him. It wasn't his master assuming power this time. It was something both inside him and that wasn't him at all. Ori tried to rise to his feet. He tried to reach out to the world around him, scrabbling for something, anything, to hold on to as terror raced through his veins faster than he could chase it away.

He dragged his eyes open and looked to the back of the room. He couldn't see into the shadows, couldn't focus. The elders were close enough to the circle of light directed toward the stage for him to make them out, but they swirled and distorted before him, their faces blurring and melting until they were barely recognisable.

Ori's limbs wouldn't work. Something moved, but all he saw was a flash of white to his side. Pain shot through him again — bright, vivid, and worse than any whipping could ever be. He collapsed forward again.

His body met the boards with a thump. He tried to open his eyes. For a second, everything returned to its usual focus. Then, very quietly, it all faded to black.

* * * * *

A hand caressed Ori's cheek. He immediately leaned

into it, relishing his master's reassurance. But the hand felt wrong. It was softer, plumper than Raynard's hand. Ori pulled away from it as he fought to open his eyes.

Men crowded around him on all sides, looming over him. Ori looked past them and between them, seeking out any sign of his master.

Raynard wasn't there. Ori tried to sit up.

A hand came to rest on his shoulder, nudging him back against something soft and yielding. "You should rest a little longer, sire."

Ori looked over his shoulder. Someone had placed a huge velvet cushion behind his back. He looked at the floor around him. There were blankets and cushions everywhere, half covering his naked body.

Swallowing rapidly as he tried to make his throat work, Ori attempted to sit up again. He automatically pulled the blankets more securely over his lap as he rubbed at his temple with his other hand. His head ached in a way he hadn't even known was possible.

He lowered his hand to his neck, seeking out the reassurance of his collar. It wasn't there. Even as panic spiked inside him, a few memories stumbled toward the front of his mind.

Raynard taking the collar back so he couldn't accidently strangle himself with it during his first shift. Stepping onto the stage. The swirling thoughts. The pain.

"My master," he managed to whisper.

The men looming above him exchanged glances as if they had no idea who he was talking about.

"Mr. Raynard," Ori managed to croak out. He focused in on Mr. Hamilton. He knew who Raynard was. "Where's my master, sir?"

Mr. Hamilton stared down at him for several long seconds, his expression very serious. "You should rest, sire."

Ori frowned. *Sire...*

His brain wouldn't work. "I need to see my master," he

repeated. Raynard would make everything fine.

Mr. Hamilton turned and spoke to someone over his shoulder. When he looked back to Ori, an annoyed expression lingered around his eyes. "One of the servants has been sent to find him, sire."

Another man crouched down at Ori's side. "A drink, sire."

Ori frowned. He didn't know what was going on. There were only three things in the world he was sure of — he was scared, he was confused, and he wanted his master. He tried to rise again. When another stranger put his hand on his shoulder to nudge him back down, Ori pulled away from him.

No one was supposed to lay a hand on him but his master. As his mind spun, that was one of the few facts that couldn't be denied. He shrugged off the man's touch, losing all ability to be polite and subtle as he did so. The man didn't try to touch him again as Ori pulled himself to his feet.

"Your clothes, sire?"

Ori hesitated. He looked down at his naked body. He was supposed to wear clothes when other people were around. He remembered that too. One by one, Raynard's rules arranged themselves neatly in his head, building a framework for him to hold onto in a suddenly uncertain world.

Ori nodded. He wanted his clothes. Raynard wouldn't like him wandering around the nest naked — not now that the shifting ceremony was complete. He'd made it very clear that this was a specific exception to the rule. The exception was over.

Pushing his way through the curtain at the back of the stage, Ori scrambled into clothes Raynard had bought for him, his hands clumsier than ever. Some hopeful part of Ori had thought that Raynard might be back there waiting for him, but there was no sign of him.

Some of the elders had followed him into the cramped little space, but they were no alternative to his master. They just stood around, useless and in the way. Ignoring them completely, Ori pushed open the door and stumbled out into the hallway. Raynard wasn't there either, but lots of other men were. A few familiar faces peeked out from the crowd; servants he'd worked alongside stood with men who'd used and abused him during the months he'd lived at the nest. But Raynard wasn't in the crowd. Turning in every direction, Ori tried to work out which way to go, but there was no path through the other men.

He lifted his hand to touch his collar the way he had so often over the months. His fingers brushed against bare skin.

A movement caught his attention. Everet, the raven who'd followed Raynard's orders and watched over him that first day, caught Ori's eye before quickly looking down.

Ori dropped his own gaze as he tried to get past the men who lined the corridors. They stepped back to let him through, making a path just wide enough for him.

"In the old library."

The words were just on the edge of Ori's hearing. They reached him as he walked past the raven. It was impossible to be sure that they came from Everet, but something of the kindness in the words reminded Ori of that day when he first met Raynard. Ori couldn't ignore the possibility they were honest. He rushed in the direction of the old library.

Throwing open the door, he staggered to a stop several yards inside the room. On the far side of the high, book-lined space, Raynard stood by a window. He was looking out over the gardens and didn't bother to turn around to see who had entered the room. Closing the heavy panelled wood behind him, Ori took a deep breath. Everything would be fine now.

Folding his hands neatly behind his back, he took up a position next to the door. Raynard continued to stare out of the window. His face was only visible in profile, but Ori could see enough to know something was wrong. Raynard's shoulders were knotted with tension; his jaw was clamped shut. Not one muscle moved as Ori watched him from across the room.

Ori's relief at finding his master drained away. Something was very wrong. While he'd been completing his shift, something had obviously happened in his master's world, something far more important than any ceremony could ever be — something bad.

"May I serve you, sir?" Ori whispered, unable to simply stand there and watch Raynard in pain.

Raynard closed his eyes. Without any thought of protocol or rules, Ori stepped forward. He broke from his rest position and crossed the room to stand at his master's side. He laid his hand on Raynard's arm, desperate to offer him some sort of comfort. "Sir?"

Raynard spun away. He strode several paces toward the centre of the room before he turned to look at Ori for the first time. His eyes moved over Ori's body, from the top of his head, all the way down to his booted feet and back up again.

"Sir — ?" Ori began again.

Raynard cut him off, raising his hand for his silence.

Ori swallowed down his plea for reassurance.

For what felt like days, Raynard didn't say anything; he just stared as if Ori was some ghostly vision that he was unable to comprehend. Finally, he spoke. "What did the elders tell you?"

Ori shook his head. "Nothing, sir. I..." He took refuge in his rest position as he realised that running away from them might not have been the best way to please his master. "I'm sorry, sir. I might have left before the ceremony was properly completed."

Raynard closed his eyes again, just for a second, as if that was the only way he could keep control of his own emotions. Turning away, he led Ori across to a little seating area nestled among the towering bookshelves. As Raynard folded his tall frame into an armchair, Ori automatically began to lower himself to kneel at his feet.

Raynard stopped him short. "Sit there." He pointed to the chair opposite him.

Frowning, not sure now just how angry Raynard was with him, Ori sat on the edge of the seat Raynard had indicated and stared across the dark bare floorboards at him.

"The ceremony didn't go as expected," Raynard said, slowly.

"Have I done something wrong, sir?"

Raynard shook his head. "No, fled—" He stopped abruptly and took another deep breath. He straightened himself in his chair, tilting up his chin and squaring his shoulders. "The partial shift you performed before the elders when you first came to the nest wasn't conclusive. Sometimes, the elders' best guess isn't accurate."

Ori tentatively felt his way forward in the conversation. "I'm not a duckling, sir?"

"No," Raynard said. "You're not."

Species scrolled through Ori's mind. Whatever he was, it didn't seem to be anything that pleased his master. He still couldn't think quite clearly, couldn't remember what species were below even a duck. He wasn't even sure if there was such a thing as a lower rung in the hierarchy.

"You're a swan—that's what the elders saw today," Raynard said, his voice devoid of any sort of emotion.

Ori nodded, then waited patiently to be told what his master thought of that development and what he should think of it too. However, no further information seemed to be forthcoming.

"You...don't like swans, sir?" Ori hazarded.

Raynard stared at him for a moment. "There's no need for a swan to use an honorific when he's speaking to a hawk...sire."

Ori felt the air rush from his lungs. He tightened his grip on the edge of the seat. He shook his head, as much at the way his master spoke to him as at the words he chose to use.

Raynard glanced down for a moment, not in submission, but as if he couldn't even bear to look at him. Ori followed his gaze. Raynard still held the collar in his hand.

The moment Ori spotted it, he couldn't look away.

He swallowed rapidly. Raynard seemed to sense what he was looking at. He pushed the collar into his pocket, the tag catching the light before it quickly disappeared from sight.

For a second, where Raynard ordered Ori to sit ceased to matter; he sprung forward and lowered himself to his knees at his master's feet. He put his hand on Raynard's leg, only just stopping himself short of actually reaching for his pocket. "Sir?"

"I neither like nor dislike swans," Raynard said, his voice stiff and formal. "I've no reason to, sire —"

Ori touched his fingers very gently against his master's lips. "Please don't call me that, sir."

Raynard took hold of Ori's wrist and moved his hand away from his mouth. Ori couldn't bring himself to struggle against his hold. It felt too good to have Raynard's hand wrapped around his skin. There was a familiarity in it that promised everything would be okay.

Gradually, Raynard's anger seemed to leave him, until there was nothing in his eyes but sadness. He settled his other hand in Ori's hair and guided him forward to rest his head against his chest.

"Everything's fine," Raynard told him. "There's nothing for you to be upset about."

Ori nodded, rubbing his cheek against his master's shirt with the movement. It didn't feel like the truth. It didn't feel as if Raynard believed it to be the truth either.

"Tell me about swans, sir?"

Raynard's chest moved under Ori's head as he took a deep breath. "Swans are... They are the purest species of avian that exists. They are good, and noble, and beautiful. They have the most exquisite spirits, the finest temperaments."

Ori frowned slightly as he waited for the rest. Raynard said nothing.

"For service, sir?" Ori hinted eventually.

"Swans don't serve," Raynard whispered, each word raw as if pushed through a throat that didn't want to let them pass.

Ori pulled away, just far enough to look up at his master.

Raynard stroked his fingers through Ori's hair again. He cleared his throat. "Swans don't serve other avians, fledgling." His lips twisted into a mockery of an encouraging smile. "By the end of the day, you're going to have a great many servants of your own."

Ori shook his head. He caught hold of Raynard's shirt, bunching the fabric within his grip.

Raynard took hold of Ori's wrist, but Ori couldn't make his fingers unfurl and release him.

"You will," Raynard repeated. "A lot of things are going to change for you now."

Another shake of the head.

"A swan's life has its course plotted out for it from—"

"Maybe they were wrong," Ori rushed out. "Maybe I'm not a swan at all—"

"Ori..."

"Maybe I really am a duck," he pushed on, fuelled by a sudden and overwhelming desperation for that to be the case. "A very big, white duck. They might have mistaken that for a swan. Or a goose—they look even more like swans. Would a goose be allowed to—?"

"Enough!"

Ori fell silent as the word snapped through the room. Standing up, Raynard dragged Ori to his feet, too. An ornate mirror filled a gap between two massive bookcases. Raynard held him facing it.

Ori stared into the glass. His master's reflection glared at him, his expression so very serious, but Ori barely recognised the man standing with Raynard.

The fluffy, mottled hair was gone. Sleek, white strands had taken their place. Each one lay neatly against his scalp in a way his fledgling colours never had.

"I was there," Raynard bit out. "You're a swan. It's not an opinion. It's not a mistake. It's a statement of fact." The words were calmer, but it was a kind of forced calm that was barely able to contain the anger that still boiled beneath it.

Raynard sat back down with a sigh. Running his hand through his own hair, he carelessly disordered the dark brown waves.

Ori swallowed as he lowered himself once more to kneel at his master's feet. While uncertainty surrounded him, he latched on to what he could depend on when all else failed. "You said you'd put the collar back on, sir."

Raynard didn't answer immediately. "If the ceremony had gone as we expected, I would have," he finally said.

"But not on a swan..." Ori whispered, as much to himself as Raynard.

"A hawk can't own a swan, Ori. It would never be permitted. And even if it were, it wouldn't be right. That's not what—*I'm* not what you need now."

Ori closed his eyes. He couldn't think. Couldn't move. Couldn't breathe. He blinked open his eyes as he felt Raynard lean forward in his seat. Raynard stood up. Ori stayed on his knees, his hands slipping down his master's body until they rested on his trouser leg just above his shoe.

Raynard stepped forward. Fabric slipped out of Ori's hold on him as he went. "Let your true nature take over, and you'll be fine," Raynard said as he crossed the library. He paused with his hand on the door handle. "The elders will take good care of you now. They'll make sure you'll have everything you want."

With that, he was gone. He closed the door behind him.

Ori's eyes fell shut. There was only one thing he wanted, and he doubted any of the elders could provide it.

He wanted his master.

Chapter Ten

"Sire?"

Ori looked up.

Mr. Hamilton stood next to him. His attention moved from Ori to the empty chair Ori still knelt in front of, and back again.

"Would you like to see your rooms, sire?"

"Rooms?" Ori repeated blankly.

"A suite of rooms on one of the upper floors has been set aside for your use, sire," Mr. Hamilton informed him.

Ori just stared at him. He already had a room—the butler's old bedroom at his master's house. "Mr. Raynard...?"

"Has already left the nest," Mr. Hamilton finished for him.

Ori closed his eyes. When he finally found the strength to open them again, the empty chair filled both his field of vision and his world. He ran his hands over the cushioned seat as if that might somehow summon up his master, like a genie from a lamp.

"Did he leave any orders for me, sir?" Ori asked, unable to make the words anything more than a whisper.

"Sire?"

"Mr. Raynard—before he left, did he leave any orders for me, sir?" Ori repeated, with all the strength he could muster. His hand tightened into a fist against the cushion top.

"You're no longer under any obligation to obey Raynard's orders."

Ori looked up at him.

"You have every avian's sincere apology for being forced to serve a lower ranking species of..."

Ori shook his head, unwilling to hear anyone speak of his time with his master that way. Mr. Hamilton trailed off. For a long time, they both remained in frozen silence.

Finally, Ori found words. "What do you think it would please my master for me to do now, sir?"

"I…think he'd wish you to see your rooms, sire." Uncertainty made the Scottish accent more pronounced, softening the words a little.

Ori dropped his gaze. Part of him was aware that he couldn't remain kneeling before an empty chair forever — no matter how much he might wish he could. He slowly dragged himself to his feet.

His knees weren't steady; they only trembled more violently as he was forced to make his way through the crowds of men that lurked outside the library door. Dozens of pairs of eyes raked over every inch of his body. The fact that he wore far more than he had while he served at the nest did nothing to reassure him. His collar was gone; his neck was bare. Mere clothes couldn't help him forget that.

Mr. Hamilton led him along corridors and up flights of stairs. He finally stopped next to a set of high double doors. Mr. Hamilton opened one door, and stepped back to allow Ori through first, for all the world as if he were the servant and Ori were the bird of prey.

"Anything that you dislike will be changed as soon as possible, sire."

Ori looked at him, then at the space around him. As Mr. Hamilton led him through one opulent room after another, Ori couldn't think of a single word to say. It was all rich furnishings and marble, all gilt and shiny surfaces. Habit made Ori look for dust and work to do. There wasn't any.

Eventually, there was nothing else for Mr. Hamilton to show him.

"If there's anything you wish for, you need only mention it to one of the servants, sire." He indicated one of the elaborate bell pulls and, with that parting shot, left the suite.

Ori gazed helplessly around the marble-coated space that linked all the rooms. He lifted a hand to his neck; his fingers were shaking. He covered his mouth with his other palm, not sure if he was fighting back a scream or sickness. Very slowly, he lowered himself to the floor.

He had no idea how long he sat there, the cold from the marble tiles seeping into both his bones and his soul. Eons seemed to pass before he gathered the strength to pull himself to his feet and stumble toward the door leading out of the suite.

Ori pushed the painted woodwork, just enough to peek out into the hallway.

A servant immediately rushed forward to open it farther. As far as Ori could tell, the man had been lingering in the corridor waiting for him to request something. The tattoo on the inside of his wrist marked him out as a pigeon. Ori stood on the suite's threshold, not sure what to say.

"Is there something you wish for, sire?" the pigeon finally hinted. "Or someone you wish for?"

Ori blinked at him.

"Any avian would consider it a privilege to—"

"No!" The word shot out of Ori's mouth, as he realised what the servant was actually offering him.

The pigeon's eyes opened very wide; he flinched as if he thought he was about to be struck. Ori recalled doing the same thing himself, so many times. But he never remembered anyone reacting to him that way.

Ori shook his head, retreating from the servant, back into the safety of his suite. At the last moment, a whispered memory tugged at the edge of his consciousness.

"Everet!"

The servant continued to stare at him, blatant fear in his eyes.

"There's a raven called Everet," Ori managed to say, a little more calmly. "I…ask him if he'll speak to me, please?"

"Immediately, sire." The servant offered him a low

bow, before taking off down the hallway as fast as his legs would carry him, his bare feet silent on the thick carpet.

Closing the door, Ori sealed himself in his rooms, away from the craziness that seemed to reign outside.

He was still pacing the marble floor of the entrance hall when a tap fell against the oversized door. He rushed across to open in.

Everet stood outside. "You wished to see me, sire?"

"Yes." One of the rooms Mr. Hamilton had shown to Ori was a formal lounge. Not sure what else to do with Everet, Ori ushered him in there and directed him to one of the seats by the fireplace.

Far too much nervous energy raced through Ori for him to think about sitting down himself. He fidgeted in the centre of the room, all the things he'd planned to say to Everet deserting him.

"You wished to speak to me, sire?"

Ori swallowed. "You know my master, sir," he blurted out.

"I'm acquainted with Mr. Raynard, sire," the raven rephrased carefully, watching Ori the way other men might watch an unexploded bomb.

"You know where he lives?"

Everet nodded. "Yes, sire."

"Will you take a message to him? I…"

Everet hesitated.

"Please, I…" Ori had no idea what to say.

Another moment of silence passed before Everet nodded. "If that's what you wish me to do, sire."

The suite was well stocked with everything a man could want. It didn't take Ori long to track down a pen and some paper. Working out what to write was far more difficult.

He stared at the paper for a long time, while Everet sat patiently on the other side of the room.

Half an hour had passed before Ori was able to carry the sealed envelope across to Everet. "Thank you, sir."

Everet said nothing as he took the message from him. On the inside of his wrist was the neatly tattooed raven's mark.

Ori looked quickly away from it, but even after Everet had left the suite, the image of the species-identifier was still fresh in his mind.

Pigeon.

Raven.

Looking down at his own wrist, Ori retraced the line of the duck's mark that his master had painted there once before. Ori had no idea what a swan's identifying mark looked like. He had no interest in finding out.

Covering his right wrist with his opposite hand, he fought down the wave of panic that idea brought with it. He was never going to have that kind of mark on his skin. Never.

He was going to be marked as a duck. That's what Raynard wanted, that's what Ori was going to be. Out of the corner of his eye, Ori caught sight of his reflection in the mirror hanging above a console table. He quickly turned his back on it. He was going to be a big white duck and he knew exactly how a duck lived while at the nest. He'd simply go back to that life until Raynard was willing to come back and fetch him.

Just having a plan allowed some of Ori's panic to fade away. What replaced it was only a pathetic imitation of the safety he felt when he was with his master, but that couldn't be helped.

Pushing the door open once more, Ori didn't give the servant lurking in the hallway time to hold it for him or offer him any other kind of service. He strode past him, only vaguely aware that the pigeon scurried along in his wake as he rushed down one set of stairs, then another, heading straight for the kitchens.

Heads turned to watch him go, but men also stepped back to clear a path for him. A flock of crows making their way into the dining room scattered at the very sight of Ori hurling down the corridor. Ori paid them no attention. Striding into the kitchen, he caught sight of the chef on the other side of the room. A moment later, he was at the gull's side.

The chef turned toward him. He was about to speak when he stopped himself short. He offered Ori a deep bow. "Sire—"

"Do you have any work for me, sir?" Ori cut in.

Part of him knew that interrupting the notoriously bad tempered chef was risking a thrashing. Maybe that was what he needed. A punishment would be a familiar landmark in a world that had tilted on its axis, tipping everything that was important off its surface. Maybe enough external pain might take his mind off the agony that already flared deep inside his heart.

The gull looked past Ori to the servants that surrounded them. The kitchen was eerily silent. Everyone was staring at them and waiting for the chef's reaction.

Ori swallowed down the instinct to beg, even though he knew he'd give in to it eventually, if that was what it took.

The chef looked down. "May I offer my humble apologies for the way you were treated before your true nature was revealed, sire."

Ori shook his head. "You...I..." He looked across the room, to the sinks he'd worked at for so many weeks. Another servant stood in his place, wearing the same scant uniform. There was no place for Ori there anymore. No one wanted a duckli—a swan. He took a step back.

The servant from outside his suite was right behind him and didn't retreat in time to avoid the collision.

Spinning around, stumbling away from him too, Ori fled from the kitchens. The flock of crows lurked around the entrance to the dining area now. The two falcons who'd stopped to speak to Raynard walked out of one of the meeting rooms farther down the corridor. They all turned to gawp at Ori.

Looking from one group of men to the other, Ori tried to think, tried to make his mind function so he could work out what his master would want him to do now.

He knew what kind of service both the crows and the falcons would want from him, that it might be the only kind of service a swan was thought capable of. He closed his eyes for a moment, as the idea of servicing any man but his master cut deep inside him, threatening to tear something out of his very soul.

"Sire?"

Hamilton. Ori felt the eagle approach and stop at his side.

"You're tired after the ceremony, sire. You should rest now."

The way he said it almost made Ori think it was what his master would want him to do too. Part of what he had written in his note to Raynard came back to the centre of his mind. He might not have his master close at hand, but Ori still had his orders. He could still follow them to the best of his ability. Ori nodded his assent.

"Yes, sir." He should rest now. That was what his master would want him to do. Turning away from both the falcons and the crows, he let Hamilton guide him back to the suite of rooms.

When he found himself alone in the bedroom, Ori lay down on the overly soft mattress and covered his eyes with his hands. His head still ached. His whole body was a mass of pain, and the worst of it all radiated out from inside his mind.

* * * * *

Raynard took no notice of the doorbell. It wouldn't be Ori, and he had little interest in seeing anyone else.

It rang again, then again, and again.

Standing by the little bar set in the corner of the library, Raynard stared down at the decanters. The amber liquid

175

called to him through the lead crystal. One of the three decanters was ever so slightly different to the others—a replacement tracked down by Ori after his lack of coordination laid waste to its predecessor.

Raynard ran his fingers over the faceted glass. It sparkled, just like everything else Ori had turned his attention to while he was under his care...

His care...Raynard shook his head. Ori would have been far better off without that kind of *care*. He closed his eyes. How could he have lived with his fledgling for so long and not realised that he was hurting him so badly by forcing him into a role he was never destined to occupy?

Raynard's own words came back to haunt him now.

There's no shame in being another man's submissive, Ori. But if you're not truly suited to it, if it doesn't call to something inside you, I'd imagine it's little better than torture...

The training Raynard had put Ori through over the last few months must have been a special kind of hell for a swan. The fact Ori had never complained, that he'd gone out of his way to ask Raynard what ducks were like, only made Raynard's answers seem especially cruel now.

Raynard shook his head at himself. What kind of bastard didn't notice that he was breaking down another man's soul bit by bit?

The doorbell rang again. In another version of the world, Ori would have answered it for him. Memories flooded Raynard's mind—making him recall the last time Ori had been unable to answer the door. Pushing himself away from the bar, Raynard strode through the hallway and wrenched open the front door, if only to make the blasted ringing stop.

Everet stood on the doorstep. He silently offered him an envelope.

Raynard stared at the rich cream paper. The coat of arms belonging to the nest was embossed on the flap.

Of course, the elders wouldn't be pleased about what had passed between a hawk and their new swan, either.

Forget how Ori had been treated while at the nest. They'd want to make it clear Raynard had screwed up in ways they found completely unacceptable.

Raynard took the envelope and nodded his dismissal, unable to raise the inclination to speak. He was about to slam the door when the raven stopped him short.

"Would you like me to wait for a response, sir?"

Holding back a sigh, Raynard left the door open as he turned away from Everet and tore open the letter.

The moment he saw the handwriting, Raynard knew it was no mere summons from the elders. He'd seen pages and pages filled with those same neat letters, line after line of the same words repeated over and over again.

Ori.

For a full minute, that was all that really sunk in. It was from Ori. Raynard reached out to steady himself against the banister. Slowly lowering himself to sit on the third stair, he forced his mind to take in the words before him.

Sir,

I don't know what the elders saw during the ceremony. I don't know what you saw either. None of it matters to me. I didn't grow up among my own species. I have no idea what I should be like — you can make me into whatever you want me to be.

I'll never shift from my human form. You can place whatever mark you'd approve of inside my wrist. I can be whatever it is you need me to be — whatever is best able to serve my master and make him happy.

I might never have given you reason to believe me, sir, but if you are willing to give me just one more chance, I'll show you that I can be the kind of submissive you want to own. I'll do anything. I'll accept whatever punishment you see fit, and I'll take any place in your life you are willing to grant me.

I am your submissive, your servant, your —
whatever you want me to be.

If you send for me, I'll come to you, sir.
Please…

Yours, Ori.

Then, a little way farther down the page, in a slightly less steady hand.

The most valuable possession my master owns is his
submissive. I will take great care that no harm comes to my
master's submissive whenever he is not there to watch over
me himself.

With his head still bowed over the paper, Raynard closed his eyes.

If there was one undeniable fact, it was that Ori truly hadn't been raised among shifters. He had no idea what any of this meant — what it really meant for a man to force another avian to live outside his true place in the world.

Well, there was no doubt he'd learn quickly now that the truth was known. The letter crumpled within Raynard's grip. Ori would learn his true place in the world, then he'd understand how much he should hate his former master, what sort of cruelty the man he seemed to think so much of was capable of inflicting.

Raynard forced himself to open his eyes. Even now he could feel Ori's affection for him slip away as if it had never existed. Ori couldn't be blamed for that. He really was the one innocent victim in the middle of it all, poor little sod.

Standing up, Raynard strode across to the door.

Everet still waited on the step.

Raynard stared blankly at him until the raven finally cleared his throat. "The return message, sir."

"You may tell your swan that there's no return message and that I've no intention of visiting the nest in the foreseeable future." He closed the door before the raven had a chance to reply.

Leaning against the woodwork, it was all too easy to remember the way his fledgling had jumped when the door thudded into its frame on the first night Raynard had brought him to the house.

Turning away, Raynard looked for some place of solace away from his memories. Wandering through the house only took him on a tour through different days they had shared there. Each room bore the duckling's...the swan's touch. The library. The study. The attic room.

Raynard paced through each of them in turn, pouring out a whole glass full of whisky as he moved through the library, before his wandering finally took him down the stairs to the servants' quarters.

The kitchen was as immaculate as ever. The floor leading to the butler's quarters as well scrubbed as all the others in the house. The little bedroom seemed to bear less evidence of Ori's presence than any other room.

It had an un-lived in feel, much like the entire house had before Ori arrived. The fledgling hadn't spent a great deal of time there for what felt like a lifetime. He'd spent every night in Raynard's bed for months.

He should never have been working below stairs in the first place. Raynard turned away from the sight of the neatly made bed.

In spite of everything, part of him wanted nothing more than to race back to the nest, to take the newly fledged swan in his arms and tell him everything was fine. Except that wouldn't make anything fine. It would just make everything worse for Ori and confuse him even further. He needed certainty now — from men who could teach him about what he really was.

There was nothing Raynard could do for Ori now but

stay as far away from him as possible. If he couldn't remain away from the nest until his return would be painless for himself, then he could at least stay away until his return wouldn't cause Ori any further pain.

Turning his back on the kitchen, Raynard tossed back the last of the whisky in his glass and went in search of the rest of the decanter.

Chapter Eleven

Frederick Raynard hadn't been brought up to believe that hawks were inclined towards masochism the way some of the other avian species were, but he couldn't think of any other reason why he'd drag himself all the way across town to visit the nest that night either. It wasn't as if he hadn't known that it would feel like his soul was being torn apart.

From a vantage point near the rear of the nest's grand hall, he studied the raised platform that occupied the opposite end of the towering space. The chairs lined up on the stage were all empty, but Raynard was acutely aware that they wouldn't remain that way for long. His hand clenched into a tight fist at his side as he tried to keep his impatience at bay. In just a few minutes, the elders would file in—and they wouldn't be alone.

Another shifter stepped in front of Raynard, blocking his view for several seconds before he continued on his way.

The whole space was full of men. A palpable air of expectation buzzed through the crowd. Every pair of eyes should have been fixed on the stage, but as many people seemed to be fascinated by Raynard's presence as by anything that might happen at the other end of the room.

Whispers swirled through the air. *Tried to master the swan... Calculated insult... Worse kind of cruelty... Servant... Shouldn't be allowed...Something should be done...* Raynard ignored them all.

Folding his arms across his chest, he tried to be patient—but with very little success. All he needed was a glimpse of his fledg— Raynard clenched his jaw. No, not his fledgling. Ori was a fully-fledged member of shifter society now. It was no more appropriate to call him that, than it would be to refer to him as a duck, or as his submissive.

Ori wasn't a fledgling, and he wasn't Raynard's *anything*, no matter what the crumpled note tucked into the inside pocket of Raynard's jacket might suggest.

Raynard took a deep breath. All he needed was a glimpse of the swan, just so he could know that Ori was safe and well and thriving in his new life—in the life he should have lived ever since he'd found his way into the community of shifters.

A commotion at the other end of the room sent a wave of chattering through the gathered men. Respectful silence followed in its wake. For several consecutive lifetimes, Raynard was unable to catch a glimpse of those who entered the hall.

With his heart racing faster and faster, he kept his gaze fixed on the steps leading up to the raised seating area and prayed.

Hamilton stepped up first. Another elder followed him, then another. Then…

Ori.

Raynard's breath caught in his throat. He'd known that Ori was bound to have changed over the weeks since his true species was revealed. Raynard had steeled himself for that. Ori's attitude, his mannerisms, everything would have altered as he found out who he was. Raynard had prepared himself to see a swan.

The image of Ori growing stronger and happier as he settled into his new position in the nest and found himself free to explore his true nature had kept Raynard going during the longest month of his life. It had given him the self-control to stay on the other side of town no matter how much he missed Ori.

But, the mental picture he'd pushed to the front of his mind every time he felt Ori's absence couldn't have been further from the reality that confronted Raynard now.

The figure that dragged himself onto the stage was no vision of health or happiness. His skin was pale, and it wasn't because his adult plumage was coming through. Dark shadows circled Ori's eyes. He'd lost weight. His body was all tension, all nerves. Every movement he made was tinged with something close to panic. The most opulent clothing in the world couldn't hide the way he was suffering.

Ori obviously didn't want to be up there on the stage in front of everyone. It didn't take a man as familiar with Ori's moods as Raynard was, to see that he was barely hanging on to his composure.

Hamilton whispered something to Ori and indicated the high-backed chair set in the centre of the row of seats — the one that looked like a throne. Ori perched tentatively upon the very edge of it.

The other elders took their positions, sitting and standing around him, jostling in an effort to demonstrate their superior rank by being closer to the nest's new swan than the others. Ori's backside had barely touched the velvet cushion before the first shifter approached the little set of steps leading to Ori's feet.

The man dropped to one knee before him. Ori's eyes opened very wide as he stared down at the top of his head. He looked terrified that the man might dart forward and bite him at any moment. Hamilton whispered into Ori's ear once more.

Ori extended a hand toward the kneeling man, who placed a kiss on Ori's knuckles. It was nothing more than one avian paying due homage to the arrival of a shifter bearing a truly exalted rank. Raynard still felt jealousy rush through him at the sight of another man laying a hand on Ori. It took every ounce of control Raynard could scrape together to stay where he was.

If it was possible, Ori grew even paler.

Another man knelt before the Ori a few seconds later. The process was repeated. Then again, and again. Any hope Raynard might have harboured of Ori settling into his chair and finding some sense of ease as the ceremony continued, faded away.

Ori stayed on the edge of his seat. His anxiety wasn't easing. If anything, it was becoming more apparent with every second that passed.

Raynard's control failed him. He stepped forward. A long line of men waited to greet the swan, but if any had outranked Raynard, they had already knelt for Ori and moved away. As a hawk, Raynard strode past those of a lesser rank without a thought. Mutters and whispers rattled along the queue, but no one tried to stop him.

There was a man at Ori's feet when Raynard reached the front of the line. Ori looked up. Their eyes met over the other man's head. Raynard knew that panicked expression. He'd seen it in the Ori's eyes before.

Ori had been about to bolt, but he froze when he saw Raynard standing before him.

The man between them moved away murmuring his subservience to the nest's swan as he went. Raynard stepped forward. He took hold of Ori's hand as he lowered himself to one knee on the top step in due respect.

Ori found a new level of tension. He parted his lips.

"Stay exactly where you are." Raynard remained bowed over Ori's hand, but tilted his head so their eyes could meet. "It's your duty to complete the tradition. You will fulfil your duty." He left no room for argument in the statement.

"Yes, sir," Ori whispered, very softly. As close as Raynard was to him, he could barely make out the words. No one could have overheard them. Raynard let the honorific pass without comment or correction, just that once.

He nodded his approval, just slightly, before brushing his lips quickly across the back of Ori's hand and rising to his feet.

Ori moved as if he intended to follow him. Raynard looked over his shoulder and their gazes locked.

Please.

Raynard heard the plea inside his head so loudly, Ori might as well have screamed it. But he couldn't answer it—not in the way Ori wanted him to.

Tilting up his chin, Raynard pinned Ori to the seat with a look, damn near daring him to disobey his order to complete the ceremony. Ori obediently subsided back against the rich velvet.

Raynard had to force himself to turn and walk away. Each step was harder to take than the last, but he finally reached the side wall of the hall. He turned back to face the stage. His choice of vantage point meant Ori would be able to see him if he was inclined to look in that direction.

If seeing him there gave Ori some sort of courage, then it was the least Raynard could do. He had no idea why Ori would ever want to set eyes on him after the torture he must have endured when trying to mould himself into someone suitable for service, but Raynard didn't need to understand it to do whatever he could to ease Ori's pain.

Hamilton stepped forward and whispered something to Ori. For the first time, Ori whispered back. More softly spoken words passed between Hamilton and a man standing just off the stage.

Raynard soon lost track of the relay of messages. He turned his attention back to Ori and watched another shifter kneel to welcome Ori to the nest. Ori was still far from comfortable, but he didn't seem quite so panicked. Raynard leaned against the wall and settled himself for the duration.

Despite all the staring, everyone had given Raynard a wide berth, but now he sensed someone step up alongside him.

"Mr. Jones invites you to stay behind after the ceremony to speak with him in private, sir."

It took Raynard several seconds to connect Ori with his surname. He glanced at the servant. "You may give Mr. Jones my apologies. I'll be leaving the moment the welcoming ceremony ends."

The servant shuffled his feet. Raynard thought the little finch might take to his heels and flee, but he held his ground. "Mr. Hamilton reminds you that Mr. Jones' rank enables him to order the attendance of any avian at any time."

The poor little bugger obviously thought he was going to get a back hander for being the unfortunate last link in the chain. Raynard offered the servant a brisk nod, forcing himself to keep any of the words he might be inclined to let fly safely tucked away inside his head until they could be unleashed upon those who really deserved to feel their sting.

The finch scurried away. Raynard turned his attention back to the stage. The queue was shorter now. Those below a certain rank would have to wait for another time and another ceremony to pay their respects. They hadn't even been allowed into the hall on this occasion.

As the last few men approached Ori, Raynard felt someone take up a position directly to his left. He looked over his shoulder. At over six foot, he wasn't used to other men being a great deal taller than him, but the hulking albatross towered over him.

"Mr. Hamilton asked me to show you to Mr. Jones' suite, sir."

Raynard bit back a curse. Unwilling to make a fool of himself by getting into a tussle with a man twice his size, he reluctantly nodded his acceptance.

Ori had barely left the room, looking over his shoulder with every step he took, before Raynard found himself being led unceremoniously out of the hall, up the stairs and to a massively oversized set of double doors.

The huge painted panels swung open to reveal a marble coated entrance hall. Every surface visible through the various doorways leading off the room glistened and gleamed.

Ori must have worked his fingers to the bone putting it in that condition.

Raynard hesitated just inside the door, mentally

cursing himself for a fool. Ori wouldn't have lifted a finger. He had an army of servants now—ready to cater to his every whim, and keep any room he wanted to use immaculate.

A matching set of doors on the other side of the room swung open. Ori walked in, flanked by several bustling servants. His steps sped up as he caught sight of Raynard. He stumbled to a halt barely a step away from Raynard, his face still pale and his hands clenched tightly at his sides.

"You came back, sir..." he whispered.

Out of the corner of his eye, Raynard saw yet another servant walk through the room and carry a tea tray into one of the rooms to his right. Turning away from Ori, Raynard made his way into what appeared to be a formal drawing room and to the little group of seats where the servant set down the tray.

Ori followed, hot on Raynard's heels. When Raynard indicated a chair, Ori sat down, as obedient now as he had ever been when he thought he was a duckling. His new found maturity hadn't yet transformed itself into grace. His movements were even jerkier than they had been when he lived with Raynard.

The servant—a pigeon according to the tattoo on his wrist—reached for the teapot.

Ori sprang forward onto the edge of his seat and snatched the handle away from him. Tea splashed from the spout, over the edge of the tray, and onto the table. "I'll do it!"

"Sire, that's really not—" the pigeon began.

"I know how Mr. Raynard likes his tea," Ori bit out. His grip on the pot tightened. His knuckles turned white.

For a few seconds, it looked as if there would actually be a scrum over the pot. Then the servant dropped his gaze. "Just as you wish, sire."

"Can...can you make them leave, sir?" Ori whispered, not once glancing up from the pot.

"Ori?"

Ori closed his eyes. "Order them to leave, sir. Please?"

Raynard looked up. Five different servants lurked

around the edge of the room, none of them with any clear purpose. "Leave."

Only one hesitated to obey his command — the same pigeon who had tried to do battle for the teapot. "Mr. Hamilton said —"

"And I'm telling you that your master wishes our meeting to be conducted in private. What an eagle wants should be irrelevant to you while you're fortunate enough to be in the service of a swan."

The pigeon dropped his gaze, backed out of the room, and no doubt rushed away to carry tales to Hamilton.

They were finally alone.

"Thank you, sir."

Raynard studied Ori very carefully. "You're allowed to give your own orders to the men who serve you," he pointed out, as gently as he could. "You don't need anyone to do that for you."

Ori gave the tea things his complete attention for a little while. A little of the hot liquid spilt onto the tray as he poured it, but when he handed the cup across the table, Raynard had to admit Ori had been right about one thing — Ori knew exactly how he liked his tea. He'd learned exactly how his master liked everything while he had been under his care.

"Everyone here is treating you kindly?" Raynard asked, more bruskly than he intended.

Ori wrapped his arms around his waist as if his grip on his body was the only thing holding him together. He nodded, but he didn't raise his eyes.

"Look at me."

Ori slowly did as he was told.

"The whole truth."

Ori swallowed. "Everyone's been very kind, sir."

"The *whole* truth," Raynard repeated.

"They won't let me do anything, sir," Ori whispered, pain creeping into his expression with the admission.

"What do you mean?"

"They won't let me work, sir."

A bitter taste rose to the back of Raynard's mouth. "It will take time for you to get used to your new life."

Ori shook his head.

"But you will get used to it," Raynard pushed on. "Over time, you'll see how well suited to it you are." Then Ori would realise just how wrong Raynard had been about anything and everything he'd offered him while he was under his protection.

But Ori obviously wasn't ready to see that just yet and Raynard found himself scrambling for anything he could say that might make it easier for his fledgling. "There are some things you like about your new life, aren't there?" He wasn't sure who he was more desperate to convince of that.

Ori stubbornly shook his head.

"You have free run of the libraries here, don't you?" Raynard said, grasping at straws. Ori had loved the library in his house, and that had been miniscule compared to all those at the nest combined. "Isn't that something you like?"

Ori frowned, never lifting his gaze above the top button on Raynard's shirt.

"And there are plenty of people to look after you, to make sure you're taken good care of."

"You could punish me, sir."

Every thought in Raynard's head scattered in a different direction.

Ori's Adam's apple bobbed as he swallowed rapidly. "If you punished me for lying to you about what species I am and—"

"Ori—"

"And, for all the things I did wrong—the things that you didn't punish me for at the time because you thought it would be cruel to expect more from a duck—you could punish me for them too." He lifted his gaze to meet Raynard's eyes for a moment. "You could expect more from me now, you wouldn't have to put up with my stupidity, or my clumsiness. I'll—"

"You will stay at the nest and get used to your new place in the world," Raynard cut in. Damn it—it sounded far too much like an order, as if he still believed he had the right to order him about.

Raynard closed his eyes for a moment. While Ori sat opposite him seeming so scared and lost, it was almost impossible to believe he wasn't that ugly little duckling the elders had thought they'd seen the first time he'd tried to shift in front of them.

"You can do anything you want," Raynard told him. "There's not a single man in this nest who can disobey you. Anything you want, your slightest whim, it will all be catered to. Don't you see you have everything now?"

"Back in the attic, you said that I was suited to service, sir, and—"

"And I was wrong," Raynard snapped. "I told you about what role *ducks* enjoy. You're a swan! The elders must have spoken to you about what that means. Swans are revered for good reason. Having a swan on the council of elders mitigates the harshness of the birds of prey. Swans are the only species who can do that—who have the strength and the compassion to do it. It's why avian laws protect you so thoroughly."

Ori didn't move a muscle.

"You're a swan, Ori. Can't you see that changes everything?"

"I know it changes the way you feel about me, sir," Ori whispered.

The other half of the sentence might have remained unspoken, but it still reached Raynard loud and clear—the discovery hadn't changed the way Ori felt about him in the least.

Raynard turned his face away, afraid of what Ori might see in his eyes if he held his gaze for too long.

"I wouldn't expect you to continue to be so kind to me,

sir."

Helpless in the face of Ori's pain, Raynard looked back to him.

"I could move back down to the servants' quarters. I wouldn't bother you or take up any of your time. I'd stay out of your way and..."

"Ori," Raynard began.

"I could take care of my upstairs duties when you were out of the house. You wouldn't even have to set eyes on me and—" Each word was more desperate than the last.

"That's not what—"

"And what you said about having more servants, you could do that, sir. You could have someone else who would be what I was to you. I wouldn't fuss about that. I could serve you both, if that was what you wanted, and—"

"Enough!" Raynard snapped.

Ori fell silent, his eyes closed very tight, his teeth cutting into his bottom lip as he bit down harshly upon the sensitive skin.

Raynard's presence in the nest wasn't helping Ori. Raynard saw that now. He'd hurt his fledgling too badly by taking him under his care and teaching him how to be someone he was never intended to become. Every extra second he spent with him, was only going to make everything worse. It would just make it harder for Ori to fight his way out of all the training Raynard had pushed on him and emerge into the man he was truly destined to be.

It was far too soon. Raynard should never have come to the nest.

He stood up.

Ori opened his eyes. He began to rise to his feet too, but Raynard put his hand on his shoulder to keep him where he was.

"Sir?" Ori asked.

"I'm sorry," Raynard whispered. It didn't fix anything, there weren't any words that could, but he said it anyway.

Then he turned, and walked away from Ori before his will to do so gave out and he became a bigger bastard than ever.

He didn't look over his shoulder as he strode from the room. He quickened his pace as he walked down the corridor, heading out of the nest as quickly as he could without shifting.

He wasn't running away. In his own mind, he was very clear about that fact. He wasn't running away. He was simply putting himself as far away from Ori as he could, before he ended up doing even more damage to his gentle soul than he already had.

* * * * *

Ori stared down at the tea tray for a long time, not really seeing it, but not able to look away either.

He was vaguely aware of a door opening and closing behind him, of someone walking across the room toward him, but it wasn't his master. Ori knew Raynard's footsteps. He knew the way the atmosphere in a room changed when Raynard entered it.

It wasn't Raynard, and Ori couldn't bring himself to believe that anyone else mattered.

Mr. Hamilton sat down opposite him, in the chair Raynard had so recently vacated. "The meeting went well, sire?"

Ori shook his head as he dragged his gaze away from the teapot. "He hates me..."

Mr. Hamilton's expression was as hard to read as always. He seemed to study Ori for a long time. "What did you hope would be the outcome?"

Ori stared down at Raynard's teacup. He'd barely taken a sip of it.

Ori sighed. What had he hoped for...? That Raynard might somehow agree to take him back. That all of this was some horrible mistake and he might wake up from the nightmare of the last month to find everything had gone back to being as it used to be between them?

"Sire?" Mr. Hamilton prompted.

"I thought I might be able to convince him to change his mind, sir," Ori confessed.

"About what?"

Ori closed his eyes. "Before he found out what I really am, Mr. Raynard said that..."

Mr. Hamilton waited with apparent patience while Ori fought against his own mind, looking for the words that might make some sort of sense of everything.

"He said that after the ceremony, he'd give me a permanent collar — I'd have a permanent place in his house."

"As his servant?" Mr. Hamilton prompted.

"As his submissive, sir," Ori whispered. "He...we..."

"You're in love with him," Mr. Hamilton finished for him.

Ori didn't deny it. The strength to lie about it wasn't in him anymore.

The silence stretched out. The tea grew cold on the tray between them and neither of them said a word.

"Perhaps Raynard merely needs to be reminded how good a submissive you were, sire," Mr. Hamilton suddenly suggested, his words sounding loud and harsh after the extended hush.

Ori couldn't meet Mr. Hamilton's eyes. As much as he wished that was the problem, it seemed far more likely that Raynard had actually had time to remember that he wasn't a very good submissive at all. "I made lots of mistakes, sir."

"If Raynard wasn't satisfied with your progress, he would never have spoken to you about a permanent collar."

Silence reigned once more. As much as Ori wanted to cling to hope, there had been a finality in his master's leaving that was impossible to wipe from his mind.

"Tell me about the time you spent with him, sire."

Ori hesitated. "I don't know what you want me to say,

sir."

"There's no wrong answer," Mr. Hamilton said, with the kind of patience that seemed to come so easily to him, now that he knew he was speaking to a swan rather than an ugly little duckling. "Just tell me how things were between you and Raynard."

Part of Ori wasn't sure if he should be talking about his master with a man he still found it hard to trust, even if they had spent a great deal of time in each other's company since that disastrous shifting ceremony.

A much larger part of Ori, the section of his mind that had been replaying all the time he'd spent with his master over and over inside his brain, couldn't resist the invitation to get some of those memories out of his head and into the real world.

They were real memories, not the idle fantasies of a submissive. Things had been that way between him and Raynard — not just for an hour or two, but for months. It was the truth, and he couldn't lose his faith in that as well as everything else.

"He was a fantastic master, sir."

Hamilton nodded for him to continue.

Still not quite sure what to say, Ori simply let whatever words came into his head pass his lips without trying to edit them en route.

"He was so kind to me, sir. Patient, and strong, and he taught me about..." He closed his eyes.

"Go on," Hamilton pushed.

"He taught me that who I was wasn't anything to be ashamed of. Submission is something a man can take pride in — it takes strength to commit to following another man that way. Loyalty is as important as leadership and..." Ori sighed. "That was before, sir...when he thought I was a duckling."

He forced himself to lift his gaze and try to get some sense of what Mr. Hamilton might think of him and his rambling recollections.

"Did he ever punish you, sire?" The question was asked very carefully.

Ori answered it honestly. He recounted the story of the china cabinet, and a dozen other memories of occasions large and small. Mr. Hamilton didn't seem to be bored. He listened vigilantly to every word, as if it were the most important conversation he had ever had with another man.

Finally, Mr. Hamilton seemed to run out of questions.

With his head swirling with all the memories the conversation had dredged up, Ori took a deep breath and tried to find the kind of mental balance that submitting to Raynard had inspired in him.

Another minute passed, and Mr. Hamilton found another question for him. "You're aware that your station in the nest means that you can summon any member of the avian community to attend you, at any time, and for any reason?"

Ori nodded. The facts of the matter had been explained to him several times, even if he still couldn't bring himself to like any of them. If a bird of prey didn't have to heed a swan, a swan would be no use on the council of elders. That's why no one could disobey him. It was the one line in the avian sand that could never risk being blurred.

"You could summon Raynard here, if you were inclined to remind him just how well you suited each other."

Ori frowned, trying to see where the joke was leading and failing.

"Do you think that's something you'd like to do, sire?" Mr. Hamilton pushed, not sounding the least bit like he was heading for a punch line.

"I don't think Mr. Raynard would be pleased with me if I did that, sir."

"Perhaps not," Mr. Hamilton allowed. "But perhaps it would be worth him being temporarily displeased with you, if it meant you'd be able to see more of him in the future? Maybe even come to some sort of an arrangement with him…"

Ori reached out to straighten the items on the tray, then hesitated as what Mr. Hamilton was suggesting sunk in. The aches in Ori's joints made freezing in position painful, but that wasn't important. "I could make things the way they used to be, sir? I could serve him?"

Hamilton nodded. "No one can deny you anything, sire. If a swan truly wants to serve, no one has any right to try to stop him."

Ori nodded very slowly as a plan started to take shape inside his head.

Mr. Hamilton smiled. It wasn't the same as having his master smile at him, but it gave Ori just a little confidence in the possibility that he was about to make the right decision.

Chapter Twelve

Ori's hands were shaking.

He stared at his grip on the heavy silver tray, but he couldn't steady his fingers, no matter how hard he tried. His nerves were as good as they were going to get. Ori took a deep breath and nodded to the servant standing by the door leading into his private dining room.

Ori walked through the door and across to the table, without looking in Raynard's direction. Setting the tray down, Ori delicately placed a plate of food between the various items of cutlery and glassware that he'd carefully arranged there earlier that day.

Raynard really had answered his... Well, Hamilton had referred to it as a summons. Ori thought of it more as a plea to be allowed to see his master. Either way, Raynard was there. Ori felt Raynard's gaze travel over him as he silently observed him from the other side of the room.

Ori stared at the plate of food he'd carried in. It was Raynard's favourite meal. It was cooked perfectly. After yet another long day of battling to set his uncle's business affairs in order, Raynard had to be hungry, but he made no move to approach the table.

"May I take your coat, sir?" Ori whispered, his voice raw with fear he wasn't capable of hiding.

Raynard slipped his jacket off his shoulders, but he laid it over the back of the chair closest to him rather than let a swan take it from him.

Ori dropped his empty hand back to his side. The movement sent pain flaring along his shoulders.

"What do you mean to prove with all this?" Raynard asked eventually.

"I'm still capable of serving you, sir."

Raynard shook his head. He seemed about to turn on his heel and walk out of the room. Desperation gave Ori the courage to speak up again.

"Mr. Hamilton said that I'm allowed to insist that you give me a chance, sir."

Raynard frowned.

Ori quickly looked down. "Just a chance, sir?" There was no word for it but begging. Duck or swan, he wasn't too proud to beg if that's what it took.

Raynard's hand clenched into a fist at his side, but he said nothing.

"Have you eaten, sir?" Ori tried. Raynard didn't look like he had eaten in days. He'd lost weight. He didn't look like he'd slept in days, either.

Raynard took a step toward both Ori and the dining table. "Have you?"

"Sir?"

"Eaten." Raynard waved a hand toward the table set for one.

Ori shook his head. He wouldn't have kept it down if he'd tried.

Very slowly, Raynard took his seat. Relief rushed through Ori, making him lightheaded with the simple pleasure of being close to his master and feeling all was right with his world.

Ori's hand shook as he poured water into Raynard's glass. It was more luck than judgment that none spilled across the carefully ironed tablecloth.

Ori stepped back. Folding his hands behind him, he settled himself to wait for another order.

His rest position, wearing the clothes his master had given him, the very sight of Raynard mingled with the smell of the food—it all combined to bring the memory of all the meals they'd shared together to the front of Ori's mind. That formal meal in the dining room before they'd visited the nest.

The first meal they'd shared in the kitchen, long before Ori had any idea that his master might one day consider him to be anything other than a simple servant. The take-away they'd shared after his first fall from grace...

"Come here."

Ori stepped forward. Raynard only had to glance at the floor at his side to have Ori kneeling there. Taking a forkful of food from the plate, Raynard offered it to Ori's lips, just as he had the last time Ori had thought his master was too angry to share a meal with him.

Ori parted his lips, and let Raynard feed him, quick to relish every hint of dominance his former master was willing to offer him and every bit of submission he was allowed to display. For just a little while, it felt as if nothing had changed.

When the last of the food disappeared from the plate, neither of them moved. The room itself seemed to hold its breath.

"One night."

Ori blinked up at Raynard as he tried to follow his meaning and failed.

"One night together, to give us some sort of...closure on what happened between us before we knew your true nature."

One night...

It hadn't been what Ori had hoped for, but he wasn't too proud to take whatever he could get from his master and cherish every second of it. If one night was all Raynard wanted to give him... Ori closed his eyes for a moment, pushing away all thought of the days that would come after that night, of all the times when his master wouldn't be there.

Opening his eyes again, he nodded his acceptance of any concession his master was willing to make.

Raynard stroked his fingers through Ori's sleek, white hair as he made him look up and hold his gaze.

"You understand that this is about finding a way to move on? It's not about going back."

Ori nodded again, if only because he knew that was the only way to get the offered night.

"And after tonight, you'll stop fighting who you really are. You'll stop refusing to be properly marked as a swan. You'll stop refusing to stretch your wings."

Ori hesitated, wondering if Raynard had stopped to speak to Mr. Hamilton on his way up to his suite.

Raynard made a rough, displeased noise in the back of his throat. "Do you really think I wouldn't notice your wrist is still bare — or how much pain you're in?"

Ori took a deep breath and nodded his acceptance of those conditions.

Standing up, Raynard stepped away from the dining table. Ori stayed on his knees, his hands still behind his back, waiting hopefully for an order — any order.

"On your feet."

Ori rose. He instinctively stepped closer to his master, but he managed to keep his hands behind his back.

Raynard stroked his knuckles down Ori's cheek, then his throat.

No collar blocked the caress. Ori pushed that fact out of his mind as Raynard slid his hand behind his neck and pulled him forward. Ori parted his lips under the kiss the moment their mouths met.

For just a fraction of a second, Raynard seemed to hesitate, to hold back. The world balanced on a knife edge, and Ori had no idea which way it might fall.

Months seemed to pass, then Raynard tightened his grip on him. He dragged Ori closer, almost pulling him off his feet. Raynard took complete possession of Ori's mouth. Holding Ori tightly against him, Raynard thrust his tongue past Ori's lips and devoured him. They tumbled off the knife and straight into perfection.

Ori let out a mewing whimper as he leaned into the kiss and tried to push himself onto his toes to bring their bodies in line. Raynard moved his free hand over Ori's body, seeming to want to touch every inch of him, to own every bit of him — duck, swan or anything else.

Ori kept his hands behind his back, even when his feet left the floor and Raynard lifted him into his arms.

"Bedroom," Raynard demanded.

Ori looked over his shoulder, toward the door. Raynard didn't put him down. Kicking the door open, he carried Ori through the marble entrance hall and into the opulent bedroom at the other end of his suite when Ori nodded toward it.

He slammed the bedroom door shut behind them, strode across the thick pile carpet and tossed Ori onto the bed. Ori sprawled on the mattress. He brought his hands from behind his back to try and brace himself, but they slid uselessly on the satiny blankets.

He was only alone on the bed for a second. Before he had a chance to right himself, Raynard was on the bed with him and covering Ori's body with his own.

"Naked."

He didn't pull away to give Ori room to follow the order. Ori had to scramble around beneath him and wriggle out of his clothes in the tiny space he was granted.

His movements only grew clumsier as Raynard started to run his hands over every newly exposed inch of skin. But that didn't matter — all that really registered in Ori's mind was that Raynard wanted to touch him — he wasn't humouring a swan because of some mistaken idea of rank. Raynard really wanted him. His master wanted his submissive.

Ori whimpered his frustration as he struggled to obey Raynard's order. It took weeks, but he finally managed to kick away the last of his clothes. Ori immediately reached for his master. And, in that moment, that's what Raynard was — his master. They both knew it. Even if they could only give in to it for one more night, it was the purest form of truth Ori had ever known.

Raynard was his master; Ori belonged to him as

thoroughly as any man ever could.

Ori's preparations for Raynard's visit had been optimistic. Lube had been placed conspicuously on the bedside cabinet. Raynard snatched up the tube and smeared his fingers. Ori pulled his knees toward his chest in offering.

Raynard didn't waste time, and Ori pushed his arse back against Raynard's fingers from the first, encouraging him to thrust them more deeply, more roughly inside him.

Raynard knew Ori's body. He worked quickly, giving Ori what he needed, nothing more. He took away his hand and smeared more lube onto his shaft.

There was no time to be wasted. That knowledge was right in the front of Ori's mind, and he could see it in Raynard's too. If one night was all they could have, there wasn't a moment to squander.

Raynard moved to kneel between Ori's spread legs. As Raynard thrust into him, hard and determined, Ori gasped. All he could see in Raynard's eyes was dominance and possession.

He thought he'd never see Raynard look at him that way again. Now all he could do was glory in it and burn it into his memory so he'd never forget how it felt. Several years seemed to pass, then Raynard began to pull away from him. Ori clung to Raynard's shoulders through his shirt, desperate not to have him slip through his fingers again.

Nothing he could do stopped Raynard's retreat. Then, just as true panic started to swirl inside him, Raynard thrust back into him. Raynard moaned his pleasure as Ori clenched tightly around him.

He didn't even try to shake Ori's hands away. He let Ori cling to him, and without Raynard's disapproval to motivate him, Ori didn't have enough strength to ease his grip on his own. His fingers bit into Raynard's muscles, and he gripped him as harshly as Raynard had ever held him.

Being in the same room with Raynard after so long had been more than enough to have Ori hard ever since he walked into the dining room. By the second thrust, Ori was already desperate.

Raynard plunged into him again. The soft mattress cushioned his movements, and Ori squirmed against the suffocating comfort that crept around him as he slid against the expensive sheets.

He closed his eyes, imagining they were back in the cold, little attic room. A hard mattress. Serviceable sheets. The chill breeze sneaking in through the open window. He gasped as Raynard's hold on him tightened.

Raynard's mouth covered his in a searing kiss. When Ori failed to instantly part his lips, Raynard nipped at them. His tongue thrust into Ori's mouth and laid its claim to him.

Ori mewed, scrabbling to control his own body even as he helplessly rocked beneath Raynard and tried to complement the rough rhythm. He tipped back his head and let Raynard take whatever he wanted from him and suddenly it didn't matter where they were.

Permission. When every other thought in Ori's head disintegrated, that one remained. He needed permission to come. In the weeks since his master had left him at the nest, he'd obeyed every rule within his grasp to the absolute letter. His hand hadn't strayed to his cock once.

He wasn't going to come without permission now.

Raynard's hold on him changed. He pulled back, breaking the kiss.

"Come!"

More a demand than permission, it raced straight to Ori's cock. He didn't know if Raynard had realised he was on the edge, he wasn't even sure Raynard cared one way or the other. Ori belonged to his master, and he'd come when he was told to.

At Raynard's command, Ori's orgasm tore through him, seeming to rip apart his mind as more pleasure than any one man could contain exploded inside him. Raynard thrust into him again, as Ori's cum spilled against his stomach.

Every inch of his skin sung out with an overload of sensations. As Raynard slammed his cock into him once more, his clothes rasped against Ori's body, a pure point of reality mixed in with all the cloying softness the elders had tried to wrap him in.

His master hadn't come.

Even as his own ecstasy rushed through him, the thought jumped up and down inside Ori's mind, screaming for his attention.

If Raynard intended to let Ori come, he almost always gave him permission to orgasm just as he was about to climax himself. Ori blinked open his eyes and looked up at his master.

He hadn't come. His master hadn't come.

Raynard slowly pulled away from Ori. Ori tightened his grip on his master's shoulders, as he tried to make sense of what was happening and failed. Fear flashed through him. Raynard really had meant it when he said he had no interest in a swan and...

Raynard said nothing as he turned Ori onto his side and spooned behind him. His slicked shaft kissed against Ori's hole again and Ori's fretting subsided. Steadying Ori with a hand on his hip, Raynard pushed into him again.

Ori murmured his pleasure into the pillow as Raynard gradually rocked his way back into him. Ori knew Raynard's body well after all the months he'd spent with him. Raynard had so much control he'd be able to keep up the slow steady thrusts all night if he wanted to. Maybe he could even maintain them forever.

Ori gripped the sheet in front of him. Forever. At one time, he'd really believed that might happen, and he'd lost himself in the way that had felt.

Raynard reached around Ori and moved his hand over his skin. He caressed and teased again and again, as if he'd missed being able to touch Ori whenever he wanted to—almost as much as Ori had missed Raynard doing that.

Ori whimpered softly against the pillow, turning his face into it, so his master wouldn't hear his weakness. Everything was going to be perfect for them. If all his master could grant him was one more night together then, Ori couldn't ruin it.

"Hush."

Raynard brushed his fingers against Ori's cheek, guiding him to turn his head and look over his shoulder. Their mouths met. The kiss was softer now, gentler. Raynard's lips reassuring as they caressed.

Ori cautiously parted his lips and let his tongue creep out to join in. Not to lead, his master would never allow that, but he let Ori play a little as he followed behind his master.

One slow, heartfelt thrust after another, Raynard brought their bodies together again and again. He was getting closer to coming. Ori could feel the change in Raynard's movements as he tensed. Raynard held back, controlling himself until the last second. A final, deep thrust and his hand returned to Ori's hip, holding him still as he spilled inside him, marking him out as his submissive in the most basic way any man could.

Ori collapsed, exhausted, onto the sheet as he felt Raynard pull away. He couldn't even bring himself to reach out and try to stop him. It was over. He knew it then in a way he'd never really let himself believe before.

Closure apparently felt like someone was driving a stake into his chest and twisting it around, not really killing him, just making Ori wish it would.

Raynard stroked Ori's shoulder. Ori opened his eyes, and Raynard gently guided him to turn around and rest his head against his chest.

"Just for a little while," Raynard whispered, not quite looking him in the eye.

Ori nodded as he snuggled in closer to Raynard's body. He'd slept like that so many times, lulled into slumber by the beat of his master's heart. Raynard pulled him closer still, as if he couldn't bear the idea being torn away from him any more than Ori could.

He closed his eyes as Raynard slid his fingers through his hair, but he quickly opened them again.

They only had a little while. He wasn't going to waste it sleeping.

"Sleep."

Ori lifted his head, just enough to glance at his master.

"I'll still be here when you wake up," Raynard promised.

Ori couldn't do anything more than stare at him. His master had given him an order; he expected him to obey it. They both knew that. Ori reluctantly lowered his gaze and rested his head on his master's chest again. Raynard switched off the light.

It was wrong to lie to his master, but Ori did his best to let his breaths fall into a slow sleeping rhythm while he remained as wide awake as ever.

A few minutes passed and Raynard's chest rose and fell underneath Ori as he sighed softly into the darkness.

"Good boy."

The words were barely a whisper. Ori wasn't even sure he'd have heard them if they hadn't vibrated through Raynard's chest directly into his ear. He closed his eyes a little tighter. His master was pleased with him.

Curling himself closer against Raynard's body, Ori nuzzled against his skin.

"Hush, I've got you," Raynard whispered.

He obviously still believed that Ori was asleep. It was wrong to take advantage of that, but Ori couldn't help but let out a little whimper — maybe as if he was having a less than pleasant dream, or as if his aching joints were even more painful than they really were.

"Hush," Raynard whispered to him again, as he gathered him safer against his body. "You're fine. Everything's going to be just fine." He pressed a kiss to Ori's temple.

Ori sighed slightly as he settled, not brave enough to keep up the pretence, no matter how much he wanted Raynard to continue whispering to him that way.

As much as he wanted to fight real sleep when it danced around the edges of his mind, Ori couldn't hold it at bay forever. It wrapped around him, blending with Raynard's hold on him and lulling him into a deeper slumber than he'd ever been able to manage when he was away from his master's side.

* * * * *

Raynard looked up when Ori jerked awake and let out a startled little whimper.

He watched as his fledgling reached out and slid his palm across the sheet where Raynard had slept through the night. When he failed to find him, Ori dropped his head back onto the mattress. His whole body shook as his fist closed around the thick satiny sheet.

"I told you I'd still be here when you woke up." *And masters always keep their promises.* Raynard had never known it could be so hard to keep such silly, sentimental words back.

Masters keep their promises; they look after their submissives. Masters…

Except he wasn't Ori's master anymore, and he never should have been in the first place.

Ori spun around, tangling himself in the sheets as he turned to face Raynard. Lifting a hand, Ori pushed his fingers through his hair, brushing the pure white strands back off his face. "Sir…"

"I've already told you that there's no need for you to call me that…sire."

Ori dropped his gaze. Raynard went back to tying his shoelaces. He'd said he'd still be there when Ori woke up; he hadn't said he wouldn't be dressed and ready to leave.

"Do you remember your promise?" Raynard asked, doing his best to keep all trace of emotion out of his voice.

Ori was still staring at the bed they'd shared when Raynard looked up.

"Ori?" he prompted.

"Yes, sir."

Raynard let the silence stretch out between them.

Ori closed his eyes. "I'm to get the identifier tattoo and stretch my wings properly, sir," he recited.

Raynard sat there for several minutes, staring down at his shoelaces as if they contained the answers to every question in the universe. "It's for the best. You'll see that over time." He couldn't bring himself to add the honorific, couldn't bear to see Ori flinch the way he did every time Raynard called his former fledgling by his new title.

Ori said nothing, quite possibly because there was nothing left for either of them to say. Raynard rose from his seat. He clenched his hand into a fist at his side as he forced himself not to walk across the room toward Ori. He headed for the door instead. His fingers were already on the handle when Ori finally spoke up.

"If you ever change your mind, sir—I'll still be here. I'll still..."

Raynard closed his eyes for a moment, but he didn't look over his shoulder. Stepping out of the room, he resisted the temptation to vent his frustration on the woodwork and closed the door carefully behind him.

One of Ori's new servants was clearing away the things from the dining room. He looked up when he heard Raynard walk through the entrance hall, but Raynard couldn't bring himself to acknowledge the servant's existence. He strode past him, as fast as he could without breaking into an actual run.

Out of Ori's apartment, he kept going, desperate to be out of the building. He had no idea where he'd go. All he knew was the longer he stayed in there, the harder it would be to resist the need to rush back, to snatch Ori out of his bed and take him with him.

"Raynard?"

It wasn't Ori's voice. Raynard forced himself to look over his shoulder anyway. Hamilton stood in the doorway leading into his office. Raynard clenched his teeth.

Ori wasn't the only man he had to answer to regarding his behaviour before Ori's first full shift. All the avians were accountable to the elders of their chosen nest. There was no way he could leave, at any pace, and let Hamilton think he was running away from that fact.

Raynard walked slowly back down the corridor, his steps calm and measured, every trace of emotion wiped from his face. In Hamilton's study, he closed the door behind him and stepped up to his desk, allowing no trace of hesitation or reluctance to creep into his body language.

"You wished to speak with me?"

Hamilton picked up a tumbler of scotch and handed it to him. Raynard stared down into the amber liquid for several seconds before tossing it back in one go.

It was a bad idea to start drinking at breakfast time, especially when he was going home to a house that currently contained a very large selection of fine spirits and no fledgling submissive.

Raynard set the glass on the desk very carefully. His hand didn't shake. When he lifted his gaze to look across the desk, his eyes didn't waver.

Hamilton stared back at him, his fingers steepled together as he rested his elbows on the well-cushioned arms of his chair. "Our swan is...well?" he asked.

Raynard was tempted to pick up the glass and pitch it at Hamilton. Ori wasn't *ours*, he was Raynard's—his and no one else's.

"Ori will be fine," he snapped. He would be fine, he reminded himself—providing his former master stayed the hell away from him.

Hamilton made a noncommittal noise in the back of his

throat.

Raynard sat down opposite him, barely resisting the temptation to tell Hamilton to get whatever the hell it was he wanted to say over and done with.

"Ori mentioned that you told him about the role ducks tend to flock toward."

Raynard shrugged. Picking up the empty glass, he turned it around and around between his fingers. The light caught against the crystal, sparkling and shining as if all was right with the world.

"What would you have told him if you knew he was a swan?"

"Obviously, I wouldn't have wasted my time telling him about ducks," Raynard bit out.

"You'd have told him about swans instead," Hamilton said.

"Of course." Raynard's jaw ached as he ground his teeth together harder than ever.

"And what would you have said?" Hamilton asked again.

Raynard pushed himself up out of the chair. If the elders wanted him raked over the coals for the way he had treated a swan, he'd take it. Hell, if they wanted him to be publicly whipped, he deserved it for hurting Ori. But not this, not Hamilton pulling his time with Ori apart, piece by piece.

"Raynard?"

Raynard shook his head as he reached the window and looked down into the courtyard below.

"Maybe you'd have said that swans are the gentlest souls of all the avian species," Hamilton suggested. "That they have to be protected and cosseted from the outside world — that they aren't suited to being thrown into society and left to fend for themselves."

Raynard swallowed down the bitter taste in the back of his mouth, wondering if there was any more scotch where that last double had come from.

"Perhaps you'd have told him that swans are too easily taken advantage of, too easily used and abused by those who don't understand their true worth. They need the constant support and guidance of those who have their best interests at heart if they are to flourish."

Raynard closed his eyes and clenched his fist tightly around the glass still in his hand.

"Or maybe you'd have mentioned to him that that's why they are generally appointed some sort of guardian — a man who is often taken from one of the highest ranking local families and — "

Raynard spun around. "You can't mean to — "

Hamilton merely gazed back at him over his steepled fingers.

Raynard strode across the room. He slammed his hands down on Hamilton's desk. "Don't you think I've already hurt him enough?"

"You consider him damaged, then?"

Raynard took a deep breath. He looked down at the desk. The glass had shattered beneath his hand as he'd smashed it into the mahogany. His palm bled where he continued to crush the shards against wood. "He's strong," he said, the words barely more than a whispered hope. "He'll heal."

"I've seen him show strength," Hamilton agreed.

Raynard took his hand away from the broken glass. Peering into the wounds, he absentmindedly checked them for splinters of glass before wrapping his handkerchief around the broken skin.

"Once," Hamilton added.

Raynard knotted the cotton in place. Red immediately seeped through it. One show of strength wasn't much, but it was something — it was a start that could be built upon.

"That day you brought him back here wearing your collar — he was strong then, strong enough to floor a bullying crow, to take a whipping from his master and enjoy every lash, strong enough to serve you in whatever way you saw fit."

"And that's what you want for him now?" Raynard bit out, barely keeping another wave of anger in check. "For a man who was never cut out for service to spend his whole life serving a man of lower rank and—"

"It makes him happy."

Raynard stared down at him, his hand clenching around the handkerchief until pain shot through him. "It's not the way things are meant to be."

"It could certainly be considered an…unconventional arrangement," Hamilton said.

"Uncon—!"

"Someone who will protect him, lead him, take care of him. Someone who will stand between him and the rest of the world and look after him. Some could say that's the very definition of a good avian master."

Raynard glared down at Hamilton, completely speechless.

"A man who loves without boundaries, an avian whose soul is so pure he wishes to give everything he is and everything he has to one person. A true submissive by any other name…" Hamilton went on.

Raynard shook his head.

"While he was under your care—"

"Swans are not suited to submission!" Raynard was sure of it. It was damn near the only thing he felt sure of right then.

Hamilton seemed to think about that for a moment. "While he was under your care, did you give any thought to what he needed, what he might want?"

"I thought he was a duckling," Raynard yelled as guilt flashed through him. "So did you!"

Hamilton rose to his feet on the other side of the desk, his hands pressing against the old polished wood opposite Raynard's. "Answer the question!"

"Yes!" Raynard spat out. "Are you satisfied now? Yes, I thought about what my submissive would want. I thought about what he'd need in order to be happy under my protection. I was wrong."

"You're sure about that, are you?"

"What?"

"Are you sure you were wrong?" Hamilton shouted.

Raynard stared at Hamilton as if he'd lost his mind.

"The elders have come to the conclusion that your initial instincts toward Ori may have been far closer to the correct method for dealing with him than we originally suspected." Hamilton sat down, and modulated his voice. "It's possible that, as a swan, he feels the need to please everyone. Having a master, one person to devote himself to, might be what he needs. Lord knows we've tried everything else since we found out what he really is..."

Raynard lowered himself to his seat.

"Do you really think this sort of arrangement was our first choice?" Hamilton asked, annoyance seeping into each word. "Everything we offer him only makes him withdraw further into himself. The only time I've seen a hint of life in his eyes is when he speaks about the time he spent serving you."

"So you try something else," Raynard demanded. "You don't give up on a man like Ori just because—"

"You're in love with him."

For a moment Raynard could only stare at the elder in slack-jawed silence. "Irrelevant," he finally said, dismissing the fact with a shake of his head as he pulled himself together.

"Hawks have always had a tendency to mate for life."

"Equally irr—"

"So have swans."

Raynard stopped short, meeting Hamilton's eyes across the desk.

"Last night, when he was with you, he was happy?" Hamilton asked.

The whole evening played through Raynard's mind.

Ori had been so relieved, so grateful for his attention, so desperate, so exhausted. But yes, he'd been happy too, so happy to be back under his master's care, if only for a little while.

"He's a swan," Raynard whispered, just in case the whole world had suddenly forgotten that fact.

Hamilton steepled his fingers once more. "The elders can't actually force you to take him on, any more than they could force a swan to accept such an arrangement. However, they wished me to make it clear to you before you left, that we would, let us say, look very favourably upon any such understanding…"

Raynard rose to his feet, turned his back on the eagle and all his stupid ideas, and strode across to the door.

Swan. Submissive. Swan. Submissive.

The two words warred against each other inside his head with every step he took, refusing to resolve themselves into one character, one man, one future.

When the door to Hamilton's office swung closed behind him, Raynard looked both ways down the corridor, toward the exit, then toward the swan's quarters, then back to the exit again.

The decision was his and, submissive or not, in that moment, Ori depended upon him to make the right choice for them both. It was all very well for the eagle to say his instincts were right.

If only the two sets of instincts warring inside him would just agree with each other, it would be so very simple.

Chapter Thirteen

"Whenever you're ready, sire."

Ori stared down at his bare wrist. He'd promised. No matter how much he hated the idea, he'd promised Raynard that if they had one last night together, he'd stop putting off getting the swan's mark tattooed on the inside of his wrist.

He ran a fingertip along the skin just over his vein, tracing out the mark Raynard had once painted on him in just the same way. That combination of waves and lines would have marked him out as a duck. And every time he'd reached out to shake another avian's hand, someone would have realised what he was, and they'd have looked at him differently. Then the orders would have started to flow and...

Ori took a deep breath and forced himself to picture another kind of tattoo on his wrist. The second he did, it was impossible for him not to imagine the kind of life that would come with it. Whenever he shook hands with people and they saw the swan's mark inked beneath his skin, that knowledge would also cause them to treat him differently.

No orders. There would never be any orders, or any work. There'd never be any chance of being taken back under Raynard's protection either.

Ori looked up.

The peacock who acted as tattoo artist for the nest had already spent over an hour patiently waiting for permission to practice his art. Ori nibbled his bottom lip. The poor guy would have probably had more luck if he'd simply ordered him to stop making a fuss and bloody well do as he was told.

Bowing his head slightly, Ori called Raynard's order to the front of his mind and nodded to the peacock.

A deeply upholstered chair stood in the middle of the room. The tattoo artist's stool was placed next to it, a tray with all his equipment laid out just to its right.

Ori settled himself on the chair and placed his elbow on the little support built into the armrest. The arrangement held his wrist out toward the tattoo artist like some bizarre sort of sacrificial offering.

"It shouldn't hurt too much," the peacock offered, as he perched on the stool.

Ori didn't bother trying to explain that his hesitation had nothing to do with that kind of fear. He doubted he'd have been able to explain the real truth of the matter anyway.

If it had been another man offering him a different sort of pain, Ori knew he'd have welcomed it. He pressed his back against the softly cushioned chair, but no hint of discomfort flared from the whip lines that had once striped his back. The marks Raynard had left on him were just a distant memory. Even his collar was gone.

Ori closed his eyes as the tattooist's needle touched his skin for the first time, not wanting to see the swan's lines appear. The machine whirred, the only sound in the otherwise silent space, until a sudden click on the other side of the room made Ori jerk his head up and open his eyes. The door swung back. Raynard strode into the room.

The peacock jerked and pulled the needle away from Ori's wrist.

Ori launched himself to his feet. "Sir!"

He covered his right wrist with his opposite hand, not sure exactly what kind of mark had already been placed there. If he was lucky, it was something that could be converted into a mark that would please his master. If he was unlucky... Ori swallowed, terrified that he might have ruined everything at the very last moment.

"Out."

Rank ceased to matter. The peacock didn't look to Ori for confirmation. The elaborately dressed young man rushed out, closing the door behind him.

Ori stared across the room at his master, unable to bring a single word to his lips.

Raynard took a step forward, then another. Moving around Ori, he made himself comfortable in the chair that Ori had just vacated. Never breaking eye contact, Ori turned to face him and lowered himself to his knees at Raynard's feet.

Raynard held out his hand. Ori remained frozen, the beginnings of the tattoo still hidden beneath his opposite palm.

"Show me."

Ori reluctantly offered his wrist to Raynard for his inspection. Raynard's grip was strong. He stared down at the curved line that had already been inked in place with a serious expression.

"Can it be fixed, sir?" Ori whispered, very softly.

"Fixed?"

"Turned into the kind of mark you'd like," Ori translated.

Raynard looked back to Ori's wrist. "What convinced you to come here and get this mark today?"

Ori dropped his gaze and stared at his wrist too.

"The truth," Raynard pushed.

"You told me to, sir."

"Hamilton told you to weeks ago—so did the rest of the elders."

"They aren't my master, sir." Ori closed his eyes as he said it, knowing he didn't have the right to call him that anymore.

Raynard slid his other hand through Ori's hair, tugging his head back and tilting Ori's face up to look at him.

"Tell me what you want—not what you think you should want, not what I've told you to want, or what rights the elders have said your station grants you. Tell me what you want."

Ori swallowed rapidly. "For everything to be the way it

217

was before. For you to be pleased with me. To be your... To be whatever I can be to you now, sir."

Raynard peered down at him, even more serious now. His chest rose and fell as he took a deep breath. "You know that a swan has every right to request anything. Any man in the nest would be expected to do as a swan wanted — even if he asked for something other than what swans traditionally desire." His grip on Ori's hair tightened. "If you really wish to belong to me, you can have what you want."

Ori dipped his head, suddenly desperate to escape Raynard's hold on him.

Raynard's fingers tightened around the silky white strands. Ori pulled away, as sharply as he could, tearing his wrist out of Raynard's other hand at the same time. He fell backward, sprawling on the tiled floor, and scrambled away until his back hit the wall next to the door.

On the edge of his chair, Raynard froze, staring down at him, anger and confusion warring in his eyes.

"No." It was the first time Ori could ever remember saying the word to Raynard. He'd had no idea he could ever sound so certain about a word, so determined.

"Ori?"

"No," he repeated.

"No?"

Looking up, Ori stared, horrified, into Raynard's eyes. "You really think I'd do that to you, sir?"

Raynard glared back at him, his expression unreadable.

"I don't want you to keep me because you *have* to, sir," Ori whispered. "I'd never ask you to do that and...and I won't let you do that either!" The words flowed out, and there was nothing he could do to stop them. Panic flared inside him — a true terror that he couldn't be strong enough to stop Raynard from making that kind of sacrifice for him. No. He shook his head. He couldn't let that happen.

"Since when do you 'let' your master do anything?" Raynard asked.

There was a teasing note in his voice, but there was also an undercurrent. Ori immediately dropped his gaze, knowing he risked pushing Raynard past what he'd tolerate from him — whatever his species. "We both know you don't need my permission to do whatever you want with me, sir."

Raynard said nothing.

Ori stared at the floor a few inches in front of Raynard's feet as he frantically tried to make his mind work, to do what was right for Raynard rather than himself. "You said I could ask you for something, sir," he remembered.

"It's a swan's right to —"

Ori shook his head. "No, sir. I mean months ago, when we first… You said I could always ask you for something if it was really important to me."

Raynard nodded his acceptance of that fact.

"I'm not asking as a swan, sir. I'm asking as a submissive." That was important; Raynard had to understand that. Not knowing what else to do, Ori glanced up to let his former master see the desperation in his eyes.

Raynard frowned, but he nodded his permission for Ori to continue.

"Please, don't…" Ori dragged a shuddering breath into his lungs. "Please don't take me back if you know there's never any chance you'll want me. If you know that I'll never be able to please you then…"

When Raynard remained silent, Ori found he had to go on. He had to find words to fill the void. Picking at the seam on his trouser leg, he pushed each word out through a throat that fought each syllable.

"If there's any way I can belong to you and please you, I'll do it, sir. I'll serve you, and anyone else, in whatever way I can. I'll do whatever you want, and I'll get down on my knees and thank you for it every second of the day, but I can't be… Please, don't take me back if you don't want me. I'd rather be miserable here on my own, than make you unhappy thinking you have to own a man you hate."

Raynard sat back in his chair, anger and confusion fading from his expression as if neither had ever existed. "Hamilton was right."

Ori swallowed, waiting to see what that verdict meant for him.

"You're stronger with your submission than without it."

Ori stared past Raynard, at the bare white wall behind him. It sounded like a joke, but he couldn't see any reason for laughter.

Raynard nodded to himself as if everything was suddenly settling into place inside his mind.

Ori watched Raynard's chest rise and fall as he took a slow, deep breath.

"Come here."

Unable to trust his knees to support him if he tried to rise, but equally unable to disobey his master's summons, Ori crawled across the floor to the base of the chair.

Raynard tucked a knuckle under Ori's chin, holding him still to be studied. "I never thought I'd fall in love with a swan." The words were slow and musing, as if he was talking as much to himself as anyone else.

Ori's eyes opened very wide as he stared up at him.

Raynard smiled slightly. "Are you really that shocked, fledgling?"

He nodded, making his master chuckle. Ori automatically smiled in response. As the rich, comforting sound wrapped around him, Raynard slid his fingers through Ori's hair and pulled him closer.

"It's not so unknown for a master to fall in love with his submissive."

Ori buried his face in Raynard's shirt, helpless to resist the temptation to nuzzle in against him, even as his brain desperately scrambled to work out what the hell was going on now. Suddenly, everything about Raynard, from his posture to the very fact he'd resumed using the word fledgling as an endearment rather than a stage in a man's life, welcomed Ori close. But at the same time... "You said..."

Raynard stroked his fingers through Ori's hair again, cradling him against his body and not even chiding him for wriggling the way he'd sometimes done when Ori had shared his bed every night.

"You said I wasn't your submissive anymore, sir," Ori whispered against Raynard's shirt.

"Apparently, even masters are wrong on occasions— not often," he stressed, his tone turning self-mocking. "But just on a few, very rare occasions."

Ori glanced up.

"Perhaps I don't know as much about what a swan's nature might make him suited to as I thought," Raynard whispered.

A slight frown appeared between Raynard's eyebrows.

"I meant what I said, sir," Ori offered quickly. "If I don't shift—"

Raynard covered Ori's mouth with his hand. "You will shift as and when you're told to, and there will be no arguing with me when I give you that command."

There was no room for negotiation when Raynard assumed that tone of voice. Pleasure rushed through Ori, just as it had every time his master had offered him that kind of certainty.

"I wouldn't let you be ashamed of your species when you were thought to be an ugly little duckling. Do you really think I'll let you hate yourself for being a swan?" Raynard demanded, his voice gaining more confidence with each word, until they began to sound harsh.

Ori traced the edge of one of Raynard's shirt buttons, around and around, again and again.

"I fell in love with a swan. That means no one, not even my submissive, is going to insult that species in front of me."

Ori blushed slightly as the words seeped into his mind, reassuring some instinctive part of him that didn't care about anything other than his master's good opinion of him. Something inside him sang out with joy and refused to care if anything made sense or not.

Raynard reached into his trouser pocket and took out a familiar length of leather. "The back of the tag will need to be marked with both our symbols."

Ori simply stared at the collar, barely daring to breathe in case it broke some wonderful spell.

"Is this what you want, fledgling?"

Ori nodded very quickly.

Raynard had the collar around Ori's neck in seconds. For the first time since it had been taken away, Ori felt his soul settle into some semblance of peace. His heart raced, but now, it was with pleasure, not panic. He looked up at his master, wanting nothing more than to make everything exactly as it was before.

"Take me home, sir?" he whispered, no longer caring if it sounded as though he was begging.

Raynard smiled slightly, but he also shook his head. "Soon, but first you have some unfinished business to attend to." He looked to the door the tattoo artist had disappeared through.

Ori quickly covered his wrist with his opposite hand again.

"No arguing," Raynard ordered, before Ori had time to say a word. "Let him in, then come back to me."

Reluctantly rising, Ori did as he was told. When he hurried back to kneel at Raynard's feet, Raynard shook his head again. He held a hand out to Ori and guided him to sit on his lap, so he could once more offer his wrist to the tattooist.

The peacock made his way cautiously back to his stool. If he thought the seating arrangement a strange one, he seemed to take one look at Raynard's expression and decide he had no wish to comment on it. By the time he had straightened up the contents of his tray, Raynard had Ori arranged comfortably on his lap.

Permitted to curl into his master's embrace and rest his head on his shoulder, Ori watched, rather fascinated, as Raynard wrapped his hand around his forearm, holding his wrist steady for the artist's needle.

"Do you know why avians started wearing these marks on their wrists?" Raynard asked him softly, as the tattoo artist bowed his head over his work.

"So everyone can know what everyone else is, even in their human form, sir," Ori whispered back.

"That's right."

"So they'd know where each man stood in the hierarchy," Ori added.

"No," Raynard said, in the slow tone of voice that meant he was thinking about what he said very carefully. "Not at first. Years ago, it was a simple statement of pride — this is who I am, this is what I stand for. There was no such thing as a mark a man should be ashamed of. That was never what these markings were supposed to be about."

Ori nuzzled closer into his master's shoulder, knowing what Raynard was trying to tell him, even if he wasn't sure he was ready to hear it.

"You're a good man, Ori — and you're a good submissive. In time, I'll see to it you become a good swan as well. And no one will be prouder of you than I will be when that happens."

Ori closed his eyes as Raynard tightened his embrace around him and the tattoo artist's needle buzzed on.

* * * * *

Everyone was staring at him. Ori tried to push the sensation aside, but the way whispers fluttered through the crowds of men was impossible to ignore. Everyone was staring and talking about him and —

"Keep up, fledgling."

Ori scurried forward a few steps to walk more closely by his master's side.

Raynard didn't even glance toward him. It was as if he knew exactly where he'd be, as if he trusted Ori to be where he belonged, and saw no need to check up on him once he'd issued a clear order.

Ori's steps faltered when he caught sight of Mr. Hamilton standing at the other end of the hallway. He turned toward them as they approached, and Ori felt the eagle's attention settle on his collar. Fear rushed through him at the idea that Mr. Hamilton might somehow be able to take his collar away, but Ori kept pace with Raynard regardless.

Mr. Hamilton shook hands with Raynard. He turned to Ori and held his hand out to him. Ori automatically looked to Raynard. He received a nod of permission.

Ori reached out and shook hands with Mr. Hamilton. The eagle tilted his hand to one side as their palms met, turning Ori's tattoo up to be viewed. The skin was still red around the edges of the swirling black mark, but the design was clear and vivid against his pale skin.

"It looks good on you, sire."

"Thank you, sir."

As he released Ori's hand, Mr. Hamilton turned his attention back to Raynard. Not having any order to occupy himself with, Ori stepped back out of everyone's way and settled himself into his rest position until such time as his master had another command for him. His movements felt so natural that, just for a few seconds, it was possible to believe it had all just been some horrible nightmare and nothing had actually changed over the last few weeks.

"We can expect you both to be at the feast this weekend?" Mr. Hamilton asked. The question seemed to be directed entirely toward Raynard, but Ori felt himself fall under the scope of the inquiry in a way he never had when everyone believed him to be a duckling.

"We'll both be there," Raynard confirmed.

The rest of the conversation didn't seem to require any sort of contribution from Ori. Mr. Hamilton dipped his head to him as he walked away, but Ori barely had time to notice the little half bow before his master was striding off again.

As they stepped into the car park, Ori hurried forward and opened his master's car door for him, before running around to the other side and taking his place in the passenger seat.

The drive was completed in what might have felt like an easy, companionable, silence, if Ori's nerves had been stronger. As it was, he just felt grateful that he hadn't actually hyperventilated by the time Raynard's car pulled up outside his house.

Getting out of the car, Ori scurried around to open Raynard's door for him again, but found himself stopped short. Raynard was already out of the vehicle. Damn. Eager to find some other way to serve, Ori turned toward the front door of the house and rushed to open that for him instead.

His hand was already on the handle when he realised it was still locked and his master was the only one with a key.

Raynard stepped up behind him. Ori tried to move out of his way, but he found his escape route blocked by a solid wall of hawk. Swallowing down his nerves as best he could, he stood very still as the heat from his master's body started to soak through both their clothes.

Raynard pushed the door open. It had taken Ori a day's work on the hinges to make the door swing smoothly and silently.

It was silly to be pleased that some little part of the service he'd provided for his master had lingered on in Raynard's home while he'd been gone, but Ori concentrated his whole mind on those hinges — it was his only chance of ignoring the other thing he'd realised as their bodies pressed against each other.

His master was hard.

The moment the door was open, Ori stumbled forward,

heading straight for the servants' quarters.

Raynard's caught hold of his arm, stopping him in his tracks. "Where do you think you're going?"

"I should start catching up on the duties I—"

"Do you think that's the best way you could serve me right now?" Raynard stepped closer, until his cock pressed intimately against Ori's backside once more.

His master had no doubt had plenty of erections before Ori came under his protection. He didn't need that from him, and Ori knew he'd already given up his right to offer himself to Raynard that way.

"I promised," Ori whispered. "I promised that I wouldn't expect things to be the same as they were before, sir. I meant it."

"You think I've lost interest in you?" Raynard slid a fingertip along the edge of Ori's collar.

Ori's eyes fell closed as he leaned into his touch. "I..."

"Or do you think a hawk's not good enough for you, now that you outrank me?"

Ori spun around, wide eyed with horror at the idea. "I wouldn't...!"

A smile played around Raynard's lips. "If nothing has changed for you, why assume it's changed for me?"

"Because you said everything had changed!" It sounded like an accusation. Ori wished he could take it back the moment it left his lips, but it was too late. The words were there, hanging in the air between them.

Raynard released Ori's arm and walked away from him. He leaned against the sideboard on the other side of the room, his arms folded across his chest.

Ori's feet stuck to the tiles, he was helpless to step forward and bridge the gap between them, even when every inch of space threatened to kill something inside him.

"I think your species changes what you're suited to," Raynard announced, no trace of emotion in his voice. "And, yes—it means you'll almost certainly prove to be better matched to a different form of submission than the one I had planned for you before the shifting ceremony."

Ori shook his head.

"The matter isn't open for debate."

Ori met his master's gaze across the room.

"You offered me your submission. It's my right as your master to ensure you practice the form of submission that brings out the best of your nature."

No matter how much Ori wanted to look away, he couldn't.

"The way you'll serve me changed the moment you completed the shifting ceremony. I won't lie to you and say otherwise," Raynard went on. "But I've never told you that the way I feel about you has changed, have I, fledgling?"

Ori finally managed to drop his gaze. The words his master had said to him in the tattoo studio still echoed around and around inside his head, too fantastical to be believed.

Submissives could easily fall in love with their masters, especially when their masters were as perfect as Raynard — Ori had known that for months. But the idea that the reverse could also happen, that his master could care for him as much as Ori cared for Raynard, was...

He looked up.

"Come here."

Ori stepped forward.

When he was a foot away, Raynard hooked his fingers through Ori's collar and tugged him forward. He collided heavily with Raynard's chest. Holding Ori there by the circle of leather, Raynard dipped his head to whisper in his ear.

"You're mine, fledgling. You belong to me — body and soul. I own you. Never doubt that."

"Yes, sir."

"And you're going to do as you're told and let me take care of you properly, aren't you?"

"Yes, sir." It was barely a whisper.

"And now, you're going to run up those stairs and strip

yourself down before climbing into my bed, aren't you?"

Ori parted his lips, but only an enthusiastic whimper emerged.

"Fledgling…"

"Yes, sir," he rasped out.

Raynard let go of Ori's collar. A sharp tap on his backside sent him on his way up the stairs.

His master had said run; Ori didn't walk. He threw himself up the stairs and into the master bedroom. His clothes seemed to fight against his need to follow Raynard's order. He scrabbled at the seemingly endless yards of fabric as he threw them aside.

The bed hadn't been made. Ori jumped on top of the rumpled sheets. He was just in time. Panting for breath, he turned toward the bedroom door as it swung open.

Raynard stepped into the room and slammed the door behind him. His eyes seemed to take in every detail as he stalked toward the bed.

He stopped at the edge of the mattress and stared down at Ori.

Ori had seen the same look in Raynard's eyes when he came in from stretching his wings. There was something wild about him, as if he could control the whole world – every bit of it, bar himself; as if there was something in him that was too strong for anyone to master, even Raynard.

"Never doubt this is exactly where you belong."

"Yes, sir. I mean…No, sir…I mean –"

Whatever he might have been destined to mean was swallowed by a kiss as Raynard brought their mouths together and took complete possession of him.

Ori tipped his head back, grabbing hold of Raynard's shoulders to steady himself as Raynard pulled him closer.

Raynard thrust his tongue past Ori's lips, sparring with Ori until Ori couldn't keep up. Ori moaned when Raynard nipped his bottom lip. He clawed for a purchase on Raynard's arms when Raynard suddenly pushed him away.

Ori's grip failed him. He toppled backward. Raynard loomed over him, his eyes serious and wild in equal measure as he joined Ori on the bed. His clothes were still between them. Raynard didn't seem to care about that as he grabbed the lube from the bedside cabinet and smeared it over his fingers.

No teasing, no time wasted, he thrust his fingers into Ori's hole, not so much encouraging him to relax and accept his master as demanding that he do so.

Arching on the bed, Ori pushed back against Raynard's fingers, trying to squirm his way farther on to them. He moaned his disapproval as Raynard's hand left him.

Raynard tugged his zip-fly down and shoved the fabric of his trousers and boxers out of the way. A nudge to Ori's side prompted him to roll over and lift himself onto his hands and knees.

Raynard pushed Ori's knees farther apart. A moment later, he settled his palms on Ori's flanks, holding him in place. Raynard's slicked cock pressed against Ori's hole. One thrust had Raynard buried inside him to the hilt. Ori cried out as pure pleasure rushed through him.

Raynard stilled. Ori scrabbled desperately at the sheet as he tried to do the same and failed. Reaching forward, Raynard put one hand between Ori's shoulder blades and pushed him down.

Ori's arms gave way, his body tipped forward. His face came to rest on the blanket as his back arched, and he offered himself up to Raynard more thoroughly than ever.

Raynard grunted his approval as he pulled back to deliver a slower and even deeper thrust.

Ori gasped as his body took over, and his mind shut down. All that existed then was Ori and his master.

Raynard's cock was buried inside his arse. Raynard's hands were holding him as tight as they could as he rammed into him again. It was impossible to think it was about anything other than dominance and ownership. Ori wasn't a swan; he was a submissive. He was Raynard's fledgling. He was simply a man who loved his master.

Permission to come not granted, Ori clung to his control as best he could. But, as his body rushed to the edge of pleasure, he found himself stopped short. His mind could think what it liked, but Ori knew in that moment, his body wasn't going to allow him to come until Raynard gave the word.

His master owned him down to the core. Such decisions were no longer his to make.

Raynard pushed into him again and again, holding him on an edge he wasn't allowed to fall from. Ori rocked against the mattress with each deep thrust. His hands clenched around fistfuls of the sheet as mewing little whimpers escaped him.

His cheek rubbed against the bedspread as he forced another breath of air into his lungs. Raynard's scent clung to the sheets, seeming to envelop Ori in his presence.

Suddenly, Raynard yelled his pleasure. The whole bed shook as he delivered a final series of rapid thrusts. Ori closed his eyes and relished his master's satisfaction as Raynard came inside him.

He remained frozen in place even after Raynard pulled away. Head down, arse up. They'd said that was a natural position for a duck. Apparently, it was a natural position for a swan, too. Ori stayed that way for a long time, panting for breath, not sure if he could move without coming.

Fabric rustled behind Ori as Raynard dispensed with his clothes. A moment later, Raynard caressed Ori's upturned buttocks, teasing the sensitive skin and making him whimper. Finally a tap against one cheek prompted Ori to try to move. Kneeling upon the bed, he turned toward his master.

Raynard was just pushing the last of his discarded clothes off the bed. He sighed his contentment as he relaxed back against the mattress. Ori nibbled at his bottom lip as he watched Raynard settle himself to rest. There was a sensitive spot on his lip, where Raynard's teeth had caught him almost hard enough to draw blood. Ori ran his tongue over it, relishing the sensations it sent spiralling through him.

"Come here."

The first word almost had Ori spilling onto the sheet. Somehow, he managed to shuffle forward without tripping over his orgasm en route. Raynard wrapped his hand around Ori's cock as Ori reached his side—his grip tight and perfect.

Ori met Raynard's eyes. There was a touch of amusement mixed in with the sleepiness and the afterglow, but all the anger and confusion from earlier in the day was gone, for now at least. Placing his own hands behind his back, Ori knelt next to Raynard and arranged himself in something as close to his rest position as he could get. With his knees spread wide apart and his head bowed, he watched Raynard toy with him.

Raynard had always liked to hold him like that, to cradle Ori's erection in the palm of his hand and know that he had complete control over him. He was treating Ori in exactly the same way he had when he thought he was a duck, and Ori had never been more grateful to be so painfully frustrated in his life.

"Come."

The word was said at his master's discretion, and according to his own timetable. Ori knew that. He also knew he'd never been more thankful to hear it spoken.

He came—lights flashing, senses spinning, and his master stroking him rapidly through his orgasm. Raynard kept pumping Ori's shaft long after his orgasm ended.

Ori whimpered, too sensitive to truly enjoy Raynard's touch right then, too lost in his submission to even consider protesting. Gradually, Raynard slowed his hand movements of his volition.

Ori managed to blink open his eyes. His cum decorated Raynard's stomach in long creamy ropes. Ori opened his eyes even wider. Raynard chuckled as he scooped up some of the semen and proffered it to Ori's lips.

Ori automatically opened his mouth to receive it, and the next few fingers-full too, cherishing the intimacy of the offering.

When Raynard slid his freshly licked-clean fingers into Ori's hair and guided his head down, Ori happily lapped the trails directly off Raynard's skin, gaining a little taste of his master at the same time. Murmuring his approval, Ori pressed lick after lick, kiss after kiss, against Raynard's body. He rubbed his face against Raynard's skin too, nuzzling him, trying to soak up his presence through his every pore until he finally fell still, exhausted, with his head resting against Raynard's chest.

"I love you too, sir. So much."

For a full minute, Ori's head moved up and down in time with Raynard's breathing and Raynard stayed silent. Ori was just about to apologise, sure he had said the wrong thing, when his master finally spoke.

"I know you do, fledgling."

Ori glanced up at him.

Raynard's smile was gentle as he looked down at Ori. Raynard didn't say anything else, but he ruffled Ori's hair, and Ori soon found himself snuggled contentedly under the blankets, tucked in close to his master's side.

For just a little while before he fell asleep, it was so easy for him to pretend he was still an ugly little duckling, nothing had changed, and everything really was perfect.

Chapter Fourteen

Ori tensed as he realised he was no longer alone. Someone was watching him. He glanced over his shoulder and spotted Raynard standing in the kitchen doorway.

Turning, Ori pushed his hair off his face with the back of his wrist. Raynard's gaze trailed slowly up and down Ori's body. Ori looked down and followed Raynard's example. Naked but for his collar, the only thing that hid any part of his skin was a good layer of dust.

There were thicker smudges here and there, where he'd managed to make himself especially dirty while throwing himself into his neglected duties.

When Ori looked up, Raynard was smiling, but there was something else in his expression as well, something Ori couldn't decipher.

"You may be the only avian I've ever met who can look happier scrubbing floors than surrounded by luxury."

Ori bit his bottom lip as he set his cloth on the kitchen table, still not entirely sure if his master was pleased with him for being the way he was, or if he quietly hated him for it.

As he waited for an order, Ori arranged himself neatly in his rest position. Raynard walked across the room, then circled behind Ori, out of his field of vision.

"How much pain are you in?"

Ori would have tried to turn and face Raynard if he'd thought there was any chance he'd get away with it. But he also knew he'd have been ordered to turn around if Raynard wanted him to be able to see his master when he gave his answer.

"The work's not too hard for me, sir," he rushed out.

"I know. The pain comes from staying in one form for too long."

Tension flooded back into Ori's body, making his joints ache more than ever.

"Shower off. It's time you stretched your wings properly."

"Sir, I..."

Raynard settled his hands on Ori's shoulders and turned Ori to face him.

Ori looked up, trying to find the right words, but the expression in Raynard's eyes quickly informed him that there were no such words. There was nothing he could say. The decision had already been made.

"Yes, sir."

When Ori came out of the shower set off the butler's old room a few minutes later, Raynard had already left the kitchen. Making his way up the stairs into the main part of the house, Ori forced himself to keep going, past the study and the library where he and his master had spent so many wonderful hours and up the main stairs toward those that would eventually lead him to the attic.

They'd spent more than a few happy hours there when Raynard returned from his flights, but that had been before.

A noise behind Ori stopped him short.

"Where do you think you're going?"

"You said..." Ori frowned, looking from where Raynard stood in the library doorway, to the attic room staircase and back again.

"Not from there."

Ori silently made his way back down the stairs.

"I can see the question in your eyes, fledgling—spit it out."

"Because I'm a submissive, or because I'm a swan, sir?"

"Because the chances of you landing successfully on a small balcony on your first attempt are very slim," Raynard said, ruffling his hair and pushing him toward the front door.

"Get dressed."

Opening the little coat closet in the hallway, Ori quickly scrambled into his clothes.

Raynard had a bag with him. He carried it out to the car and set it in the back seat before Ori could even open the door for him. Sitting uncomfortably on the passenger side, Ori glanced across at Raynard several times, but he still couldn't read anything in his expression.

"Are we going to the pool, sir?" he finally blurted out, unable to bear the silence a moment longer.

"No."

Ori fidgeted with the seam on his trouser leg.

No further information was offered, until they pulled up at a big set of iron gates in a part of the city Ori wasn't familiar with.

Raynard took a key out of his trouser pocket and passed it to Ori. There was a padlock on the gates. Ori eventually made his brain add one and one together. Hurrying out of the car, he unlocked the heavy metal chain from the fancy ironwork. By the time he turned back to his master, Raynard was out of the parked car, his bag in his hand once more.

He strode through the gates ahead of Ori, and nodded for him to relock the barrier behind them both. Trapped in the park with Raynard, Ori scurried to keep up with him as he walked swiftly down one of the paths that wound away between the trees.

Far too busy wondering what the hell was going on to take much notice of the trees and bushes that filled the grounds, Ori came to an abrupt halt as they emerged from the foliage. A wooden bench was set in a clearing, looking out over a large lake.

Ori stared at it as if he'd never seen such a body of water before.

"Keep up, fledgling."

Raynard put the bag on the bench and sat next to it,

looking out over the water. Ori stepped closer, until he was standing directly before his master.

"Strip."

"Sir?"

Raynard looked up at him as if he couldn't see what the problem was. Ori wasn't sure he knew what the trouble was, either.

"The park is owned by the nest. We let humans use it during the day, but they know better than to venture in here once it's locked for the night."

"It's not that," Ori muttered. "If you ordered me to strip in front of the whole nest, I would."

That much was true. Ori felt as if he'd already spent half his life naked in front of Raynard, and he didn't care about anyone else's opinion. But that didn't change the fact that, for the first time in so long, he found himself clinging to the protection his clothes offered him.

Raynard couldn't order him to shift while he was still dressed. If he hadn't been willing to let him shift in a collar, there was no way he could command him to change forms in a tangle of trousers, shirt and boots.

Raynard leaned back in his seat.

Ori shuffled his boots against the leaf litter. Not one word, no recriminations, no condemnation. Raynard didn't need to say anything. Ori knew when he was failing to obey his master. He knew when he was being a bad submissive.

He held out all of three minutes before he started to remove his clothes. Folding them neatly, he set them on the seat next to Raynard, until he stood naked bar his collar.

Raynard reached out to relieve him of that too.

Ori wrapped his hand around his master's wrist, as if some stupid little part of him thought he could actually stop him. "Please, sir…"

Raynard took no notice. In a second, the collar was gone. Raynard took Ori by the hand and led him into the centre of the clearing facing the lake.

"Your collar will still be here when you get back."

Ori blinked up at him.

"So will I."

Swallowing all his protests, Ori dropped his gaze to the ground between them.

Raynard tucked his knuckles under Ori's chin and tilted his head back, demanding Ori look him in the eye. "Belonging to another man means accepting that there are times when he knows what is best for you—that he's doing what's best for you, even if it doesn't feel like it."

"Yes, sir."

"You're going to stretch your wings."

Ori nodded, looking to the side so his master wouldn't see his reluctance.

Raynard tapped him on the cheek with the tip of his finger. He was smiling when Ori looked back to him. "I don't expect you to like it, or even pretend to like it. But, swan or not, I expect any man who offers me his submission to do as he's told."

Ori managed another nod.

Raynard walked back to the bench. Standing alone near the water, Ori looked over his shoulder toward him.

"Try to land somewhere near this edge of the lake when you come back."

Ori stared out over the water.

His master didn't want a swan, and now he was going to watch his submissive morph into one before his eyes. Ori instinctively reached for the comfort of his collar.

It wasn't there.

The sooner he got this whole stupid thing over with, the sooner he'd know if it really would be waiting for him when he got back.

He glanced at Raynard one more time. Nothing to hide behind, nothing to disguise what he was...

Ori looked down at the tattoo on the inside of his wrist, before quickly closing his eyes.

The mental door that he'd opened inside himself when he was on the stage before the elders was still there. It had been trying to push itself open more and more insistently over the last weeks, as pressure built up on the other side of it and leaked out as an ache that seeped into every muscle and joint.

Even as Ori mentally glanced in its direction, the door inside him sprang open. Sensations rushed into his body, faster than he could process them. Pain and pleasure mixed together so thoroughly it was impossible to tell where one began and the other ended.

For one glorious moment, it felt like everything he was and everything he could be existed in the same universe. Almost too soon, he felt the side of himself that he was the most familiar with fade away. Reaching out, he tried to grasp at it with the farthest edges of his mind, but it raced away from him until it was difficult to see it over the mental horizon, hard to remember there was even anything that had gone.

Ori lifted his arms, but his shoulders didn't move the way he expected them to. He tipped his head back, stretching out an unexpectedly long neck as he looked up toward the sky.

He took a step forward. His legs weren't the same as he remembered. Everything was different. The world had changed.

The breeze blew against him, seeming to call to him. He stepped forward again, a little closer to the lake. Instinct took over. Arms stretched out as if they were wings, he ran forward. The edge of the water was right in front of him, then the air suddenly caught against his arms and the ground was falling away beneath his soles and he was climbing higher and higher into the atmosphere.

Even as his mind looked in wonder at the world below him, the landscape shrank a little more. The sky was wide above him, pulling him up with each movement of his arms. A flick of his fingertips was all it took to turn in large lazy circles high above the lake and the bench at the edge of it.

* * * * *

Leaning back against the rough wooden bench, Raynard craned his neck and stared up into the sky. Ori was little more than a white dot as he reached the far end of his circular path, but he never once strayed entirely out of Raynard's sight.

Smiling up at the spectacle, even as he felt something inside himself crack and break at the sight, Raynard tracked Ori's progress, around and around as his fledgling started to experiment with his new found freedom, dipping and swirling in the atmosphere above the park.

It was impossible to tell from the way he flew what kind of man he'd be when he came back to the ground. If there was no trace of submission in him when he landed then...

Raynard took a deep breath. If that was the case, then it wasn't Ori who needed to change. If Ori needed him, and couldn't have him as a master then, somehow, Raynard knew he'd have to learn how to be something other than a master to him. He'd have to find some form of submission inside himself, some way he could serve the needs of the swan.

The chances of a hawk doing that and keeping his own sanity intact were slim at best, Raynard knew that too. But, if there was no other way...

Another deep breath failed to bring Raynard any comfort as Ori continued to circle above him.

If nothing else, he'd been right to think Ori was strong. He stayed in the air a lot longer than most men could ever hope to manage on their first attempt. Over an hour had passed before he descended toward the lake.

Raynard watched, his heart racing faster and faster as he realised Ori was coming back to him, that it was now mere moments before everything would be settled once and for all.

The swan glided down toward the edge of the lake, all grace and fluid movements. Ori was barely a foot above the surface of the water when tension flooded back into his body. After that, the landing was…interesting.

A flurry of wings and webbed feet splashed and crashed into the edge of the lake. One moment there was a blur of feathers, the next, a beautiful naked man appeared in the shallow water closest to the bench.

Raynard perched on the edge of the seat, studying, watching, waiting for some sign. Shaking the water out of his hair, Ori immediately turned toward Raynard. Their eyes met. Raynard's hand tightened around the collar, his breath caught in his throat, prayers rushed through his head, and all he could do was hope against hope.

Ori stumbled up onto his feet under Raynard's watchful gaze—his arms and legs all going in different directions as he tried to control a body that wasn't entirely sure what shape it was.

He splashed his way to the edge of the lake. Again and again he stumbled, but he kept pulling himself upright and pushing forward, making his way determinedly back to Raynard's side.

The edge of the lake was muddy. By the time Ori emerged from the water's edge, he was smeared with dirt. Earth and leaf litter clung to his coating of mud as he scrambled up the bank.

He tumbled to his knees at Raynard's feet and reached out to him. Seemingly unable to scrape up human words, Ori whimpered his pleasure and rubbed his face against Raynard's body in a way that seemed to promise Raynard that everything really would be fine.

Wet, muddy, and affectionate in equal measure, Ori snuggled against him.

The wildness that was so familiar to Raynard from his own returns to a human form was conspicuous in its absence. Ori was all…

Raynard closed his eyes for a moment. There was only one word that fitted and he was almost too afraid to use it.

Ori was all submission.

As Raynard encouraged him even closer, Ori's lips moved to his fly, kissing and licking him through the fabric, desperate little noises escaping from the back of his throat as he fumbled at Raynard's clothes and clung to whatever material he could wrap his fingers around.

Every movement cautious and measured, Raynard slipped his hands between them, nudging Ori away slightly so he could undo his fly and free his cock.

Ori didn't appear able to comprehend what he was trying to do. He turned his attention enthusiastically toward Raynard's hands, licking and sucking at his fingertips, slowing him down with every nuzzle and kiss.

Raynard smiled at his antics, relief racing through him, turning him as silly and lightheaded as his fledgling seemed to be. As Raynard finally managed to pull his fly down, Ori dived on him. His hands fluttered over his cock as he sucked around the tip of his shaft.

The stream of whimpers and moans turned into a flood. Raynard stared down at Ori as his cock slid deeper into his mouth. No technique, no control, Ori was running entirely on adrenaline and instinct, and he was stunning.

A true submissive. It didn't matter what it said on his fledgling's wrist. No avian could hide who he really was when his species was so close to the front of his mind. Swan or not, Ori was all submission.

Ori dipped his head again, begging Raynard with his lips and tongue to come in his mouth. Holding back, Raynard instinctively made him work for that pleasure. Ori's eyes were closed. He seemed content to stay there all evening. He knew Raynard so well, and his conscious memories seemed to be coming back to him. He knew what would please his master, what would push him to the edge, and he didn't hesitate to display that knowledge.

Not even a hawk could hold back forever. Ori moaned his pleasure as Raynard relented and gave him what he wanted. He spilled into Ori's mouth, tangling his hand in Ori's hair as he held him close to receive everything he could give him.

Ori bucked as he tasted his master, and Raynard had no doubt that his fledgling had found his own pleasure in servicing him. Even when they both fell still, Ori didn't pull away. He stayed exactly where he was, suckling gently around Raynard's shaft.

The collar was still in Raynard's hand. He fixed it carefully around Ori's neck. Ori murmured his pleasure as he finally let Raynard's softening cock slip from between his lips.

Reaching into his bag, Raynard pulled out a huge towel and wrapped it around Ori's damp body. Sleepy and sated from his climax, Ori snuggled against Raynard as Raynard rubbed the towel against his skin.

A few minutes passed before Ori blinked open his eyes. He frowned at Raynard's clothes. "You're all muddy, sir…"

"Hush," Raynard chided, encouraging Ori to snuggle against him however much he wanted regardless of all the wet and dirt he'd brought with him.

Ori didn't need much convincing. He had complete trust in his master right then. Raynard smiled down at him as a full breath finally made it into his lungs. All submission, all what Raynard had thought he was from the very first moment Ori came into his service.

Very slowly, the guilt from everything he'd thought he'd inflicted on a man not suited to submission began to fade. There was no cruelty in teaching a submissive about submission.

"Good boy."

Ori blinked up at him, a tiny touch of confusion making it back into his eyes.

"You have no idea how glorious you looked up there, do you?"

Ori smiled at him, even more beautiful there than he had been up in the sky.

Raynard pushed his fingers through Ori's damp white hair, studying him intently. "You have no idea how much I love you, either, do you?"

"Even though I'm a swan, sir?" Ori whispered, fear creeping back into his eyes.

"You're you, and you're mine. Nothing else matters." For the first time, there was no doubt in Raynard's mind as he said it. "When you're with me you're not a swan, or a duck. You're my fledgling."

Ori seemed to sense Raynard's complete certainty about every word. All his fears appeared to fade away as easily as Raynard stroked his hair. "Yes, sir."

Raynard smiled down at him once more. "Ready to go home, fledgling?"

Ori nodded and smiled up at his master in return. Swan or not, he was obviously as content in his submission as any ugly little duckling could ever be.

Also in the Avian Shifter Series
Coming in November 2015

Magpie — 2nd Edition

Everet has found his perfect place in the nest. As a raven, he's ideally suited to his new role in the nest's security flock. Some of the jobs it entails have been far more enjoyable than others, but when he's called to retrieve a magpie, who's got himself into trouble in a local human club, it becomes a truly life changing experience.

Magpie shifters have always been looked down on by other avians. Just as attracted to shiny things in their human bodies as they are in their avian forms, everyone knows they'll do anything for money — and they're not above stealing what they can't get by more honest means.

Kane knows what being a magpie means, and he's got the bruises to show for it. When Everet rescues him from his latest scrape, Kane knows better than to believe the raven will actually take an interest in him and his welfare, but it's just possible that Everet is different to any other man Kane has ever met.

Other books by Kim Dare

Series

Werewolves & Dragons
The Avian Shifters
Kinky Cupid
FIT Guys
Thrown to the Lions
Rawlings Men
Sex Sells
Sun, Sea and Submission
The Whole A-Z
Pack Discipline
G-A-Y Lust Bites
Perfect Timing
Collared
Pushing the Envelope
Kinky Quickies

Kim Dare has also written a number of free short stories.
You can find these on her website.

About the Author

Kim is a bisexual submissive from Wales (UK). First published in 2008, she has since released over 100 BDSM erotic romance titles ranging from short stories to full length novels. Having worked with a host of fantastic e-publishers, she moved into self publishing in 2013.

While she occasionally enjoys writing other pairings, most of Kim's stories focus on Male/Male relationships. But, no matter what the pairing, from paranormal to contemporary, and from the sweet to the intense, everything she writes will always feature three things - Kink, Love and a Happy Ending.

You can find out more about Kim's books on her website, follow her on twitter, catch up with her blog, and email her directly using the links below.

Website: **www.kimdare.com**
Twitter: **www.twitter.com/KimDareAuthor**
Blog: **www.kimdare.wordpress.com**
E-mail: **kim@kimdare.com**

www.ingramcontent.com/pod-product-compliance
Lightning Source LLC
Chambersburg PA
CBHW031314170626
46807CB00001B/416